T0151813

GHETTO GIRLS

5
TOUGHER
THAN DICE

ESSENCE BESTSELLING AUTHOR
ANTHONY WHYTE

WHERE
HIP HOP
LITERATURE
BEGINS...

AUGUSTUS
PUBLISHING

© 2013 Augustus Publishing, Inc.
ISBN: 978-0982541562

Novel by Anthony Whyte
Edited by Parijat Deasai
Creative Direction & Design by Jason Claiborne
Photography by BigAppleModels.com

Augustus Publishing paperback June 2013
www.augustuspublishing.com

GHETTO GIRLS **5** TOUGHER THAN DICE

Dedicated to Will Teez, the lion of Inwood...

Like the one who writes your checks, I'm just trying to be your
favorite author. Getting at-cha... Feeling like I'm back... GNA... I'm
already that...

ANTHONY WHYTE

1

"Your score is two hundred, Uncle E. You've, without a doubt, stepped up your bowling game," the excited teen said in a mock, stern tone. "But everyone in Harlem Lanes will get the new memo informing them of how your niece destroyed you by twenty-five points," she laughed.

Deedee Ascot was in a good mood at the end of an exhausting six-game set of bowling at the Harlem Lanes. Quickly she and her uncle, Eric Ascot, changed shoes. They packed away their bowling balls. Deedee's face was glowing, as she handed her uncle the bag containing her ball.

"Losers treat," she smiled at her uncle.

"Yeah, you won, but my game was a little off today. I needed that last pin, but it just wouldn't fall," Eric countered. "Anyway, like you said, my game is getting a little better."

"Practice, practice, practice..." Deedee smiled, wagging her finger.

"Okay Ms. Show-off, I gotta give credit where it's due. Lunch's on me."

Deedee walked alongside Eric to the café, rocking tight black Cavalli jeans and boots. The pair was quickly directed to empty seats.

"Whew, these seats are great for resting my tired feet," Deedee exclaimed, flopping on the red cushion seat.

"C'mon, I'm the one who's out of shape. Remember now, you were just teasing me about that," Eric smiled, sitting down.

"I could eat a huge burger right now," Deedee laughed.

"Winning takes a lot of energy, huh, Dee?"

"Uncle E, you couldn't possible know how tired I am. And I'm still cramping too. Men don't know anything about menstruation."

There was a long pause. Deedee studied the embarrassed grin on her uncle's face. She let out a schoolgirl's snicker before continuing.

"You right," her uncle sheepishly said.

"Uh-huh, bowling was great. I was able to get rid of some of my aggression."

"Look out, world. Deedee's an aggressive bowler."

"But I keep it in my lane, not in the gutter," she laughed.

"Let's get you some food before you go delirious."

Light chatter continued while Eric Ascot and his niece perused the menu. The relaxing sounds of Coltrane wafted over the Sunday afternoon crowd in the Harlem Lanes café. The waitress arrived with glasses and filled them from a pitcher of ice-cold water. After taking their orders, the waitress zipped off. Eric shook his head, grooving to the sound of jazz piped through the sound system.

Eric Ascot had a monthly bowling game with his niece, Deedee. They had bowled since he began teaching her at age seven, and since she had begun living with him. He reached for a *Vibe* magazine, thinking about the games he played with her dad—his brother, Dennis.

Despite the fact that his younger brother had lost his life at the hands of the police, Eric had found the strength to smile. Both he and Deedee were able to survive the pain. As Eric turned the pages of the leading urban magazine, a photo of Coco caught his eye. He glanced up at Deedee casually sipping water.

"Well, look-a-here, look-a-here. *Vibe* did a piece on your girlfriend and my new artist," he said.

"Oh my God! Let me see it Uncle E," Deedee said, reaching across the table and snatching the magazine away from her startled uncle.

"Hey now, be easy..."

"Sorry Uncle E. I just have to see this," Deedee said as she dove into the story of Coco. "I completely forgot *Vibe* was doing this piece. She's gonna be surprised!"

In no time, Deedee was completely immersed in the article. Lunch was served and Eric requested another copy of *Vibe* from the waiter. He chomped down on a turkey burger with fried onions. The article was basically a puff piece—a brief introduction to Coco the artist, described as the latest phenomenon coming out of Gotham onto the music scene. Eric ate while reading, but Deedee ignored her cheeseburger. When he was finished eating, Eric glanced over at his niece. Deedee still had not touched her food.

"That cheeseburger will be cold if you don't eat it."

"I'm sorry. I got caught up," she said. "*Vibe*'s a real cool magazine, and they did a nice piece on Coco," she said.

Eric pointed to the meal in front of Deedee, and raised his

eyebrows. "Eat up, Dee. I have to make a stop at the studio."

She glanced around, and seeing the rush of the afternoon crowd, she replied, "Ok, Uncle E." Some of the patrons were dressed as if they were coming from church. With the sounds of Dizzy Gillespie and Coltrane mingling with boisterous chatter, the scene was reminiscent of the early days of the Harlem Renaissance.

Donning their shades, niece and uncle left the lanes, exiting onto the buzzing sidewalks of Seventh Avenue. Sunlight shone bright outside, throwing light on the post–Saturday-night. They walked across 125th Street to where Deedee had parked her new BMW. They jumped in and headed to the West Side Highway. Approaching the Hudson River, she dropped the top.

"Did I tell you how I love this car, Uncle E? Thank you very much," she smiled.

Deedee raced onto the south lane of the Henry Hudson Parkway as her uncle looked on in surprise.

"Hey Dee, slow down, girl. Take it easy. Let's enjoy the ride," Eric cautioned.

"Okay Uncle E. Let's enjoy the ride," she sighed, shaking her head.

Moments later Deedee parked and they alighted from the car. Both walked to the building and nodded to the security personnel stationed in the lobby.

"Good afternoon, Mr. Ascot. Are you gonna be long, sir?"

"No, I'll be out in a few," Eric answered, walking with Deedee.

"You always say that, Uncle E," Deedee smiled.

They continued to the elevator and waited quietly. Minutes later, Eric Ascot was in the office of his recording studio. Deedee sat alone at the receptionist desk, reading *Vibe* again. About half hour later, there was a buzz at the door of the recording studio. Deedee was still engrossed in the magazine. The buzzing continued. She finally looked up and before she could answer, Deedee saw it flying off the hinges and what seemed like an army of police barged in.

Shouting and banging noises carried through the entire studio. Eric walked out of his office and was greeted by officers with their weapons drawn. In a New-York minute the recording studio was shut down, ready for search and seizure. Detectives and dogs were everywhere taking everything. Standing outside his office, Eric was stunned. It took him a long time to fathom the depth of his situation.

A detective accosted him, "Who are you?"

"Eric Ascot. What is all this about?"

"You are under arrest!"

"For what...? I haven't done anything, and if you put those handcuffs on me you better have a good reason."

The dogs, preoccupied with sniffing, suddenly began barking. The commotion brought a smile to the officers' face and a hush among the employees of the recording studio.

"I guess the dogs found it," a detective shouted after a tension-filled pause.

"Found? Found what?" Eric asked, perplexed.

"I got something here that will put you away for good."

"What...?"

With a scowl on his face, Eric glanced in silence at an officer standing next to a dog. The animal was joyfully wagging its tail while the officer petted its face. He pointed to a plastic bag being zipped by two officers and answered.

"Atta boy, doggie. You found the smoking gun."

Deedee was placed against the wall and patted down by an officer. Other officers quickly searched Eric Ascot and said, "You're being charged in the death of a police officer..." Eric was taken by surprise and couldn't focus. He was abruptly handcuffed, and arrested. Sounding like a preacher delivering a eulogy, the officer read him his Miranda rights.

"Don't worry, Dee. Get home and I'll call you later," Eric said with conviction.

"Uncle E, I..."

"I'll be alright. Call Sophia and tell her what happened. I'll be out soon."

"Sure you will," an officer offered, sarcastically.

The small army of officers and their dogs laughed. Eric was efficiently escorted out of the studio and into a waiting elevator. Deedee was left thinking, watching from the window as her uncle was led out the building. A band of reporters were already on hand downstairs. Camera bulbs flashed, recording the moment for the city's dailies.

In tears, Deedee gathered herself and dialed rapidly from the office phone. Holding the receiver to her ears, she waited while the call rang to a voicemail.

"Hey Sophia, this is Deedee... The police just arrested Uncle E and he wanted me to let you know. You can call him direct—he has his cellphone. I'll try to reach you later. Bye."

Deedee put the receiver down and plopped into the big office chair behind Eric's desk. She spun the chair around, glancing at platinum plaques her uncle had earned. There were pictures of him and her father. Eric and his younger brother seemed so young and innocent back then. A whirlwind of events flashed across her mind.

She found herself recalling her father's death as he was being arrested. A case the police claimed was a drug deal gone wrong. Eric Ascot's older brother, Dennis, had been caught in a sting involving a drug kingpin. No one was ever tried for his death. Those life-changing events had brought her and her cocaine-addicted mother to live with

Uncle Eric. Eric Ascot was a top record producer. Well-respected in the music game, he had parlayed his talents into the movie industry. Despite the tragedy she lived through, her uncle had allowed Deedee to enjoy the fruits of his success.

Her thoughts of happiness with Uncle E were quickly interrupted by memories of her mother's sudden disappearance. No one had seen or heard from Denise Ascot in over twelve years. Eric Ascot had been her primary parent. He and his on-again, off-again fiancée, Sophia, had guided her from childhood through high school. She was now college-bound. Deedee put her head on the desk and sobbed quietly.

Exhausted and unshaven, Eric Ascot sat in the holding cell. He had not spoken to his attorney. The police had allowed him to keep his cellphone. It seemed like an eternity and he was still waiting for his lawyer to call back. He glanced at his phone, thinking of calling Sophia, his now-ex-fiancée, at her office. He had tried reaching out to her last night after the arrest, but to no avail.

Eric heard shuffling noises coming from outside his unexpected confines. The first person to stop by this morning was the same officer who had allowed him to keep his cellphone. Eric watched him thinking the officer had probably returned early to confiscate the phone. Wiping his lips of breakfast, the heavyset, uniformed man stared at Eric for a minute. The officer cleared his throat and continued eyeballing other prisoners in the cell silently. His intense frown became a sardonic smile before he spoke.

"I guess your over-priced lawyer hasn't called yet, huh?"

The disheveled Eric shook his head wordlessly. To prevent his anger from spilling over, Eric bit his lip.

"He must be a busy man," the officer smiled. "Hope your battery doesn't run out with you waiting and all," he laughed, walking away. "Get your Armani's ready—the cameras are gonna start rolling soon. Another officer will be here to transport y'all down to Central Booking in a few. He'll let you know if you can keep that PDA."

There was no fronting about this situation. Eric contemplated how right the officer was—his lawyer should have called back by now. The high price of retaining Max Roose might come with the best representation, but it also better came with no waiting. He had left several messages requesting to speak to Roose, only to be told over and over that he had gone fishing. Mr. Roose would get back to him as soon as possible.

Eric closed his tired eyes momentarily, and made a silent wish. He wanted to be somewhere on an open range, fishing, hunting. Instead he was stuck in a cramped holding cell waiting to be booked. Banter came from the riffraff sharing the small space. Eric found himself fuming at the delay, the backchat, and the unbearable stench.

Despite leaving messages for Roose that it was an emergency, Eric remained trapped. His brow furrowed in a cliff of frustration. Agitated, he angrily smashed the keys to dial his attorney's cellphone yet again. Once more his call went straight to voicemail. He left another message, his mind working overtime.

The afternoon raid by the police seemed too neatly wrapped. Everything appeared to work in concert to ensure he wound up in a cell. Even the question posed by the doorman at the building lobby now hung eerily in Eric's head. Eric tried to piece together how his gun had left his home and gotten to his office.

"I never took my gun out," he mumbled.

His cellmates' ears perked up. Eric glanced at them to find they all wore blank stares.

The possibilities seemed unlimited. Eric was determined again to speak with his attorney. The bizarre afternoon raid had become an overnight jail stay. Not sleeping all night long and waiting all morning was enough to make him explode. But he remained calm.

He wanted badly to skip back into opulence. His marbled shower, warm water spraying from the silver nozzle washing him free of all the dirty slurs, was what he craved. He would settle for simple peace and quiet. Eric had endured the loud voices all night. In silence, he vowed never again to wind up in a cell. He stared at unknown faces and smelled the sweat. He yearned to be cleared of all this.

The new morning brought no light on the inside of this dank hole, built for one and occupied by four. Eric sneered at the three smelly drunks sitting close to him. Maybe it was paranoia, but when his hand went to his pocket, Eric realized he had surrendered everything except this PDA he clutched. His thought shifted gears as he stared at the instrument in his grasp, but all he could do was wait.

Still Eric's mind roamed, covering all the possibilities of how the gun got into his office, a gun that was used to kill a detective.

He knew his legal mess had started with the rape of his niece. His thoughts turned to a fateful call he received from an old friend of the family, Busta. Eric was driving home when his cellphone rang. It was Busta calling to inform him of a grievous error. Seeking street justice for the attack of his niece, Busta and Eric had engineered the death of the man they thought was involved in Deedee's sexual assault.

Sitting in the cell, Eric stared at his cellphone like it was about to ring, and Busta would call again. Maybe this time he would make the right decision. His mind fell back to the time and place when he met the street informer known as Rightchus. He was on his way to Gee's night club. Back then, his brother's best friend, Busta was alive. Nether of them had calculated the full consequence of their actions. They had no clue that such actions would set off a chain of events which would eventually lead to Busta's demise, and Eric's present circumstances. Spurred by emotions, Eric's thoughts went back to the time he first met with Rightchus.

He gazed at the flashing low-battery signal. "Shit!" Eric yelled and then concentrated on the traffic. Within minutes he was at Gee's club. He went through the heavy red wooden door, past the beefy security. Inside, Busta beckoned to him. Eric felt a trickle of sweat down his spine. He smiled uneasily and made his way to Busta.

"Hey E., what's up?" Busta greeted, giving him a hearty hug and a closed-fist shake.

"What's poppin', Busta...? You better cut down on your visits to the kitchen," Eric said, watching the large man chomping down on fried chicken.

"No, see, when I get nervous I eat a whole lot more fried foods. Chicken...? Send us a bucket over to the booth, honey."

Busta gave his order to a passing waitress. Then he walked to a booth in the back of the busy café with Eric.

"A bucket...?" Eric echoed.

"Yeah man, a muthafuckin' bucket. They have some good stuff up *in here. Why? You have a problem with that?"*

Busta sounded husky, threatening. He returned to sipping from a glass of beer, saying nothing further. Eric had to do the talking.

"Okay, okay Busta. Do you?"

"We buried the wrong man. You know wha' I'm saying?" Busta said, glancing around.

"No, I don't know what you're saying. So please tell me what da fuck you're talking about, Busta."

"I'm talking 'bout that hit, E. We... That guy, Deja wasn't da one who raped your niece. He was just a well-connected, small-time drug dealer," Busta said, his voice lowered to a raspy whisper.

The mellow sound of a clarinet, in the form of a jazz riff, came through the speakers. It collided head-on with Busta's heart-stopping message. Eric sat back and glanced around at the other patrons, as if waiting for someone to read him his rights. Had he done something wrong? He tugged at his nose, where sweat had suddenly formed. Busta noticed, and so did the waitress who brought Busta's chicken.

"May I get you something cool to drink, gentlemen?" she asked.

"Bring us couple beers and some extra napkins," Busta said to the waitress. Then he turned to Eric. "E., don't sweat that. Shit happens daily, man. I mean—"

"Busta, Deedee was calling this guy's name in her sleep," Eric said. He raised his brows. "She was screaming, 'get off me ... get off me ... stay away from me, Deja.' She told me he was trying to rape her again. I'm sure it was this fucking drug-dealing Deja. It had to be him or his peoples. Either way, somebody had to pay."

"E., let me tell you, man. I got da word. I mean..."

"What word, B.?"

"E., I got da fucking word," Busta repeated.

Eric Ascot's attention drifted back to the music piped into the nightclub. He wanted silence. For once, the music haunted him. It sent chills down his back and he broke out in sweat. Patrons laughed and drank. He thought of his brother and how the police had done nothing.

"So what...?" Eric asked after a few beats.

"So what...?" Busta asked while attacking a piece of chicken.

"Well, we got to do da right muthafuckin' thing. Know wha' I mean, E.?"

Eric watched Busta who was still grubbing away as if his life depended on every bite.

"What are we gonna do?" Eric finally asked.

"We gotta break da right muthafuckas off a piece," Busta said, waving the chicken leg. "I mean, niggas can't be running free, raping, unsafe sex, spreading all kinds of germs and shit. They're out there E. and your niece might not be their only vick. We got to make those dirty muthafuckas pay." Busta burped. The music from the club masked the guttural interruption. "Listen E.," he continued. "I'm a show you somebody with the knowledge on all that shit—like, why your niece was raped and all that. He might even tell you who did your brother. Believe it, E.; I'm telling you, right now, I could bring him to see ya."

"Are you serious, Busta?"

"Eric, when do you know me to be joking?"

Before Eric could answer, Busta was on his cell phone, his chicken-stained fingers pressing buttons. Then he yelled into the phone, "Pick up that kid Shorty-Wop. Yeah, Rightchus, or whatever da fuck he wants to call himself. Bring him downtown to Mr. Geez."

"You sure you don't want a piece?" Busta asked, hanging up.

He gave Eric a long look, and ripped into a piece of chicken breast. Eric stared back lit a cigarette and sipped his brew. He took a deep drag and exhaled to the accompaniment of a jazz riff while Busta finished all the chicken.

"Let's go," Busta said finally, as he placed a large bill on the table and got up.

Eric rose as if he was about to greet a bad verdict. His steps came tentatively. Eric felt like he did not want to move, but did anyway. Like a prison guard leading the long walk to the chair, Busta led Eric to a parked van. There were two men inside, and the pair joined them.

"Give us a minute," Busta said to the driver.

"Shorty-Wop, this is—" Busta said. The door slammed behind the driver.

"I know who this is, man. You don't have to tell Shorty Wop nada, know wha' I'm saying? This da hottest brother out there mixing down R&B tracks, kicking Hip-Hop shit all over da place, just blowing shit up, know wha' I'm saying? Shorty-Wop be keeping up. Nah mean?"

"Yeah, no doubt about that... But Shorty, I want you to tell him sump'n. Shed some light on da scenario you kicked to me earlier."

"Eric Ascot, you all this an' you all that... Da beats, da drums, da music. That shit is on. And if you need a new emcee, up and coming, like myself included, shit, I'll be your man. Not even who...? Silky Black...can do it like I can. What! I'm saying I'll rock the mike at the drop of a dime. And R&B, that's me all day. Sang all the way through high school... Now I'm old school. Shit, but lemme do my thing. Even R. Kelly be listening. You wanna hear me bust a few rhymes or break it down R&B style, even Reggae...?"

"Yeah, that's all good, but..." Busta said, calming the hyper Shorty-Wop. "We wanna hear 'bout that rape thing, ya know wha' I sayin?" Busta said, his annoyance showing now.

"Shorty- Wop ain't gonna front. Eric, as God is my witness, da wrong man went down, see? It was these knuckleheads that should be dead and stinking."

Eric lit another cigarette. He offered one to Shorty-Wop. He quickly grabbed it and Eric lit it. The man took a drag and his mouth was running again.

"Them niggas kill you at the drop of your jaw. You mouth off to any of them niggas an' that's it. Ka-pow, ka-pow!" Shorty-Wop pointed two fingers. "I can't afford that, Mr. Ascot, you know wha' I mean? I got a family. Seeds, ya know. So I'm a tell y'all this. Hit me wid some dough, record contract, whatever. Put me on, cuz I'm an aspiring rap star. I know it. I can feel all that."

"Shorty..." Busta said, running out of patience. "Just tell us what da fuck you know an' get hit wid some dough, a'ight?"

"Eric, your niece was gang-banged by two knuckleheads. Lil' Long and Vulcha, them's da muthafuckas. Two, not one," Shorty-Wop, a.k.a. Rightchus said.

Eric cringed at the news. His lips uncurled as he snuffed out the cigarette. He stared at the street character, almost hating him.

"I don't mean to be so blunt, but that's wha' happened. Deja was trying to fuck wid her in da club, but when she and Coco—"

"Coco...?" Eric asked.

"Yeah, you know her? She a singer, actress, da dancer... Now she got a lil' sump'n going on, I'm sort a like her advisor. I be showing her moves that helps her when she be performing, know wha' I mean? So your niece rolls up wid Coco and her girls in this bad-ass car... A Mercedes, black one... And when they went outside, boom! Them niggas gun-butt Coco, knocked her young ass out. Da bitch lay on da street, nose bleeding, swollen up like Santa's reindeer. They took your niece and da ride. Them muthafuckas were dead wrong."

"Really..." Eric said.

"Yeah, and they's da ones who hit your brother, know wha' I mean? He was paying off someone. He was fucking 'round wid Xtriggaphan. Them fake-ass gangsta rappers, wannabes. Them niggas had beef wid everybody. They owed Lil' Long dough, see."

"Hmm, I hear you..." Eric said.

"So when Lil' Long went to get his dough—Boom—He sees your brother fuckin' wid them niggas. Lil' Long and Vulcha start beating down the Xtriggaphan niggas. Your brother, may he rest in peace. Your brother steps up to them, and it's like, don't fuck wid Lil' Long `n' Vulcha. Your brother did, an' just like that, he was killed. Just like fucking that," Rightchus said, snapping his fingers.

"What about the musicians? Xtriggaphan...? The drugs...? All that shit the police ignored. Why didn't you say anything before?" Eric asked.

"Nah, nah, he was fucking some girl on da low. Bebop. Some girl who was killed wid Deja. I could a fucked wid her, but every man she fucked get killed. No disrespect, know wha' I'm saying?"

"I hear you," Eric said.

"Them niggas, Xtriggaphan, they s'pose to be out in Cali or Cleveland. Lil' Long hit them niggas wid some dough and I heard they paid da bitch, Bebop. Your brother was strapped and they killed him, right? Nobody crosses Lil' Long or Vulcha. They not having it! But see, they did ma boo Deja, see, an' that was dead wrong. All he was doing was just grindin' tryin' a get his. But them niggas, they ain't no joke. Da police don't even fuck wid them."

"A'ight, a'ight Shorty-Wop. Hold this," Busta said, slipping a fifty-dollar bill into Shorty-Wop's huge hand.

Eric stumbled out of the van. He searched his pocket. He found a cigarette and quickly lit it. He needed satisfaction, but nicotine was not the cure.

"Shit! Fuck it!" He cursed, throwing the smoke away.

"Remember, if anything comes up...you don't know me," Shorty-Wop said as the van pulled off.

Eric waved and dismissed any thoughts of Shorty-Wop, except

for his message. He now knew the men who had murdered his brother and raped his niece. Father and daughter were the victims of the same people. Yet they still walked around free as the wind. Anger boiled in Eric Ascot. The sound of retching distracted him. As he raised his chin, Eric saw Busta leaning over the curb, vomiting. He rushed over to him.

"You a'ight, B...?" Eric asked.

"Yeah, I'm good. Fucking chicken bones," Busta said, his eyes were teary as he coughed.

"We got to get rid of those muthafuckas, Busta."

"That's how I feel, too, buddy. I'm wid you on that."

"How much...?"

"I can't say right now, but I know their fucking days are numbered."

"Fuck it. Let's end their shit now," Eric said gritting his teeth.

"Ease up, E. Chill, chill. Grab a hold of yourself. Cool out," Busta said, gingerly removing his neck from Eric's strong grip. He coughed and spit out a chicken bone. "Fucking chicken bones! Word is... Ugh, ugh," Busta said, holding himself steady, careful not to lean on a still angry Eric Ascot. "Word is Lil' Long and Vulcha, them muthafuckas down wid da law. They involved in some sort of informant-type shit. Them muthafuckas you got to be careful wid. It's gonna take a lotta dough. But they can be reached. They ain't da fucking Untouchables, hiding behind them fucking tin badges."

"Let's do it, Busta. Just set that shit up. Set it up right now," Eric said.

He swung his arms, swiping at the air, slapped Busta's chest, and then his own. Busta nodded solemnly. Their right hands slammed together and with that, the deal was sealed.

"Where you parked?" Busta asked as they crossed the street.

They walked to the oversized red doors of Mr. Gee's, where notoriety was the valid I.D. card.

"I'm gonna go back inside for a minute and chit chat. How's Sophia?"

"Sophia...Oh, shit, I have to do something with her tonight. She's a'ight, Busta. Go ahead, B. I've got this thing, some kind a dress-up party to attend. I really just wanna fucking get drunk, just tore up, assed-out, like ol' times and shit."

"Yeah, I hear you, E. But you got things to deal wid. I got some business to take care of, myself. We'll do this some other time, know wha' I'm saying?"

"Cool. Call me, B. Set it, then call."

"A'ight, I'll do that, E. I'll see ya, man."

Eric ran to his car. Busta disappeared through the club doors, headed straight to the bar and ordered a drink. He stared ahead as he sipped. He winked at three women close by. Energy seeped into his groin area and alerted his scrotum.

"Ah yeah," he said. "I'd love to be hitting those panties tonight."

"We did the wrong nigga, Busta," Eric heard himself muttered aloud.

"What you did...?" one of his cellmates curiously asked.

Sitting in the tiny cell, his thoughts in a swirl, Eric slowly realized that he had fiinally drifted off to sleep. His thoughts had emerged in a dream and he was talking in his sleep. Eric scratched the shadow of an unshavened beard, and opened his eyes to see an inmate eyeballing him.

"I ain't said nada, nigga!" Eric retorted, eyeballing the man.

"What da fuck you want, huh?"

"Sound like you talking in your sleep," the bum said. "I ain't trying to be all up in your B. I. but you might need a priest. It sounds like you got some confessing to do!" The man laughed, and couple other inmates joined in.

"Yeah, he pillow-talkin'," one of the inmates joked.

"I hear you. What y'all in here for...? Bad comedy or y'all fucking bad taste in clothes?" Eric asked, looking the man up and down. Then shaking his head, Eric frowned and said, "Get away from me. It stinks in here!"

The nosey inmate could hear the sarcasm dripping from Eric's mouth and he walked away. He joined the other inmates huddled in discussion, and their loud laughter continued. Staring in their direction, Eric slowly realized he had been dreaming and his mumbles must have brought their unwanted attention on him. When his cellphone began buzzing, his thoughts veered to his niece.

"Hey, Dee," he said, excitedly answering the call.

"Hi, Uncle E, how're you doing...?"

There was deep concern in her voice. So far she had been resilient throughout his legal ordeal. Ascot smiled and answered in a steady voice while wondering how his niece was holding up through this latest traumatic change.

"I'm making the best of this situation. How're you doing Dee...?"

"I'm hanging in there, Uncle E. I tried reaching Sophia last night but couldn't. I'm on my way to her office right now."

"You are driving and talking on the phone? That's not safe, Dee..."

"Uncle E..."

"Dee, hang up and call me back when you're not driving. It's dangerous out there. You can't be driving while on the phone, girl. C'mon now—safety first. Call me back."

"Okay, I'll call back as soon as I reach Sophia's office."

"Okay, bye."

"Talk to you later Uncle..."

Ascot stared at the instrument and a pronounced wince formed on his unshaven features. His body tightened, clearly agitated by the news. Ascot didn't want to reveal his feelings since three pairs of bloodshot eyes were on him. His expensive jeans, silk shirt and boots made him feel like a target. Scowling while looking at the phone in his hand, he willed it to ring. At the other end would be his high-priced attorney, but Eric couldn't express this feeling. His fellow inmates, now looking him up and down, rolled their eyes toward each other and back, like they saw food. A loud sigh slipped through Ascot's clenched teeth.

He tried to still his breathing, but it was becoming increasingly difficult. Annoyed, he sat while his mind churned. Eric jumped to his feet and began pacing. The rattling of keys disturbed a pensive Eric Ascot from exploding.

"C'mon, Ascot, it's time."

His cell phone chimed simultaneously with the command. Ascot felt a moment of relief wash over him when he saw the number: his attorney.

"Man, what took you so long. I be paying you that phat retainer for you to be here for me. Right now, I need you and I heard you went fishing...? C'mon man, get me outta here! I'm in a fucking cell... I'm giving you one hour."

"Times up, Ascot, you know the routine. Let's go do this perp walk for your media friends," the officer laughed, opening the door. "Turn around, and put your hands behind you."

Ascot did as commanded. He bit his lips when he felt the handcuffs binding his wrists. Ascot was shaking his head as the officer led him outside. The boys in blue lined up and escorted him like he was public enemy number one. The clicking of shutters by the cameras of the paparazzi was under way. Newshounds rushed him despite the strong police presence.

"Mr. Ascot, do you care to make a statement regarding the gun found in the office of your recording studio...?"

Eric stared at the reporter and said nothing. As cameras continued to take photos, other reporters stepped forward with their questions.

"A gun used in the murder of a detective from the city's police department. Was the gun yours, Mr. Ascot...? You're facing murder charge, and you have nothing to say to that...?"

Ascot kept his lips sealed and wore a sarcastic smirk as he was finally led away to the awaiting police transporter. The three drunks were being interviewed and probably had plenty to say about his phone conversations. From the window he glanced at the crowd and the whole event seemed arranged. It would sell on the news wire, and go viral. Eric's thoughts moved quickly while sirens and flashing lights of the police vehicle loudly signal take off.

About fifteen minutes later they were downtown at central booking. A sense of relief washed over him when he saw his attorney doing what he was being paid to do. He was busy shaking hands and finding a way to get out of this gloom. Eric sat in the holding pen for what seemed to be an eternity. Hours later, he finally heard his name being called. He couldn't wait to be out of this circus.

Deedee guided her BMW through a busy Monday-morning Manhattan rush. She thought she had left early enough, until she saw the heavy traffic, and arrived to meet Sophia later than planned. Deedee parked in a garage and quickly walked down the crowded city sidewalk. A fly girl, down to her Gucci heels, Deedee felt the crush of busy pedestrians making tracks to places of employment. Slipping Gucci shades on, Deedee, unfamiliar with Sophia's midtown office, navigated her way to the building.

After being scrutinized by security, she made it upstairs a whole hour later than planned. A rotund secretary greeted Deedee.

"Good morning. May I help you young lady?'

"Good morning. I'm here to see Sophia Lawrence—"

"I'm afraid that's impossible at this time," the woman said.

Deedee noticed the secretary was wearing her eyeglasses on the tip of her nose, and she slowed her roll.

"We spoke and—" Deedee started to say, but the woman interrupted.

"Did you have an appointment, ah...?" the secretary asked sharply.

"Deedee, its Deedee Ascot. She was expecting me."

The woman flipped the bifocals from the edge of her nose to her eyes and covered her bulging eyeballs. She held the glasses in position with one hand while the other leafed through a list of names. Glancing down at note sheet filled with names, she shook her head.

"I don't see your name anywhere here," she answered, her eyes still skimming the sheet.

"It was kind of personal. So I don't know..." Deedee's voice trailed when the secretary looked up at her. Her eyeglasses had slid back into the same position on her nose.

"Then why didn't you say that in the first place? Have a seat—she's busy with a client. I'll let her know and see if she can fit you in... Have a seat."

"Thank you," Deedee smirked.

The woman haughtily watched Deedee strutting to the waiting area. Deedee sat, reading magazines. After waiting for over an hour, she finally spotted Sophia emerged from one of the offices.

"Hey Dee, how are you?' Sophia said, reaching out.

"Hi, Sophia," Deedee responded with a hug and a kiss on Sophia's cheek.

She was led past the frowning secretary and into a medium-sized office. There were a couple of desks and several chairs. There was no one else around, making the place seem like an interrogation room.

"I apologize, Dee. But you caught me when I'm really busy, and my office is in chaos. So I had to bring you into this office. Before we start do you want some coffee or hot chocolate?"

"Sure, I'll take the hot chocolate."

Deedee watched Sophia disappear out the door. Sophia was gone, and this allowed Deedee time to settle down and think. She remained standing while mentally going over the story of her uncle's arrest. Sophia returned with two hot chocolates in white, medium sized Styrofoam cups.

"Let's sit over here, Dee" Sophia said.

She ushered Deedee to a desk outfitted with a two chairs across the empty office area. They walked over in silence and sat. Sophia handed Deedee a cup. She took a sip from her own and smiled at the beautiful teen. An uneasy silence ensued. Deedee watched Sophia slowly sipping the hot liquid and waited for eye contact. None came. After watching Sophia take couple more sips, Deedee dove in.

"I don't think I've seen you since your graduation. Congratulations," Sophia said with a smile.

"Thanks, Sophia," Deedee quickly said.

"So, you're here to see me because..."

"I don't know if you've heard, but Uncle E has been arrested again by the police. They—"

"Raided his office..." Sophia said, interrupting Deedee. She stared, but not with sympathy. Deedee was surprised by the deep resentment she saw welling inside Sophia. It grew into an angry outburst. "I'm so damn sick and tired of all this!" Sophia said.

Deedee was not prepared for Sophia's agitated response. Her eyes blinked rapidly. Struck by a heavy dose of reality, Deedee tried to refocus as Sophia continued.

"Eric should have known better than to get involved in all this, Dee. He should have known better and I can't help him. My job, my position will be on the line. I've got all the police documents on my desk. I work for the government, the DA, and I can't go against that. Your uncle has to figure this out."

"But he isn't involved in anything—"

"Dee—"

"Sophia, you're his friend. You're close to him and you know that he's been setup by the police. They've been after him all this time."

"Dee, trust me on this. Eric is involved and that's that. The law has caught up to him."

"The law is corrupt!" Deedee shouted.

There was a pause and she looked at Sophia pleadingly. The attorney was dressed in a blue skirt suit with black heels, her face pretty with a little makeup. Deedee wished she could take back what she had just said, but it was already out.

"Oh Dee, please don't be fooled. I think your uncle was wrong taking the law into his own hands. I guess when a man reaches a certain status in life the only thing that matters is money. But I'm not gonna judge him. Only a court of law can bring him—and you—justice. And I'm sure he will get his. There's nothing I can do to help him, Dee," Sophia calmly said.

She shook her head and the room went silent. Deedee took it all in but stared at Sophia in disbelief.

"Well, I guess I won't take anymore of your time," Deedee said and stood.

She placed the cup of hot chocolate on the desk, untouched. Sophia was standing, her mouth agape but nothing came out. They stared at each other in an uncomfortable silence.

"Goodbye, Sophia," Deedee said and walked out of the office.

"Dee, I'm sorry but—"

Sophia was left standing alone when the door slammed and Deedee kept walking. Even with her Gucci shades on, the fat secretary could see tears rolling down Deedee's cheek. She whisked by without a nod or wave. Shaking her head, the nosey secretary watched Deedee quickly get on the elevator.

"These teenagers have no manners," she hissed under her breath.

Outside, the sun shone brightly and Deedee made her way to the garage. She adjusted her makeup, paid her toll, and drove out of the parking lot. She turned the music on and tapped in time with the rhythm of the song playing on the car radio.

What a difference a day makes
Twenty-four hours a day...
Brought the sun and the flowers
Where there used to be rain...

Esther Phillips moaned her way through an up-tempo version of the Dinah Washington classic while Deedee guided the car through the busy streets of Manhattan. Later, she pulled into the parking lot under the building housing Ascot Music Group. Her father was gone, her uncle was arrested, and Sophia, a person she thought she could turn to, was not available. Deedee was now in charge of running the family business, which included a recording studio.

She walked inside the building, ignoring the doorman in the lobby. He was always staring lecherously at her ass. Now that her uncle was not with her, she wanted to keep the doorman further away. She remembered that he was present on the day of her uncle's arrest.

"Good morning," he greeted.

"Good morning," she returned and kept it moving.

"Great day we're having..."

Deedee was already on the elevator, checking her floor and thinking of the work ahead. School was out and if it wasn't for the chaotic nature of things in her life, running a business could be a great summer gig. It was a huge undertaking and there would be so many important decisions to make. She had spent time arming herself with understanding all the nuances of a recording studio. Her uncle had been her best teacher. The business aspects she would have to learn on the fly. Deedee contemplated her options as she walked out of the elevator.

Walking toward the office of the recording studio, she saw what looked like a confrontation in progress. She couldn't hear what was being said, but things looked pretty explosive. Deedee hurried inside.

She saw Coco and Tina locked in a heated exchange, Tina seated at a receptionist desk, Kim hovering over her. By the time Deedee reached them, the two were having a staring contest. Not a second later, Kim arrived, talking loudly on her cell phone.

"Shyt girlfriend... You done know da deal already! We back doing our thang like the second comin' o' crack!" Kim screamed, giggling into the headphone hanging around her neck.

She waved royally in the direction of Deedee. Then she froze in her tight-jeans, pranced, and flashed a smile. Coco pretending not to have noticed, kept a cold stare on Tina. Meanwhile a smirk was registering at Richter scale–high on Tina's face. Kim's brow furrowed briefly then quickly went to a frown.

"Hmm, hmm...Hold up, sump'n look like it's about to jump-off up in here. Lemme handle biz real quick, and I'll call you right back and shyt. Bye..."

As Kim's cell phone conversation ended, she saw Deedee trying to get Coco's attention, waving a hand in the girl's angry grill.

"All I did was asked her in a nice voice to sign in," Tina said.

"Nah, she ordered me to sign in, yo," Coco countered.

"Shut your face! I told you everybody have to sign in," Tina shouted.

"Alright, okay. That's enough!" Deedee said.

Tina walked away and left Deedee and Coco standing next to each other. Kim was still in earshot.

"What's going on, Coco...?" Deedee asked.

"Miss Recording Artist just came in and been ripping everyone," Kim disdainfully said, walking away.

"Who ask you anything, yo?"

"Coco, do you wanna go get some breakfast?" Deedee offered. "I sure could use some."

"Yeah, let's go real quick, yo. I'm getting kinda sick up in this piece."

"What's the matter?" Deedee inquired with concern.

Coco remained tensely silent. Deedee stared at her best friend for a few beats. She seemed to be caught up in thinking exactly what to say. Coco was finally ready to open her mouth when suddenly they heard loud yapping.

"She be acting like she somebody!" Kim said.

"You right. She can't sing, can't rap. Don't know what the fuck she can do," Tina said.

They were yapping loud enough for Coco and Deedee to hear. The conversation between Kim and Tina was enough for the rekindling. Coco knew they were talking about her. Deedee shook her head and sighed heavily.

"It ain't me so much, yo. It's these bitches, running around here with their stink ass."

Coco's vociferous response caught Deedee off guard. Salvo from Kim and Tina's had been fired in the general direction of Coco.

"They want it? They can bring it, yo!"

The place was about to return to normal office mode, but Coco dropped the proverbial bomb. It was a direct hit. Everyone and everything stopped moving. It was as if she had unplugged the very lifeline of Ascot's recording studio. The only thing lacking was the long beep at end.

Tina, who was popping gum loudly, quickly hung up the phone call she was on. She was the first to respond.

"Shut da front door! No this bitch didn't!"

"Nah, nah, wait a minute, wait a minute. Did this hater-ass, dyke-bitch just call me a bitch...?" Kim asked.

"Hmm, hmm... Oh yes, I think she did," Tina said, sliding over closer from her desk.

"Yeah, I said that, yo. And I do mean, stink bird-ass types, yo," Coco said, nodding, and pointing at Kim and Tina.

They were the two business assistants hired by Eric on the recommendation of his lawyer. Kim and Tina were archenemies of Coco from their days growing up on the same block. Coco was the little wiry girl, with the great voice back then. Having won a talent show, Coco joined the recording studio to work with Eric Ascot, music's hot producer. She took offense at being in the same vicinity with her former foes. Tina, who was sitting at the receptionist's desk, jumped up.

"Shut da fuck up! I know you ain't talkin' to moi...? Cuz that be just one more reason to be up in ya fuckin' ass!" Tina said.

"Nah, nah, nah, bitch, see don't let me start akkin' ig'nant up in here and shyt!" Kim said, looking Coco up and down with the dirtiest of stares.

"You can't even rap you—just a fucking foul-mouth bitch!" Tina said.

"Who you talkin' to, you Spanish ho'?"

"No you didn't! Shit, push come to shove, I'll just say fuck everything and you and me go at it, right here. I'm a bitch of my word," Tina said, coming around the receptionist desk.

Coco met her half way. In a hot second Coco and Tina were again squaring off in each other's face, ready to go at each other.

"We ain't gotta whip her ass right here. Don't forgot bitch, we from da same hood and shyt!" Kim said, stepping into the fracas.

"Alright, everyone take a chill pill, breathe, and fucking relax," Deedee said, interceding.

"Go ahead, yo. You a bitch of your word, right?" Coco said, standing directly across from Tina.

"Don't let this ghetto girl push you to do nothing, Tina. Take her out da hood, but she still don't know how to act..." Kim laughed mockingly.

"Your friend got killed and now you got heavy problems, huh hood bitch?" Tina said.

"Better listen to your bitch, yo!"

"Who you callin' bitch...? Oh God, what's gotten into this bitch? Bitch, I'll set your ass on fire so fast, you'll know what beef is," Kim said, jumping back in the fray.

"Yeah, you got a match, yo? I got a lighter right here," Coco said with a smirk.

She smiled then removed a Bic lighter from her pocket. Taunting Tina and Kim, Coco sparked the lighter.

"Bitch your ghetto-ass be's nobody and shyt..." Kim said,

waving her arm.

"That's real rap. You ain't shit, will never be spit, and your mother is a crack-head bitch!" Tina said, laughing.

She was now standing directly in front of Coco, chuckling cruelly. Deedee watched keenly, flinching at their impious laughter, but she held back. Instead she glared at Kim and Tina. It was clear that Deedee had enough.

"Everyone just shut da ef up!" Deedee screamed waving her arms.

The verbal sparring came to an immediate halt. All the combatants glanced surreptitiously at each other. Coco would not back down. Brazen, she was on high alert and primed for whatever went down. A warrior, she was ready for battle.

All of a sudden, the loud sound of flesh colliding harshly with flesh violently rang. The smacking sound ripped out like quarters hitting an empty collection plate. Tina's cheek stung. She tried lunging at Coco, but Deedee quickly tripped her. She fell in an embarrassed heap on the tiled floor.

"There'll be no fighting here. This is a place of damn business and not some store in y'all's hood!" she said.

Kim wanted to jump, but only harrumphed and helped Tina up. Deedee saw Tina was back on her feet and staring at Coco with blood in her eyes. Deedee stepped in front of Coco then addressed Tina and Kim.

"Look I know y'all don't like each other. But for now y'all gonna have to learn to get along with each other. Comprende...?" Deedee barked and glared at both Tina and Kim.

Tina regained her composure and Kim backed down. The grimace on Coco's face said she was still ready to go.

"Anytime any of you want it, yo just set it I'm ready!"

"Coco, please—" Deedee shouted to Coco.

"Please what...? They started this, Dee."

"There's no need for your outburst— just apologize now and end this ghetto squabble."

"Ghetto what...? A'ight, yo! I'm out," Coco said, walking away. "I came here to record. I ain't gotta put with this shit! Later for this, yo!" she continued toward the exit.

"Coco, I didn't mean to offend you, but we have work that needs to be done around here. And you know my uncle isn't here and someone have to take charge."

"A'ight, yo. Holla at me when your uncle get back up in here. I'm out."

"Coco, look..."

The precocious teen ignored Deedee's attempt to stop her. Coco was coasting to the lobby with her familiar bop, on her way. A young man, rushed in just as Coco was going out the door.

"Hi," he said, and hurried to where Deedee, Tina and Kim were standing.

Coco's outburst had left them dizzy, whirling in the aftershock and trying to comprehend how this had begun. Deedee was scolding Tina and Kim when she noticed the young man standing in front of her.

"What do you want?" Deedee asked, irate.

"Good morning, I'm Reggie Mills and I'm here for the studio engineer position," he said calmly.

Reggie Mills pulled out a copy of his resume. Glancing at Kim and Tina as if he was seeking mercy, he sheepishly handed his resume to Deedee.

"I saw the ad in the new *Vibe* mag and decided to take a chance and—"

"Good for you! Listen I'm kinda busy. Give your resume to Kim and I'll give you a call."

With a glance, Deedee ushered Kim and Tina back to their positions at reception. She quickly started out the door. "Oh yes, and Reggie you can come with us," Kim said.

"Yes, she gotta run after her dyke girlfriend," Tina added dryly. "Oh Coco, you're such a star..."

"That was Coco? The rapper...?"

Tina and Kim stared at Reggie like he had just let out a loud fart. They made gas faces, before continuing.

"I heard about her. She's dope..." he continued, looking around for some type of confirmation.

"Don't get all excited, she ain't all that..." Tina dryly said.

In the lobby, Deedee hopped off the elevator. She was racing by the doorman trying to get the door for her.

"Have a nice day," he said.

Outside Deedee looked around and finally spotted Coco strolling down the busy midtown avenue.

"Coco!" she shouted. "Coco could be soo ghetto," Deedee hissed under breath.

Walking quickly in her direction, Deedee watched Coco come to a stop and turn around. She smoked a cigarette as Deedee hurried to where she stood.

"Please spare me the lecture yo," Coco hissed.

"I wasn't planning on giving you a lecture—although you deserve it," Deedee said, shaking her head.

"A'ight, so then what do you want, yo? I can't fucking work with those bitches."

"I wasn't gonna talk about them bitches, or the fact that you can't be slapping the employees either," Deedee smiled. "I was gonna say what about breakfast? Are you still down?"

"A'ight, I'm hungry as a bitch in heat, yo."

"When you're hungry, you are a bitch in heat."

"Who are you calling a bitch, yo?"

"You..."

"I guess you're a friend. I'll let you get away with that one, yo."

"Yes, please don't slap the taste out of my mouth. Here's a café. They're serving breakfast."

"Let's try here then. I'm mad hungry, yo."

"Yes you are."

"You don't have to agree with everything I say just because you're a friend."

"Yes, I know..."

"You are impossible, yo."

Coco held the door and Deedee walked in with Coco behind her. The smiling maître d waved them to a vacant spot inside the café. The late Monday morning rush was over. Coco and Deedee sat quietly at the table for two, perusing the menu. Coco looked up and stared longingly off into the distance.

Deedee observed her quietly and went back to perusing the menu. After a few minutes, Deedee raised her head and spoke.

"I'm trying, but I don't see anything here that I'd like. What about you?"

Coco cocked her head in a gangster sway. She studied Deedee

for a moment before answering.

"You know all the rappers with 'Big' in their names were dope, but they all died early. There's some science to that, yo."

"What do you mean?"

"You know Big L, Biggie Smalls and Big Punisher...? They were all dope but they all just died real fast, yo."

"I'd never think about something so morbid prior to breakfast. But I got it, you won't name yourself Big Coco in the fear that you're gonna die young, huh...?"

"I'm just saying, those artists... Those rappers were really ill. Soo ill they died real young, yo."

"On second thought, I'll skip the big breakfast and just have some hot chocolate to drink."

"Yeah, I think I'll go for some of that too..."

"That's good we decided on breakfast. Now we've got to decide on working with those two or not."

Coco held a blank stare as Deedee drank from a glass of water, waiting for an answer. She was still in limbo when the waiter returned to take their orders.

"Did you guys decide yet or do you need more time...?" he asked.

"I'll have pancakes with eggs and a hot chocolate," Coco said.

Deedee was surprised by Coco immediately answering his query, but had not responded to hers. A loud sigh escaped her lips before she placed her order.

"Okay, I guess. I'll have another hot chocolate with waffles and strawberries on the side," Deedee said.

The waiter walked away. "Coco are we gonna get to an understanding on how to deal with the issue with the employees? My uncle is locked up and—"

"Yeah right, you were telling me about that before we were rudely interrupted by them hood rats in the studio."

Deedee stared at Coco for a beat, trying to decide where to begin. Coco interrupted Deedee's thoughts.

"So, where the cops rolled up on him, yo?"

"It was yesterday. We went bowling and then we were supposed to visit my father's grave, but Uncle E had to make a stop at the studio. He wanted to get a disk he left in his office. So we went upstairs and I was chillin' in the lounge while Uncle E went to his office. Then it just turned into a nightmare. Coco, there had to be about ten cops. They were all over the studio and then..."

The conversation paused when the waiter arrived with their hot chocolates. He walked away and the girls sipped. Deedee recounted her uncle's arrest.

"Music producer arrested on weapon charge..."

Police following up on anonymous tip found the gun that was involved in the killing of police detective Jim Kowalski. The detective was a six-year veteran and was the lead detective involved in the investigation of the music producer, Eric Ascot.

"And have you seen how every newspaper in the city ran with the story this morning? The police made it up. They want him to be convicted in the media so he won't stand a chance in court. My uncle didn't kill that detective and then bring the gun to back his office. That's so fucking crazy, Coco. I can't even begin to fathom it," Deedee said.

She held Coco's gaze and the two looked at a world they had been introduced to. The loss of her friends had Coco's mind going. And she knew what Deedee had been through. In that moment a connection was made. They both knew it. Coco held Deedee's hand.

"That shit is wild, yo. I mean, damn it, seems like what madukes been saying all along. She always telling me there's a lot of bodies falling. And things ain't always what it seems out in da streets. Five-oh setting up your uncle is just another example, yo."

Deedee took a deep breath before continuing. It was clear as the strain showing on her face. She was deeply concerned about her uncle's fate.

"It gets worse," she said, taking another sip of hot chocolate.

"Say word...?"

"Word, listen to this, I called Sophia—who's supposed to be on my uncle's side, mind you—and she told me, 'Oh it's unfortunate, but I'm afraid I can't help him.'"

"Damn, cut you off like that, why...?"

"I really don't know. Of course she tried to explain why, but yeah, like that."

"That's fucked up, yo. She was just with us after he had gotten knock the last time. What's up with that, yo?"

"Oh she explained, very lengthily, that her job is quote unquote 'with the DA and I do not work for your uncle'. Those were her exact words. She was the woman who was supposed to be marrying my uncle at one point, not so long ago."

"Damn, that's really fucked up. Where did the love go...? She ratchet, yo... I mean she just gonna do him like that? What about the time they were together, yo?"

"I guess that doesn't mean a damn thing. Sophia says her boss told her she had to cooperate with the DA or face disbarment."

"Damn! What you said to her, yo?"

"Coco, I was like, 'Can't help? Honey, you're supposed to be his ex-fiancée and been talking about making up! I was like, 'Whoa. Hold up, sweetheart!' She didn't want to discuss it. She was quick to remind me that my uncle had a criminal attorney. So I've been calling his office and I'm yet to speak with him."

"Damn, yo..."

"I mean of all the people I thought would turn their backs on my uncle, Sophia would not have been one of them."

"I hear you, Dee. She's slipping. They used to be crazy tight. There must be sump'n else behind all this, yo."

The girls sipped in silence for a while.

"I'm telling you Coco. It stinks like a setup, and I'm gonna get to the bottom of it."

"But what are you gonna do, yo?"

"I don't know yet. Got any ideas?"

"Hmm, we could check Rightchus—he used to know everything that goes down, but that nigga dead, yo."

"Didn't he have friends...? Someone he trusted like his girlfriend or maybe family—"

"Matter of fact he did, yo. He had this Puerto Rican chick. She used to go on missions with him, yo."

"Missions...? What kind of missions?"

"Crack-head type... You know, 'Beam me up, Scottie...'"

"Coco, you're being silly. Where can we find this Puerto Rican chick?"

"I think she still comes to my building, her peeps live there."

"Think we should give it a shot? I mean what would she know?"

"True that nigga dead, but he could've told her something. I don't know, yo."

"You're right. It's worth a try. Let's go see her now. This breakfast is taking too long."

"Real talk... It's lunchtime and they still ain't served us breakfast yet, yo.

"Let's go, later for that," Deedee said, standing and gesturing to the waiter.

The girls were about to walk out when the waiter arrived. "Oh, I'm sorry! We're still waiting—we ran out of strawberries," he said.

"Please don't worry yourselves. I'd like to cancel our order. How much do we owe?"

"It's all good. The hot chocolates are on me. Your uncle, he always comes here. Tell him we're all behind him one hundred percent."

"Thanks," Deedee said. "I'll make sure he knows."

They walked out of the café and hurried down to the garage located below the recording studio. The valet quickly handed Deedee a set of car keys, and the girls jumped into Deedee's new car.

"This is your uncle's BM or yours, yo?"

"Oh, that's right. I'm sorry, you were in the hospital and... Anyway, it just totally occurred to me, you haven't seen my new car. Uncle Eric bought it last week for me," Deedee smiled, starting the engine.

"Huh...? Oh shit goddamn. I didn't know, yo."

"Yes, it's a 2004 BMW 545i. I think it's super hot."

"I'm with you on that. This really a dope ride, yo!"

"Uncle Eric gave it to me for my graduation gift."

"This shiny black color is soo fly, yo."

"Metallic black, girl," Deedee smiled, high-fiving with Coco.

"Go girl..." Coco laughed.

"Yes, I really liked the white one too, but they didn't have any in stock. So they gave me this one and when the white one comes in, I can take this one back if I want."

"No, yo, keep this. It's the shit. Haters are gonna die. You better have a good alarm. You can never be too careful, Dee."

"The alarm system is intensely complex. Plus it's got lo-jack through the dealership."

"Yeah, but what about niggas who wanna take your shit cause they think you're a girl and can't defend yourself. I mean you been around long enough to know how niggas be hatin' on a girl who got hers."

Deedee reached inside her Birkin bag and pulled out a small nine millimeter. She pointed the gun and Coco stared in awe.

"I got a little something for them too," Deedee smiled.

"Yeah, please put the gun away. We're safe right here, yo."

"Yeah you right," Deedee agreed, putting away the gun

"Is it loaded—lemme see it, yo?" Coco asked.

She took the small handgun and examined it while Deedee continued talking. "Yes, this car has a remote twelve-play CD changer, TV, and heated seats."

"I meant the gun. I see it is, yo."

"Of course, Coco. Ten rounds in the magazine... Yeah, I think the black one is cool," Deedee said, slipping her Gucci shades on and whizzing through the parking lot.

"The gun or the car, yo...?" Coco asked, quickly passing Deedee the gun.

"The car silly," Deedee laughed, returning the gun to her bag.

They were waiting to join traffic when Deedee pressed a knob, and the top dropped. Coco was visibly impressed when the car went convertible. She smiled when the engine roared with power as Deedee raced into the busy late-morning traffic.

"This shit is awesome, yo. Your uncle..." Coco said, making a circle with her thumb and index finger. "He's mad cool. He really hooked up. You'll be styling going to college, yo."

"That's why I have to do all I can to help him."

"I hear you. Let's go see if Rightchus' girlfriend is hanging in the building. You know a lot of crack heads be in my building and they all know each other, yo."

Deedee thought for a beat and kept driving. She wanted Coco to know that she understood her mother's situation. But Deedee remembered how Coco had slapped Tina, and thought better of it.

"So what's her name?" Deedee gunned the engine and asked.

"Your mother died from drug overdose, right yo?"

"Yeah, cocaine, not crack—"

"What's the difference—it still drug addiction, yo."

"You're right Coco," Deedee said.

She stared ahead and kept driving. Coco eased back in her seat with her arms folded. Deedee bit her lips and without looking at Coco, she spoke.

"My mother died of a drug overdose. The important thing is your mother is still living."

"Yes, but as long as she keeps using crack she's barely living, yo."

"We could help her. She has a chance."

"Yeah, but she always go back to that bullshit, yo."

"I hear you Coco, but you can't give up on her. I gave up on my mother."

"Anyways... fuck all that bullshit, yo," Coco said and was about to light a cigarette.

"Hey you can't be smoking in my car without offering me one."

"My bad, yo," Coco smiled, pulling out another cigarette.

She lit both cigarettes and handed one to Deedee. Pressing a knob, Deedee produced an astray.

"So what's the name of Rightchus' girlfriend?" she asked, taking a puff.

"They call her Tuttie," Coco answered, looking at Deedee.

"Tuttie...?" Deedee asked with a smile. "That's it?"

"Yeah yo, that's it. I really don't know her, but I know who does."

Deedee turned the music on from the control on the steering wheel. A hard-knocking hip-hop beat rang out.

"Aw shit, taking it back old-school style. Blast that Apache shit, yo."

I need a gangsta bitch yo (a gangsta bitch)
I want a gangsta bitch (a gangsta bitch)

"This reminds me of the first time I'd met you, Danielle, and Josephine outside that nightclub," Deedee said. What was the name of it again?"

"Club Deep," Coco answered. "I remembered that night, yo. You were such a geek," she laughed, and Deedee joined in.

"I was. But y'all had been kicked out of Deep, and were outside smoking," Deedee said.

"Yes, then some fools started shooting and we broke out in your uncle Benz."

"Yes, I remembered that night soo well, Coco. Like it was yesterday," Deedee said.

"Me too, we was wilding outside Deep, then you showed up with that nice ride, yo."

The girls' chatter fell silent, each of them replaying that fateful night in their mind.

Coco, her friends, Danielle and Josephine, the crew as she called them, started to walk. They had just been tossed from a jam for teens

thrown by Disco Dave at Club Deep, caught lighting up a blunt. Now they stood around outside, at 23rd and Fifth enviously checking out all the happenings. They watched the party people stepping into the club, some they knew and some they didn't. It really didn't matter; they were outside scheming on getting back inside when headlights hit them.

"Yo, check out that fat Benz," Coco had shouted.

Danielle, Josephine and Coco all made tracks for the corner to take a better look at the sleek black ride.

"Damn! Now that whip is P-H-A-T. Now I could see jacking a nigga for sump'n like that."

Danielle placed her hand under her shirt like she was gonna pull out a gun. They saw Deedee approaching them.

"If this bitch comes out of her face, I'm a have to smack her down."

"You're soo hood, always thinking mean and shit," Josephine said.

"Them security chumps just kick my ass out the club, I could've met some cutie tonight. You think I should be welcoming people and all that, bitch?" Danielle retorted.

Deedee had walked into their bickering before Josephine could answer.

"Can I get a light?"

The driver was a tall and beautiful dark-skinned sister and wore a sexy red DKNY outfit. She popped out from nowhere, scaring the girls. Coco tried to size the girl up as she stepped closer to her. She didn't look like she was a hood-rat.

Is this bitch packing, or can she be jacked? Coco wondered. The girl appeared to be sixteen or seventeen, taller than Coco, but much thinner. If it came down to a fight, Coco was sure she could kick her ass.

"Yo, are you gonna give me a light, or what?"

The girl stood a couple feet from Coco. One hand rested confidently on her hip, and the other held out a cigarette. Coco gazed at her, smirked and decided, She trying to act Ghetto. Moving past the girl, Coco went back to admiring the car.

"Wow this shit's nice! How much does a whip like this cost?" *Coco demanded.*

"Don't ask me," *Deedee replied.* "It's my uncle's, and he's outta town, so I'm driving it this weekend."

"So I know you got a lighter in that whip," *Coco said with a wry smile.* "That shit cost too much cheddar not to have a lighter, yo."

Coco then removed the cigarette dangling from her lips and handed it to the newcomer. The girl lit hers.

"Yeah, but it ain't all that," *Deedee replied, returning Coco's cigarette.* "Have y'all been inside the club yet?"

"Yeah, it's a'ight. But we—"

The conversation ended abruptly as a volley of shots erupted. The blast of the bullets rang out and all the girls hit the dirt, except for the newcomer. She was frozen to her spot. Coco yanked her down.

"If you wanna keep driving this weekend, you better get your black ass down here with the rest of us," *Coco said.*

All of the girls scrambled on their stomachs back to the Mercedes 600. Another volley went off as they raced to get inside the car, slamming the door.

"Shit! Is the whip bulletproof?" *Coco asked.*

"You mean this car? I don't know," *the newcomer said.*

"I think we should be ghost," *Danielle shouted.*

"Yeah, we should definitely be leaving this spot," *Coco agreed.*

The driver put the car in gear and slammed on the accelerator. She barely avoided hitting another car. She swerved wildly to the middle of the street.

"Damn this thing can really fly, yo," Coco exclaimed from her place, riding shotgun. "Oh, um, I'm Coco, and that's Da Crew, Josephine and Danielle."

"I know who y'all are! I mean, I've seen y'all in L.'s last video."

"Yeah, we were in that joint dancing our asses off. But we're coming out with our own style now, yo."

"I'm Deedee..."

"What's up, Deedee? You cool with me. Good looking out on the ride. What kind of biz is your uncle into, yo?"

"Music biz," Deedee smiled. "He's a music producer."

"That's a'ight," Coco smirked, pointing at McDonalds. "Yo, make a left and go through the drive-thru, Deedee. I want me some fries."

"Yeah, I could go for some fries, too," Danielle added. "But what I really want is a chocolate shake."

"I'm with that," Deedee said, turning into the McDonalds entrance. "Y'all wanna chill here or go to the drive-thru?"

"Drive-thru, no doubt, we could be chilling, listening to music and all that." Coco said, checking out the restaurant.

"Ain't no niggas worth sump'n sitting up in there," Danielle said.

Deedee pulled up to the drive-thru window and let her window down.

"Welcome to McDonalds. May I take your order, please?"

"Yeah, let me get four orders of large fries and," Deedee looked back. "And what, four chocolate shakes?"

"Three chocolate shakes and one vanilla," Josephine said.

I got it, y'all," Deedee said, reaching for her wallet.

Pulling out a twenty-dollar bill, she stuck it under the cup.

"Do you have twenty cents so I can give you back a ten?" the cashier asked Deedee.

"Nah, take it out the twenty," Deedee yelled, trying to sound hard.

It was smiles all around. The four girls sat in the car listening to music. Their fries and shakes hit the spot.

"Wu-Tang has mad, mad flavas, yo," Coco said, demanding agreement.

Da crew nodded, but Deedee didn't agree.

"Yeah, too many," Deedee said. Then her eyes met Coco's stare of indifference, and her voice trailed off for a second. But Deedee didn't blink. She continued, "There's too many emcees, and they all wanna let off their rhymes at once."

"Shame on a nigga
Who try to run game on a nigga
Who's buck-wild wid da trigger..."

The lyrics of the Wu vibrated from the car's speakers, and Da Crew nodded their heads to the music. Coco stared at Deedee's manicured nails, resting on the wheel. Besides an occasional glance in the rearview mirror, Deedee kept her eyes on the road. Flashing lights went by as the sound of the police proceeded in opposite direction.

"Do you know much about da business?" Coco asked with that same stare.

For a moment, Deedee thought of elaborating, but decided to wait. Coco continued to stare. She checked out Deedee's features against her dark skin, and decided that Deedee was not an ugly duckling. The Mercedes came to a halt at a red light. The car speakers blared the hype lyrics of "Protect Ya Neck." Deedee lit another cigarette and checked the time. She felt some kind of weird alliance forming with this shotgun.

"What time is it, yo?" Coco asked.

"One forty. It's still early. Anything y'all would like to do?" Deedee smiled, looking at her Gucci.

"Yeah," Coco said, smiling. "Let's rock and roll uptown, yo."

The rest of the girls glanced at her. "We're always downtown. I'm saying let's give Harlem a try, yo."

"A'ight, a'ight, we with all that," Danielle and Josephine shouted in agreement.

Deedee smiled and lifted her foot off the brake and slowly pressed on the gas. The sleek car began to move toward the downtown lane, the sound of the Wu-Tang Clan in tow. Deedee smiled, enjoying the sense of camaraderie. Coco stared straight ahead, nodding her head.

It was a sunny day in the city, and Deedee drove the BMW through midday traffic. Coco was caught up rapping along to the chorus. Both girls reminiscing on the time they first met. Now best friends, they were chilling.

I wanna Gangsta boogie! With my gangsta bitch
I need a gangsta bitch I want a gangsta bitch...

"Things done change," Coco smiled.

"Yes, I agree," Deedee said with a wink.

Deedee glanced at Coco and quietly shook her head, while continuing to drive uptown Harlem.

With the top dropped, Deedee wove through the busy streets to Coco's block in Harlem, and hit the turn signal. Coco strummed an invisible guitar in the passenger's seat.

"Get that spot right there, yo," Coco said excitedly. "You're not gonna see too many spots like this close to my building. It's summer too. These peeps don't know what to do, yo."

Deedee steered the car into a parking spot. It was mid-June and shaping up to be a hot summer. People milled outside the entrance to the apartment building. Kids dressed in shorts and tees jumped double-dutch outside. Others scooted about while others played hopscotch on the sidewalk. Pitchers were posted up in front and fiends darted about trying to score their next hit.

All eyes were on the girls as they stepped out of the new auto. Deedee hit the remote alarm to her car, and kept moving. Most of the crowd stared in admiration at the shine on her ride. Some kept an eye on Coco, her familiar bop immediately identified by regulars and residents.

"Oh, it's Coco. What up, girl?" one of them greeted.

"Keep up the good work, Coco. Your new joint is hot!" Another said.

"I heard your shit on the radio earlier today, Coco. It's hot, Coco," a young teenage boy said, throwing up two fingers in a peace sign.

"Coco, your friend is she a video girl or model?" another inquired.

"I'm neither. I just run things," Deedee said with too much sass.

"This Deedee. She do her thing, yo."

"Hey what's poppin, Deedee? You're a dime. Damn you fine, girl," the young teenage boy smiled. "Those some Gucci heels...? They look real nice on you."

"Hey you..." Deedee said.

"Them heels looks soo nice," a young girl shouted, taking a closer look at Deedee's shoes.

"I didn't know they make shoes like that?" another young girl asked.

"Where you buy those at?" another girl asked. "That's that Donna Karan sarong skirt I like too."

"Coco, I like your new song," someone commented.

"I can't wait for you to finish your album, Coco. That's gonna be a chart topper," another person said.

Greetings were shouted at the talented teen and Coco gracefully returned the favors. She nodded and offered daps to all. Deedee walked by Coco's side, smiling and nodding at the people milling in front of the building.

"Wow, Coco, they were really showing you mad love," Deedee said when they were inside the building.

"But don't let them smiling faces fool you. Some of them same smiles could be waiting to jooks you," Coco said.

Deedee nodded knowingly as the elevator arrived. The girls hopped inside. Coco pressed the button and they rode it in silence. The girls got off on the third floor, and walked a couple of feet down a hallway littered with overnight trash. Coco opened the apartment door she shared with her mother.

"Let's see what it is with madukes, yo."

The girls entered the apartment, and inside the place reeked of cigarette smoke. Her mother seemed dazed sitting in front of the television with a grinning man. He was also smoking and laughing while *Sanford and Son* played loudly on the television. Coco guided Deedee to the kitchen and signaled to her mother.

"Ma, can I bother you for a second, please," Coco said, opening the refrigerator door. "See what I'm talking 'bout, yo," she said to Deedee, while pointing to a couple of forty ounce bottles sitting in the refrigerator.

"Hello Miss Harvey," Deedee greeted the emaciated woman walking into the kitchen.

Coco was still inside the refrigerator with the door wide open. She was unaware that her mother had walked into the kitchen.

"Why must you be in the refrigerator so long, Coco? What're you looking for? And what's up with this 'yo' biz? I told you before, not in my house, Coco."

"Ma, why you gotta be up here with him...? And what's soo funny? Y'all laughing like you haven't seen that episode of *Sanford And Son* six times already?"

"What I chose to do with my time, Coco is my biz. You just worry about what you gotta do. Didn't you leave outta here talking 'bout you gotta go to the recording studio to work on a song...? What happened to that? Hello to you too... Ah..."

"Deedee," Coco said.

"Deedee...? I ain't talking 'bout no damn Deedee. I said, didn't you leave here going to a recording studio? Now you're back checking up on me and talking 'bout some damn Deedee. What's the matter with you, child? You think you're grown, but you just lost all your sense or what? You must think I'm a fool or sump'n?"

"Ma, I didn't say you're a fool. I just don't like that man. He be up here giving you crack, yo—"

"I'm not your damn 'yo'! I'm gonna slap that street lingo outta your filthy mouth if I gotta say it again. I'm your mother," Ms. Harvey said to her daughter. Then she turned to her male guest and shouted, "Dontay, get over here!"

The man went from smiles to hobbling into the kitchen. He nodded to Deedee and Coco while licking his lips lecherously.

"Hey, how y'all doing...?"

"Hi, how are you?" Deedee greeted.

Coco turned her head and stared out the window without acknowledging the man. His smile had completely faded. Miss Harvey hit Coco with her coldest stare before speaking.

"Dontay, have we been smoking any drugs up in here?" Miss Harvey bellowed.

"No, no, we been drinking a few brews and watching TV, that's all..."

"Get Dontay outta here," Coco said in an angry outburst. "I can see it in his eyes that he's straight up lying—"

"Coco, do not show out your lil' damn self and disrespect my guests!" Miss Harvey shouted, cutting Coco off.

Deedee went over and stood by Coco. She attempted to touch the angered teen, but when Coco turned away she thought better.

"Dontay, please excuse me. Lemme straighten sump'n out with my daughter, and I'll call you later," Miss Harvey said.

"Can I get my half of the beer before I go?"

"Here," Miss Harvey said, charging to the refrigerator, and getting the bottle. "Take this and get the fuck up outta Dodge," Miss Harvey continued, throwing the bottle at Dontay.

He grabbed it before the bottle could hit the floor. Then Dontay turned, stormed out of the apartment, slamming the door behind him.

"Don't slam my door, you fucking rat!" Miss Harvey shouted. "Back to you Miss Coco, why you think you can come up here with the attitude disturbing my peace of mind with your false accusations, huh?"

"Cuz..."

"Cuz what?"

"Cuz I don't like that man around you. He's a known crack head and he'll have you doing that shit again, that's cuz."

"Oh really, is that it?"

There was a long pause. It was as if Coco's words had sucked the air from the place. Deedee stared at Miss Harvey and Coco tilted her head toward the window. She saw the hustlers plying their trade and customers running back and forth. Coco turned her gaze away and stared at her mother. The strain showed on her face.

"I don't wanna lose you, mom," she said, with tears stinging her eyes.

"You're not going to, sweetheart," Miss Harvey said.

Deedee watched with tears welling in her eyes. Miss Harvey was hugging her distraught daughter.

"You're concerned for nothing, Coco. You just worry 'bout going to school and being somebody. Your mommy will be just fine... A'ight?" Miss Harvey pulled away and smiled. "Isn't that how y'all say it...?

"Mom, you know they killed Rightchus—"

"Girl, whatcha saying? Rightchus done packed up and moved to South Carolina."

"What?" Coco and Deedee echoed in unison.

The girls stared at each other in disbelief. Not knowing what to think. This information was new and they both realized that it would have them rethinking this caper.

"I heard Tuttie in her own words saying how he was a changed man, been going to church, and all that."

"Mom, are you serious? I mean he was supposed to have been shot and now you said his girlfriend said?"

"I didn't say 'his girlfriend.' Don't put words in my mouth. I said Tuttie said he was in some parts of South Carolina."

Coco glanced at Deedee and then back at her mother. She seemed to be fighting doubts about what was revealed by her mother. The older woman quickly added.

"If you don't believe me, go ask her. She lives on the fifth floor, 5G," Miss Harvey said.

Again Coco glanced at Deedee and waited before she heard her mother's words.

"Oh go ahead. Go ahead. You'll see that I'm not lying."

"What floor?"

"Fifth floor, Coco..."

"C'mon Dee, let's go," Coco said, grabbing Deedee by the arm.

"Bye, Ms. Harvey," Deedee said on the run behind Coco.

"Coco, I know you're nosey and all, but don't go up there getting me involved in no she-say bullshit. Just ask in a polite way. Okay?"

They were already out the door and making their way up the stairs, as Coco's mother called out. The girls paused in the stairwell to chat.

"Why didn't you just come out and ask your mom straight up about Rightchus' chick?" Deedee asked.

"Cause I know my mother well and I knew if I made her start guilt trippin', she'd tell me everything. Otherwise, she'd be cursing me out. Like, 'Why you wanna know?' So this way, I'm in charge and she not only gave up the info, but she actually told me to go see for myself. Now when I go and check, if it is the way she said it was then she thinks she's earned my trust. It's that crack head mentality, yo. I've learned that game."

The girls reached the fifth floor and Coco opened the door to the hallway and searched for the right apartment.

"They get good service on this floor. Hallway is cleaned and the lights are working," Deedee said changing the subject.

"You see that too, yo," Coco said, before ringing a doorbell. "I'm telling you these owners are shady..."

They immediately heard the rattling of locks from behind the door. Then slowly a young child opened the door and said, "Hello, can I help you?"

Before the girls could answer, there was a sound of hurried footsteps and an inquiring adult voice in the background. "Who is it?"

"Hi, we're looking for Tuttie. Is she here?" Deedee said.

"What for...? Who're y'all?"

"We ah..." Coco began but Deedee cut her off.

"I'm trying to find her to ask her about something that Rightchus could've—"

"You got the wrong apartment. I don't know no Rightchus. Who are you, po-po or sump'n? No, I recognize you. You that chica from downstairs... You a rapper..."

"You are Tuttie, right?" Deedee asked.

"No, I don't know who fuck Tuttie is, and I don't know nobody by that name."

Other occupants came out of their room and descended on Coco and Deedee. Six pairs of eyes appeared with cold and inquisitive stares.

"It's that rapper chick from the building, Tee-tee," a young boy said, pointing to Coco.

"Mind your business!"

The cutting order was direct. Both Coco and Deedee stared at each other momentarily assessing the situation.

"I'm Deedee and this is Coco," Deedee said.

"So what ya want?" the young Latina woman asked.

"I came here looking for help. I wanted to know if anyone knew Rightchus..."

"You po-po?" the boy asked, gazing Deedee up and down.

"I told you to mind your business already," the Latina woman said, looking agitated.

She shot the young boy a cold glance before directing her focus back to Coco and Deedee. Two older Spanish women stood silently behind the young Latina woman.

"Why are you here?" the Latina woman spat in disgust.

"I'm here trying to help my uncle get out of... uh, trouble," Deedee said.

"What uncle...? Who are you? I don't know you or your uncle."

Deedee paused for a beat trying to diffuse the situation. During the quiet—that seemed like too long a pause—Coco glanced casually at Deedee, trying to catch her attention. But Deedee's eyes were riveted at the angry-looking young woman. Deedee sensed that the young Latin woman's rage was getting hotter and every second was slipping by, but she didn't see Coco winking at her.

"Trouble...?"

"I'll pay you for—"

"Pay...? How much?" the boy asked.

"Didn't I tell you already that this ain't none of your fucking business, huh?" the Latina screamed at the young boy.

She turned and stared the kid down. Then she turned her focus on the two older women. The daggers coming from her green eyes chased the rest of the household gathered behind her.

"That's none of your business. Go back to y'all's rooms," she bellowed.

They could have been family members the way they seemed interested, gaping at Deedee and, every now and then, glancing at Coco. Deedee breathed a sigh of relief when they all walked away. The person left standing was a petite, light-skinned Spanish woman. Seemingly like the person Coco had earlier described when they had talked about Righteous' girlfriend. The woman's green eyes darted about the room then she focused on Deedee. When she was sure that all the others had left the room she addressed the girls.

"Why didn't you say that at first? We know Rightchus. I'm Tuttie," she smiled. "I thought y'all were the police, but... You said money's involved, right?"

Her eyes were beaming when Deedee nodded positively reaffirming her query. There was a collective sigh of relief. Coco,

Deedee and Tuttie were left alone. Tuttie waved to the plastic-covered sitting area. Coco and Deedee followed her lead and sat down next to her.

"Me and Rightchus go way back," she offered. "I ain't his girl or nothing like that. We were just cool like that. You know? He be telling me a lot of things. I ain't the type to snitch out anyone. So you already know how I feel."

Coco and Deedee nodded, looking at the young woman. They were busy looking around at the plastic-covered décor when the woman spoke.

"So how much you willing to pay...? Rightchus told me before he left the city that a whole lot of peoples wanted him dead. So whatever info he had told me must be worth some kind a change. I like your outfit."

"Thank you," Deedee smiled. "Ah Tuttie, why don't I buy you an outfit just like this, and give you a few dollars to go with it...?"

"Okay, that sounds good. I'm not greedy," Tuttie said.

"I've gotta go and get the money," Deedee said.

"I'll have all that info for you when you come back with the dress and some nice shoes," Tuttie said, smiling.

Coco and Deedee hurried out the apartment door, closely followed by Tuttie.

"I'll see you in a few," Deedee said.

"Okay, I'm petite small...six-seven..."

"Okay," Deedee said.

Coco nodded at Tuttie and walked toward the stairs. Deedee quickly followed behind her. They walk down a few flights before Coco spoke.

"Didn't you see me winking when you mentioned money, yo?"

"No I didn't," Deedee answered taking her time down the

stairs. "I was too busy looking at Tuttie. Why what were you trying to say?"

"I was trying to tell you not to give that crack head any money. But then you already did."

"I have not given anyone money, yet," Deedee countered. "She liked my dress and I told her I'd get her one."

"That shit cost some cheddar. It's one of them high-end joints, right, yo?"

"Nothing but the best, Coco."

"That's what I'm talking 'bout, yo. You might as well give her the five bills cuz that's about what a dress like that cost. And you offering her more dough, plus you gonna buy the shit for her. I heard of philanthropy, but I think this is crazy, yo.

The girls walked down the stairs and stopped in the lobby. Deedee turned to Coco and smiled softly.

"Coco, you know all the street angles, but let me handle this my way," Deedee said, looking directly at Coco.

It had been two years since they had met and a lot had gone down between them. Through the bad times and unpleasant happenings, Deedee and Coco had formed a strong bond even though they were standing at opposite ends of the economic scale. Coco was streetwise and hip to all the ways of the hood. Deedee had been living in grand style with her uncle who was deep in money. Coco was concerned that Deedee flaunting money opened herself to being hoodwinked.

"A'ight, yo. As long as you know what you doing," Coco said, throwing her hands up.

"Trust me, Coco. I do."

"Okay, yo."

They stood in front of the heavy, transparent plastic walls of the building's lobby. Coco and Deedee could see the exterior, and the street. Deedee spotted a couple of kids sitting on her new car. She pushed the door and quickly exited. Using the remote starter, she turned the ignition on. The car engine roared startling the teens. They remained sitting on the new car, looking around in surprise. Deedee hurriedly made her way to her new car.

"Please get y'all ass off my car," she ordered.

The kids all glanced yawningly up at her. They gave her the once over and smiles replaced frowns. Then they slowly got off the car.

"You fine, ma," one of them complimented.

"Thank you," Deedee said, getting inside. "Are you rolling?" She asked Coco.

Coco was standing behind her, nodded to the guys, and jumped into the car. Checking her rearview mirrors, Deedee peeled off.

"You don't need me to go to the bank with you, do you?"

"I don't have to go the bank. I just need you to come along to see what I'm gonna do. Catch my drift?"

"A'ight, I feel you. Do your thing, yo."

Coco was standing next to her when Deedee paid the cashier thirty bucks for the knockoff dress. She bought Krazy glue and they started back to the car. The green sarong dress was a dead ringer to the one Deedee was currently wearing which was valued at three hundred dollars. Coco smiled and nodded to Deedee. Later they jumped into the car and Deedee asked Coco to remove the original label from the dress and switched it to the knock-off using Krazy glue. Coco was laughing when Deedee peeled off again.

"I guess you're really not going to the bank, yo."

"You got it, Coco. Now I'll give Tuttie twenty dollars and she'll tell me all I need to know."

"Okay, I feel you, yo."

"Coco, I told you, I needed you to come along with me to see what I'm gonna do. Catch my drift?" Deedee laughed.

The girls slapped high five and their laughter boomed louder. Coco glanced at Deedee smiling, bobbing and weaving through traffic. In a hurry to get back the source with the information to help her uncle, Deedee drove faster than usual.

"A'ight, I feel you. Do your thing, yo," Coco said, admiring how Deedee had grown.

She was so much smarter than the girl she had met nearly two years ago. Deedee was now using street tricks. It was a step up and Coco laughed.

"You turned into a con artist, huh? Let me find out you got game, yo."

Deedee parked the car in front of Coco's building. There was a small crowd of people along with the same group of boys from earlier that the girls had encountered sitting on the car.

"You could leave the key. I'll watch it for you."

Deedee strutted past the group while Coco was busy glad-handing with other friends. She didn't see one of the teens that had been sitting on the car walk menacingly toward Deedee. She along with everyone else was surprised by Deedee's response.

"Nigga if you don't get outta my face, I'll shoot you!"

The chilling warning rang disturbingly clear in the friendly atmosphere. For a moment there was enough tension as everyone stared at Deedee. Ignorance brought confusion and someone pulled out a gun.

"You ain't gon' shoot anyone!" the pistol holder said, confronting Deedee.

"Let's all chill, yo," Coco said, getting between Deedee and the guy holding the pistol. "This my girl, y'all peeps. What's up...?"

"What's up with your girl, Coco?"

"She's overreacting. You guys can't overreact. Everything's good, yo. She ain't got no gun."

"You mean she just running her mouth? A'ight..."

The situation became calmer and everyone seemed to share a collective sigh of relief. The guy holding the pistol put away his gun.

"No harm no foul," he said, walking away.

Coco and Deedee continued into the building. They were inside the lobby before Coco spoke.

"Dee, you gonna have to know when to chill, yo."

"I do have a gun and I would've shot his ass right there, if he would've tried anything," Deedee said. "Coco, you're sleeping on me, girlfriend."

They took the elevator to the fifth floor and rang the bell of Tuttie's apartment. Coco stared in disbelief at Deedee. She was silent through the exchange once the door was answered. Deedee took charge.

"Hi, is Tuttie home?"

"Ma, it's the model and the rapper," the kid screamed.

"Coco and Deedee," Deedee smiled.

Tuttie hurried to the door and invited the girls inside. They walked to the same corner of the living room, and Deedee went into action.

"Here's the dress as promised and here's your twenty dollars," she said, removing the knock-off item from a fake shopping bag.

Tuttie took the dress and immediately checked the label. She saw the price tag and hugged the dress to her petite frame. She smiled and spun around as if she was dancing in the dress.

"I know this dress cost a lot but can I have forty dollars instead of the twenty?"

Coco and Deedee stared her down for a minute. Deedee sighed and pulled out forty dollars. Tuttie pulled out a piece of paper with two out-of-state numbers scribbled beneath Rightchus' name.

"You can reach him at these numbers," Tuttie said. He's living in Charlotte, South Carolina."

Coco and Deedee looked at each other. Coco shrugged her shoulders. Deedee saw the frowns of doubt on Coco's face. It made her pause and she wondered about Coco's concerns. Batting her long eyelashes in rapid succession, Deedee passed a signal to Coco.

"Do we know if these numbers are real, and not some fake-ass digits, yo?" Coco smirked.

"Uh-huh, and when I call these numbers and they don't work, I can't reach you," Deedee added. "Where can I reach you Tuttie?"

"I'm a real woman. I don't play games. Those are the numbers I used when I last spoke to him about a week or so ago. Just call me if you don't reach him. Here's my number," Tuttie said, scribbling down a telephone number on the piece of paper.

Deedee took the piece of paper, gave Tuttie two twenties. She strutted out the apartment with Coco and the information. They skipped down the stairs, laughing. When Coco and Deedee hit the lobby, they burst out laughing. Hitting the street, Deedee waved at the guys who were previously sitting on her car.

They got in the car and Deedee drove away. A few blocks later, she felt the rattling on the outside of the car. They were at an intersection and Deedee was about to pull over when a passerby pointed at her tire.

"I think you got a flat, Miss," he said walking away. "Nice car."

"No shit!" Deedee said, getting out of the car. "Oh no Coco, I know one of them niggas from your block punctured my tire."

Coco got out of the car and walked to where Deedee stood at the rear of the car. They both were standing there shaking their heads when along came a man. He was shabbily dressed and unshaven. Cautiously, he made his way to Coco and Deedee.

"I don't mean to offend you and all, but it seems like you got a flat and I could help you for a small fee."

It was six in the evening, but Deedee stared at the man like he had showed up at midnight. A frown immediately descended on her already rankled forehead.

"Thanks but no thanks," she shot back. Pulling out her cellphone, she said, "I got roadside assistance, and I don't need no bums messing with my car. Furthermore, you could be the one going around messing with—!"

"Chill, yo," Coco said, jumping between Deedee and the man. "Lemme holla at you a for few, yo."

Coco grabbed Deedee by the arm and pulled her away from the man. He glanced at the girls and backed up, waving.

"Take your time," he said. "Can I get a cigarette?" he added when he saw Coco lighting up.

The girls had walked away to the other side and shared a cigarette. Deedee was on her cell phone calling for roadside assistance.

"It's gonna take a whole damn hour just to get here," she said.

"Let homie over there do it, yo. He might be able to... Plus you hit that nigga with like twenty dollars and no one will ever puncture your tire in the hood ever. He's gonna be looking out for life, yo."

"Okay, Coco, I'm gonna take your advice and we'll see," Deedee answered.

Once the man went into the motions of doing the job, Deedee felt more comfortable. Leaving him alone with Coco, she walked away. Deedee pulled out the paper with Rightchus' number scribbled on it, and dialed. Someone answered on the third ring. Putting Deedee on hold, the person set off to get Rightchus. Deedee waited with the phone to her ear. She watched Coco talking with the man. When she heard Rightchus voice on the other end, Deedee waved for Coco.

"I'm telling you I don't have any family in New York...Hello, Deacon Rightchus here..."

Deedee put the call on speaker. Before speaking, Coco nodded, affirming that it was Rightchus on the other end.

"Rightchus, I mean Deacon Rightchus this is Coco, what's really good?"

"I don't have any relatives by the name of Coco," Rightchus said.

The girl looked in amazement at each other. Then all they heard was the sound of dial tone. Coco and Deedee laughed.

"No he didn't just hang up on us."

"Yes, he most certainly did, yo."

Deedee tried calling back and both numbers rang and rang. No voicemail and she couldn't leave a message. Frustrated, Deedee put away her cell phone. By then, the man had finished changing the tire. He was smoking a cigarette he had bummed off Coco.

"You did a good job. How much I owe?" Deedee asked.

"Give me ten," he modestly said.

"Give him a tip too, yo."

"I think ten is good enough," Deedee pulled out the ten spot.

She handed it to the man. He bowed gracefully, and was turning to walk away. Deedee pulled out another fifteen dollars and handed it to the grateful man. He waved a couple times and disappeared.

"You saw how quickly he did that?"

"Hmm, hmm, I was here, yo."

"That leads me to thinking that he might just be the one going around messing with peoples' cars, puncturing the tires and all that..."

"I hear you, yo. On the street, there's a racket for everything. You want it the streets got it for you. All you need to do is want it badly enough, yo."

Deedee drove back to the office and parked. They made their way inside the building. The doorman was still there ready to stare.

"This nigga always staring at my ass," she said, standing in the lobby.

The girls were waiting for an elevator, but the doorman was still in earshot. He got up and took another lecherous peep.

"That muthafucka on some pervert shit, yo."

They got on the elevator and went upstairs. Inside the studio, they saw Tina and Kim sitting at the receptionist desk. Without saying anything Coco bopped through the hall, and went into the office. Deedee stopped to speak with Kim and Tina.

"Who da hell she thinks she is and shyt...?" Kim asked.

"She's Coco," Deedee smiled, handing Kim recent copies of *Vibe* magazine. "How's everything going so far?" she asked.

"So far so good. We took Reggie Mill's application and told him to come back," Kim said.

"Your uncle called. He said to give him a call when you get back," Tina said.

"My uncle called? You should've told me that first!" Deedee said running off to the office.

"Uncle Eric is out," Deedee said to Coco who was already in the office.

Coco watched her as she grabbed the phone and started dialing. In the quiet studio office, the phone rang loudly. Every chime seemed to pound as fast as Deedee's heartbeat. Her skinny dimpled cheeks moved in anticipation of the conversation. It ranged through to his cellphone. Deedee left a message.

"Uncle E, it's Dee... I'm very happy to hear the news. Please call me back..." Deedee said.

She hung up, pulled out the piece of paper, and dialed Rightchus' number on the office phone. The phone rang and Deedee eased herself into the big office chair.

"This Ascot Studio calling me? It better be for a recording contract. But wait, I've gotta tell you and I hope you're not disappointed. I don't do gangsta rap anymore...None of that street stuff glorifying drugs—I only do religious-type music...I got me a new faith and belief in the Almighty, who has blessed me with another day to serve him..."

Rightchus answered and spoke without taking a breath. Deedee held the phone and quietly switched it to speaker.

"Recording contract, yo...?"

"Oh no, Coco is that you stalking me... I'm gonna have to get an order from the court blocking you. I hear you poppin and all that, but your sinful lifestyle don't really hold my interest. I'm a changed man, and I'm gonna have to hang up this—"

"We aren't talking recording contract, we're talking money..." Deedee hinted.

There was a long pause. Coco smiled and gave Deedee the thumbs up. The sound of money still made Rightchus's ears ring. He was fumbling for words when he finally spoke.

"I don't know, but what kind of money you talking 'bout?"

"Real money, my man," Coco and Deedee hummed.

They were fully aware that Rightchus was glowing. He was totally hooked when he eagerly blurted, "When can I get this money...? What do you want to include me for...?"

"You may be able to help my uncle," Deedee said and continued to explain the situation to Deacon Rightchus, formerly Shorty-Wop.

Coco smiled when Deedee closed the deal at a reasonable amount of dollars. She knew that Rightchus would do anything for a dollar. He agreed to come back and meet secretly with the girls when the money reached him. He gave his mailing address and got off the call. Satisfied that everything was going well, Coco and Deedee were left smiling. Deedee dialed her uncle's number, and it rang until she heard his voice.

"Uncle E...Yeah! We're at the studio...Coco and I... We'll wait until you get here... See you soon."

"Hey, Uncle E!" Coco shouted.

She hung up, wearing a huge smile. Coco walked over and hugged the clearly overjoyed Deedee. They slapped high fives, and exhaled in the celebration of Eric Ascot's release from jail.

"You know what Coco...?"

"What Dee...?"

"I think we're gonna solve this shit," Deedee confidently said.

"I hear you, yo."

"I'm gonna send Rightchus the price he's asking."

"I thought he was dead...Think we can trust that con man, yo?"

"I don't know, but we gotta give it a shot."

"Rightchus be all up in everybody's biz. He might be worth it, yo."

The girls bumped fists. Coco sat down while Deedee dialed Western Union. The money Rightchus had requested was a reasonable sum she could easily afford. Even if the information obtained led nowhere, Deedee convinced herself that she was doing it on behalf of her uncle. If she was in trouble, Deedee could rest assured that he would have made any sacrifice to alleviate it. The money would reach Rightchus overnight and he would call Deedee as soon as it was received. Deedee had questions and figured Rightchus may provide the answers. As Coco sat down, she caught sight of the *Vibe* magazine.

"Oh you're gonna cherish that issue," Deedee smiled.

"Why, yo...?"

"Keep reading."

"A'ight already, yo—"

Coco delved into the different articles in the magazine. Skipping through pages, she kept on eyeing Deedee. After searching through the pages of *Vibe*, she made a startling discovery and Coco screamed in delight.

"Oh shit! They wrote about me, yo!"

Eric Ascot parked his Benz inside the garage and smoked a cigarette while walking to the midtown building that housed his recording studio. He had vowed to stop smoking, and had not taken a puff in a couple years. Then all the problems started. As he puffed, he reminisced about the pact he had made with Busta. It had cost Busta his life, and now it was threatening to curtail Eric's own freedom. Maybe he should have cooperated with the police investigation when Deedee was raped, when his brother was killed and Deedee's mother mysteriously vanished. His thoughts were churning loudly again.

Eric stopped on the corner of the busy midtown intersection. Wearing a blue Armani suit with a tan shirt and blue tie, he could easily pass for another businessman. Eric was unnerved by the level of trouble caused by the accusations that swirled around him. He wanted it all to go away but knew he had to pay. Staring at the building, Eric knew he had the resources. Shaking his head, he threw the cigarette away, and walked into the lobby. Then the security personnel greeted him.

"Good evening, Mr. Ascot. Good to see you, sir," the man said.

Eric Ascot stared at him for a good minute before speaking. Then he said, "If any police come to this building to see me, I don't care if you have to use your cellphone. You call my office and let me know."

"Those cops—when they came here the last time, they just barged in. They didn't tell me where they were going," the man answered.

"Oh, really...?"

"Yes, really, Mr. Ascot. I had no clue."

"Then why did you question me about how long I was gonna be in my office?"

"It was a Sunday and the building supervisor requested that we find out."

"Only on Sundays, huh...?"

"Sometimes on holidays, too," the man said.

Eric stared at him for a moment until he heard the bell announcing the arrival of an elevator. He got on quickly, leaving the man staring at him. Sitting down at his desk, the doorman picked up a phone and dialed quickly.

"He went upstairs to the studio," he said then hung up.

The nattily attired Eric Ascot got off the elevator and walked into the studio. Tina and Kim were both wide-eyed.

"Hey, how are you ladies doing?" he asked going by them.

"Fine, thank you, Mr. Ascot," they echoed.

"Wow you're looking really good," Kim whistled.

Eric smiled and kept walking, wondering whether they were also part of this conspiracy or not. He needed a break, he thought, as he continued to his office.

"See that's how things go when you have a well-connected lawyer," Tina winked at Kim.

"And when you're well paid and shyt," Kim smiled.

Walking into his office, he was greeted with a huge hug from Deedee. Eric returned the embrace while Coco, who stood apart from them, was smiling. He motioned for her to join them.

"C'mon over here Coco...Group hug," Eric said.

"I know you were only gone for a minute, but you were sorely missed, yo."

"Are you insinuating that I wasn't doing a good job?" Deedee laughed.

"No, I'm just saying...I'm happy that Mr. Ascot is out and..."

"Uncle E. to you..." Deedee laughed, and they all shared the joke.

It was a good moment. An album deal was part of the prize for a singing talent competition Coco had won. She was the only surviving member of her group, Da Crew. First Danielle then Josephine was no longer in the picture. She stood with Deedee and embraced Eric. He was a successful music producer and was about to launch Coco's music career. It was a moment she had been working to achieve. While huddled together, Coco could hear Deedee uttering a prayer.

"Thank you, God, for bringing us all together again... Amen."

"Okay, let me go over some paperwork and we'll go out to dinner. Everyone's down...?" Eric asked, glancing at Coco and Deedee.

"I'm cool with that, yo."

"Then you got—ah, we got ourselves a date," Deedee smiled.

Eric sat in his office chair and checked his phone messages.

Deedee went to get his mail from the reception area. Coco sat down and continued reading *Vibe*. A few minutes later Deedee walked in with a small stack of mail.

"Thanks Dee," Eric said.

"You're welcome," she said, walking toward Coco.

"Oh-ma-God! Did you see this? Have you seen this, yo?"

Coco jumped up again, pointing to the magazine. Deedee had a wry smile on her face. Ascot was listening intently to his messages and didn't seem fazed by Coco's outburst. He had seen it all before with Deedee.

"The piece written about you in *Vibe* magazine...?" Deedee smiled. "I reacted just like you did when I first saw it," Deedee said.

"Oh, but this mad cool, yo. I'm gonna be recognized for doing my thing. I love it, yo."

She was hugging Deedee and dancing around to an imaginary beat. Eric sat at his desk, watched and laughed while listening to his messages.

"That's great!" Eric shouted. "The budget has been approved. Ladies, let's go celebrate," he excitedly announced.

Later when they left the studio, Eric rode in the back seat of Deedee's car, and Coco sat upfront with Deedee. They drove across town to Sardi's to chow down on some of the city's finest steaks. Inside the restaurant, Eric glad-handed with the owner, and they were immediately seated.

"Always good to see you and your lovely niece, Eric," the portly Italian man said, pumping Eric's hand. "And you have one other guest...?"

"Yes, this is Coco, a future star," Eric smiled, nodding at Coco.

"Very beautiful, nice to meet you Coco," the man said to Coco. He turned to waiter. "Bring him a glass of our best," the man said, waving.

"Bring me the bottle," Eric laughed. I'm not driving tonight."

When they had all settled at the table, a bottle of wine arrived. The waiter carried three glasses, and was about to pour, but Eric stopped him.

"Hold on. I'll pour my own and you can leave the bottle," After putting away the other glasses, he turned to Coco and said, "What kind of soda are you having, Coco? I know Deedee drinks 7 Up."

"We can have alcohol. We graduated from high school, yo."

"Not under my watch," Eric laughed. "Like I was saying, what flavor soda...?"

Later when they were finished eating, the three diners sat back and relaxed. They engaged in after-dinner chatter, and Eric kept drinking wine.

"You know I got this movie thing that I'm working on and earlier I found out it was a go," Eric said. "I was thinking of giving the both of you a part in it."

"Oh, that sounds real cool!" Deedee immediately said. "I think that's really huge."

Deedee was clearly excited, Coco seemed more reserved and reacted more in disbelief. Eric saw through her insecurities.

"It's gonna be titled, *Angels at the Gate,* and I need two female leads—teenagers like both of you. So basically you'd be playing yourselves. Young teenage girls with an urban background...facing crucial, life-changing decisions..."

"Hmm that definitely sounds like us. Don't you think Coco?"

"Yeah, but I've never acted before, yo," Coco said, looking at Eric. "But I guess it couldn't be that hard being me."

"Exactly... Now you're seeing the picture. I didn't plan it this way, but this is how it worked out. Perfect, we'll do the paperwork later."

"This seems all like a dream, yo. So I guess that means I'm gonna be a movie star, yo."

"I think we could have a drink to that, Uncle...?"

"Yes, sure we'll definitely have a drink to that," Eric laughed.

The girls were excited and smiling. Deedee looked on in disbelief as her uncle filled two glasses with ice-cold water, and one with wine.

"Here drink this—it'll wash down all that food you just ate, and it's great for digestion too. Here's to good health and success."

Their frowns quickly changed back into broad smiles, and Coco and Deedee raised their glasses of water. They clinked in toast with Eric's wine glass.

"To the movies," he said with a relaxed grin.

"Here, here..." Coco and Deedee chimed.

"I can't believe that we're gonna be in a movie, Coco," Deedee said, walking into the studio.

"I can't believe I'm gonna be in a movie called, *Angels at the Gate*. I'm no angel, yo. What am I gonna do—fly around all day?"

"So we'll be flying around all day," Deedee said.

"I may not be an angel, but I can always act like one, yo," Coco laughed.

They walked by the receptionist area where Kim and Tina were sitting. Deedee waved and Coco held her head straight ahead. If looks could kill Kim and Tina would be on murder charges. Their cold stares send daggers at Coco's back.

"She ain't fly," Kim whispered to Tina.

"Shut da front door. The boss' niece is real fly. She can brag, but the other one ain't nothing but a ghetto girl," Tina said.

"Did you ever hook her mother up and shyt, like you said you would?" Kim asked.

"I sure did. Check this out; I turned her ass over to that crack head Dontay. I gave him three pieces of rock and told him to hook her ass up for real," Tina said and the both laughed.

"You are soo sick with it," Kim laughed.

"Dontay, you know he got game and he gonna bring that ghetto girl's momma some o' that special K, and fuck her ass raw," Tina chuckled.

"But he got the monster. His days are numbered..."

"Shut your face! So what...? If her mommy wanna give him some pussy after he tighten her up with some jumbo, who is to blame...?" Tina questioned.

"Hey...No one, I guess," Kim said.

The two receptionists laughed. They nodded at each other and went back to the business at hand.

Meanwhile Ms. Harvey heard her doorbell ringing and she quickly got to it. She was expecting his arrival and immediately opened the door to her apartment. When he walked in and shut the door, she smiled eagerly.

"We can't smoke here, Dontay. School's out for the summer and my daughter could walk in at any time," she said, leading him through the apartment and to her bedroom. "I don't want her to catch me smoking rocks."

"We can't smoke?" Dontay asked, opening his hand and

showing her the two pieces of crack.

"Oh hell yeah, and these look really nice," Ms. Harvey said, grabbing the rocks.

"One is for you, and the other we can smoke."

She hurriedly retrieved her pipe and torch from the closet and blazed the first piece up. Ms. Harvey inhaled with vigor and hissed loudly when the vapor passed through her lungs. She exhaled and her bedroom was filled with a cloud of white smoke.

"Yeah, it's my time. Let me do this," he said, smiling.

Dontay took the pipe and torch. Sucking on the stem, he blazed up the rock with a click of the torch. Ms. Harvey's face glowed when she saw the rock burning. It was her turn again, and when she sucked, her face was nothing but veins. Her lungs were filled with the intoxicating hallucinogenic drug. Ms. Harvey's blood vessels transported the effects of the high to her brain. She was reeling in delight brought on by the cocaine-induced euphoria.

Her mind was swimming in the sea of smoke from crack. She fell back against the bed and didn't move. Dontay quickly unbuttoned his pants and let them fall to the floor. He was out of his underwear and in a hot second he shoved his penis into Ms. Harvey's gaping mouth. Her body succumbed to the sexual delight. She moistened her dry lips, massaging his member between her jaws. Spitting and rubbing his dick to hardness, Ms Harvey fingered her pussy while Dontay removed the rest of his clothing.

"You have a condom, right?" she asked.

Dontay didn't answer. He undressed Ms. Harvey and immediately pushed her back onto the bed. Dontay quickly penetrated her moistness and was lodged between her opened thighs. Ms. Harvey moaned in pleasure.

"Uh... Oh yes," she said.

Their bodies were intertwined in ecstasy. She was holding on tightly to his shoulders as his body shuddered over and over again. Then she was on top of him, straddling his torso, and riding his hard dick.

"That's all you got?' she kept asking.

In mid-stroke, her body seemed to freeze. Ms. Harvey tossed her head back and her muscles tightened when she felt the release of an orgasm.

"Oh, oh ooh... Ah..."

She rolled off the man, took the pipe and walked out of the room. A few minutes later, she returned with a fresh piece of rock and lit up. Dontay was smoking a cigarette and watched as Ms. Harvey razed the rock with the torch. He smiled when she handed it to him.

"You gotta get up. You can't smoke in my bed."

He stood and they smoked the rest of the rock to yellow ash. Grabbing her by the waist, Dontay pulled Ms. Harvey down on top of him and they fell together on the bed. Another round of heavy sex ensued. Dontay swung her around and entered her from the rear. The pace of his strokes quickly increased and before long his body was shuddering. She could hear his breath quickening then he exploded.

"Ah... Shit!" He grunted.

"Damn! You cum already...?" Ms. Harvey asked in disbelief. "Don't tell me, you're a two-minute-man?" she asked frustrated.

Ms. Harvey turned around trying to get some more but Dontay was completely exhausted. His limp dick wouldn't budge.

"You need Viagra or sump'n," she said.

"I got some o' that—"

"Tell the doctor the prescription ain't working."

Ms. Harvey jumped up from the bed, and walked out of the room to the bathroom. Dontay got up and put his clothes back on. He was fully satisfied, and dressed. Dontay was leaving her apartment when the bathroom door opened.

"I'll see you again," he said.

"Yeah next time double up on the Viagra," she said.

"That pussy you got is hungry and tight. That shit took everything outta me," Dontay said, kissing Ms. Harvey.

"Whateva, save that for the birds," she said.

Ms. Harvey shut the door and got busy. Opening the window, she began frantically cleaning up the place. After sweeping the apartment, she sprayed the entire apartment with air-freshener then turned on the television. Ms. Harvey sat quietly, licking her lips and staring at the screen. She was still in her drugged-up state of mind and nothing else seemed to matter. Ms. Harvey closed her eyes and sadness enveloped her emaciated body.

She had tried to stop smoking crack, but it seemed like an impossible thing for her to do. For a couple of months, it felt like she could escape the deadly vice, but Ms. Harvey had slipped again and now felt the futility of her situation. Her mind craved the drug and her body reacted. She felt her skin crawl and unconsciously her hand moved to ease the irritation.

Soon she was scratching like she had a skin rash. Ms. Harvey got up and went to bathroom. She showered and dried. Then she scratched some more. She applied body lotion and still the irritation continued. It irritated her body and ravaged her mind.

"God grant me the serenity to accept the things I cannot change, courage to change the things I can and the wisdom to know the difference...Lord, help me to understand the things I cannot deal with and...Oh Lord," she started to whisper.

Then discarding all the principles she had learned in the rehab program, her mind gave in. The immense craving overtook her thoughts and she knew what she had to do. Quickly, she got dressed and went out the door in search of more drugs to fix her aching.

Outside the building, she could see the players. The pitchers and lookouts were awaiting her return to the fold. They saw the desperation welling in her eye and knew exactly what was on Ms. Harvey's mind. The dealers had the rocks she craved and were prepared to serve her. Ms. Harvey went to the dealer she was familiar with, and copped a couple of crack rocks.

"This good shit, right?" she asked.

"You already know," he answered.

She didn't wait to hear his response. Ms. Harvey was ghost. Hurrying back inside her apartment, she immediately launched into action, setting herself in position to be beamed up.

Deedee stopped at the red light and several people walked by greeting Coco. The popular teen flashed the peace sign at them and Deedee smiled.

"So when you become a movie star, you're gonna have to move from here," Deedee said, continuing up Lenox Avenue. "You're gonna be all the rage."

"Yes, for sure... I'm gonna have to get Madukes up outta this hood for real, yo."

"I can't wait for us to be in the movies, Coco."

"I hear you. I'll see you tomorrow, and we'll talk some more about that, yo."

"Alrighty then..." Deedee said, pulling over to stop in front of

Coco's building at a Hundred-and-Tenth Street.

"It's ten O' clock, I gotta go see what Madukes is up to, yo," Coco said, getting out of the BMW.

"I'll call you on your cell," Deedee said.

Smiling, Coco waved as Deedee drove away. Greeted by a throng of people in front, she walked into the building. She ran upstairs and felt her heartbeat increase as she tried the door and saw that it was opened. Her heart was pounding in her chest when she raced inside the apartment, and then to the bathroom.

She could see her mother curled up on the floor next to the bathtub. Her mother's neck was hanging in an unnatural position and her eyes were closed. Ms. Harvey looked like she had fallen asleep and Coco shook her mother. Ms. Harvey didn't respond. Her body collapsed on the cold bathroom floor when Coco released it.

"Ma, ma, ma…!" Coco shook Ms. Harvey's body again, and again no response came. Coco's eyes widened and she raced to the phone. Nervously lifting the receiver to her ear, her fingers rapidly dialed emergency. Requesting an ambulance, she gave her location and name to the operator. Then Coco raced back to the bathroom and struggled with her mother's limp body back to the sofa. Coco found a blanket to cover her mother's unmoving body with. Wandering through the apartment, she saw the crack pipe and torch. Coco grabbed the apparatus and threw them out the window. Then she sat with her mother and the tears flowed.

It seemed like a lifetime before there was knocking on the door. Coco opened and saw the emergency workers. She allowed them entrance.

"She's over there, yo," Coco said, pointing to the sofa where her mother's body was laid out.

They quietly walked over to the woman and examined her

closely. Then they strapped her to the gurney and spoke to Coco.

"She's suffered a cardiac arrest. She had a heart attack," one of them announced. "Are you related to her?"

"Yes, my name is Coco Harvey. I'm her daughter, yo."

"We're gonna have to take her to the hospital."

"Is she gonna make it, yo?" Coco worriedly asked.

"What was she doing when it happened?" the emergency technician asked.

"I don't know, yo," Coco said, tears streaming down her face. "When I got in, she was lying on the floor. Is she gonna be alright?"

"We'll have to transport her to the hospital. We'll need you to answer some more questions. You can come with us."

Coco walked out of the apartment with the two emergency medical technicians. Her mother's body strapped to the gurney, they made their way to the elevator.

"I don't know if it works, yo."

"We took it coming up and what goes up must come down," the EMT said, smiling sarcastically at Coco.

The door of the elevator slowly opened. It was a tight squeeze, but they filed inside. Coco held her mother's hand all the way down. She let go when the EMT's hoisted the gurney into the back of the emergency vehicle. Coco jumped inside. The wail of the siren announced another change in her life. Helplessly Coco watched time slip away as she regained a hold of her mother's hand.

Sitting in the back of the speeding ambulance with an EMT, Coco glanced out of the window. The small crowd in front of the building became blurry and seemed surreal to her tear-stained eyes. Her mother was lying motionless. She could hear still hear Eric Ascot's voice resonating in her head.

"*I need two female leads for this movie, teenagers like both of* you," he had said, pointing at both her and Deedee. "So basically you'd be playing yourselves. They sould be young, teenage girls with urban background... Just like you two, facing crucial life-changing decisions..."

It was after 11 pm when they arrived at Harlem Hospital. Her mother was checked into the emergency room and Coco wandered through the visitors' area. She had called Deedee when the ambulance first arrived at the hospital. The paramedics had rushed her mother to the emergency room for immediate medical attention. Coco waited despite being told that she could go home.

The paramedics and medical professionals had asked her a whole bunch of questions, and she had tried to answer as accurately as possible. Then after filling out a number of forms and signing some documents, the admission phase was done. Coco made a few phone calls and dozed off in the waiting area.

It was after midnight when Deedee arrived. Her coiffure and

gear were in place, and she strutted to the information area looking like a runway model. She saw Coco reclined in a metal chair. Deedee went over to her friend and the two girls hugged.

"I wanted to call you back to get the name of the hospital you were at," Deedee said. "But since she was here before I took a wild guess and just came directly here, " Deedee continued.

Coco's furrowed brow spoke volumes and Deedee felt the compassion for her friend. Deedee was aware of the love Coco had for her mother. This situation required tough love and Deedee recognized it.

"If your mother recovers—"

"If she recovers…? You mean when she recovers, she's always doing fucked-up shit like this, yo," Coco said in an exasperated tone. "She's been in and out the damn hospital because of fucking crack. I mean they been told her she's got a weak heart."

"Well, when she recovers you've got to get her in a program where she can stay for a long time. And I mean a really long time," Deedee said, extending her hands.

"Let's go hang out, maybe have real drink," Deedee suggested.

"Ah man, Dee, I don't know, yo."

Coco seemed reluctant at first, but apparently changed her mind when they walk outside the hospital. The night air smacked her sleepy face; she was fully awake.

"A'ight, yo, where you wanna hang?"

"Let's go to your spot and cop—"

"I got some of that weed left. I haven't smoked weed since that last time in the hospital…" Coco's voice trailed. "Josephine crazy-ass and you almost got me kicked out before I was due to be released, yo."

"Yeah, I remember. Coco, you think you should be—"

"Fuck it, yo. A night like this it's anything goes."

"That's what's up. Let's go hang and then we can go back to my place and chill. You don't wanna go back home alone, do you?"

"That sounds a lot like a pickup line, yo."

"Who says it isn't," Deedee answered with a mischievous smile.

"Don't be practicing on me, yo."

"Who better to practice on...?"

They got in the car and Coco rolled up before Deedee drove off. Heading south, the BMW purred through the streets of Manhattan. Deedee and Coco were riding high while puffing on a blunt. They were at club Amnesia where the legendary Disco Dave was spinning hot music.

The dance floor was crowded for a record-industry Tuesday-night party. Coco and Deedee were waved in by security. Floating high from the weed smoke, the girls immediately gravitated to the dance floor. Coco fell in her groove, and soon carved her spot with her moves. A few rounds later she was still sparring with the rhythm. Like a skilled boxer shadow boxing, there was no competition. Coco freely showed her skills dancing as Biggie flowed.

"I go, on and on and on and
Don't take them to the crib unless they bon'in
Easy, call em on the phone and
platinum Chanel cologne and
I stay, dressed, to impress
Spark these bitches interest
Sex is all I expect
If they watch TV in the Lex, they know
They know, quarter past fo'
Left the club tipsy, say no mo'
Except how I'm gettin home, tomorrow..."

While Coco took center stage with *Nasty Girls* from the Notorious BIG, Deedee slipped away and returned with refreshments. She came back with drinks, two-stepping and watching Coco in her element. The talented teen was dancing and having fun with other dancers. Suddenly Coco stopped moving, apparently woozy. She staggered off the dance floor and gingerly walked away. Onlookers applauded like it was part of her routine. Drinks in hands, Deedee followed closely behind her.

"Are you okay, Coco?"

"I don't know, yo. I was good then everything just started getting hazy. Felt like I couldn't see nothing for a minute, yo."

"Here's a drink. You might feel better," Deedee said, handing Coco a glass.

"I don't know, yo. Maybe that weed got me twisted."

Coco took the drink and sipped. The music played on. She shook her head around and smiled. Her expression was not one of satisfaction, but more delirium. Deedee watched her closely with concerned enthusiasm.

"Feel any better?" Deedee asked.

"I think it's wearing off, but it's my eyes, yo."

"What's up with your eyes?"

"Ever since the surgery, whenever I smoke, I get this feeling like I'm losing my vision and going blind or sump'n. I get hazy and—"

"It's the haze we were smoking on the way here," Deedee giggled. "I feel hazy too like my mind is riding a wave."

"That's not funny, yo," Coco said, trying not to laugh.

After thinking about it for a moment, Coco shook her head and said, "You funny Dee. You missed your calling, yo. I know I'm supposed to feel high and wavy, but my sight be getting cloudy too."

"You sound like the weather man. Your sight is gonna get cloudy and a few raindrops..."

Deedee broke out in a giggling fit and Coco had to do everything not to join her. The humor had lightened the mood, but Coco knew she had to eventually see her doctor.

"He, he, he, very funny, Dee... But not like this. I think I be having temporary blindness and shit, yo."

"It might just be your paranoia acting up. You know they say smoking marijuana does that to you."

They were conversing when two good-looking thugged-out guys approached the pair. Coco and Deedee were standing close to each other, but the guys purposely bumped into the girls.

"Pardon me, beautiful," one of them said to the Deedee.

"I'm sorry Miss," the other guy said to Coco.

"That's alright, yo," Coco said, looking at the guy.

"Y'all 'just watch where y'all going," Deedee said. "You damn near spilled the drink on me. Da-yum...!"

"My bad, well my name is—"

"I really ain't trying to know your name because I'm not gonna remember it," Deedee said.

"You ain't gotta be acting like a bitch and all!"

"Oh shit, the truth is out. You walked over here, deliberately bumped into me, and I'm the bitch, huh, scrub?"

"I can buy you many drinks, the whole fucking bar for that matter!"

He pulled out a knot and shoved it at Deedee's face. Then he slowly peeled off some Lincoln's and threw them at Deedee's feet.

"Right... Cheapskate, pick up that small change and keep it moving. Go buy your boy a drink," Deedee laughed.

"You's a fucking bitch!" the other guy joined in.

"A'ight, yo... We came here to chill. We don't need to be standing around calling each other bitches," Coco said, stepping between Deedee and the guys.

She took Deedee by the arm and was about to walk away when one of the guys said, "Fuck you, dyke bitch!"

Coco turned around and stepped to the guy. Toe to toe, she was in his face, sizing him up.

"So that's the deal, huh, yo? You can't get no play and I'm a dyke bitch, huh? Well fuck you! You shallow homo-thug!"

"Who you calling a homo, bitch?"

Coco reeled back to slap at the guy, but Deedee was able to grab her in time. The small-scale commotion had drawn the ire of the club's security. A couple of burly bouncers rushed over while Deedee quickly corralled her now irate friend, and dragged her away.

"Hold up, Dee!" Coco shouted.

Deedee was able to hold on to the now excited Coco. They headed to the dance floor while the bouncers escorted the thugs toward the exit door.

"Call me when you off your period...Bitches!" one of the thugs shouted as they girls walked away.

"Everything all right over here?" a burly bouncer asked, smiling licentiously while gawking at Deedee's backfield.

"Yes, we cool, yo. But get them hard-up boys outta here."

"They must be feeling on each other," Deedee laughed, strutting away.

Indulging in a couple more rounds of alcohol, the teen girls danced together and laughed. Coco and Deedee hung out on the dance floor for a couple more hours, until they were feeling good and exhausted from prancing. The whole incident with the two thugs was way past them.

"I'm ready to be out, yo."

"Yes, I've had it too."

Before leaving, they hit the ladies room to refresh themselves. Deedee fixed her makeup while Coco disappeared into a stall. Finished with all their bathroom actions, the girls, with a distinct inebriated sway to their steps, made their way out of the club. The bouncers stared at them leaving. Coco caught one smiling at Deedee's shapely ass.

"Hmm, ah... Lemme walk you to your ride. You never know what might be out there," he said.

"Nah, we good, yo!" Coco snapped.

"Thanks for looking out, but my ride is not that far. Good night," Deedee smiled.

The girls were buzzing and the air was warm but fresh outside. They made their way to the BMW parked on the street near the club. Coco started to slur as she spoke.

"Why you nice to that nigga? He was busy ogling your ass like he wanted to eat your shit—"

"Damn Coco why you gotta always have to be so mean...? He can't help but look at my fine ass," Deedee said.

"Niggas ain't 'bout shit but ass, yo."

Deedee deactivated the remote control and was about to open the doors when they heard the shouting from behind them. The girls tried to quickly jump inside the car, but two thugs were quickly all over them like hungry jackals.

"Yeah, bitches!"

"Whassup, dyke?"

Coco felt the cold steel on the side of her spine. She whirled around and a hard slap to the cheek staggered her. Deedee jumped to her rescue before the young thug could place his Timberland in her rear.

"Be easy now," Deedee said.

"Get in the car bitch!" one of the thugs ordered.

When Deedee hesitated, he showed her the gun and her jaw dropped. She opened the door and got inside the car, he sat next to her. The other thug shoved Coco into the back seat, holding the gun.

"Drive bitch!" he ordered. "This a nice fucking ride!"

"Yeah, now what you gotta say dyke bitch?" the one sitting next to Coco asked.

She stared at him not answering. He stared back menacingly at her. Deedee drove the car and tried to concentrate on the road amidst all the chaos.

"You a good-looking dyke," the one sitting next to Coco said. "And you staring at me like you wanna suck on my dick!"

He was undoing his jeans and Deedee swerved as if she was out of control. The shotgun was watching her closely.

"What the fuck you doing, bitch? Wanna get po-po on us or sump'n? Put your seatbelt on and drive safely!"

The young thug in the back seat with Coco had his jeans undone and pulled his penis out. He pointed the gun at Coco. She shook her head and looked away.

"Bring them juicy lips over here now, bitch!"

His friend was in the front seat and was looking back, laughing. The thug in the back put the gun in Coco's face then he tried pushing her head down onto his dick.

"Yes, ha, ha," his friend laughed. "Give that dyke bitch some o' your lollipop."

The back-seat thug was pushing Coco's head down and although she was resisting, he was stronger and was forcing her down on him showing her the gun. Then there was a loud squeal.

"Ugh-ah-ah! The bitch bit my dick head!" he screamed.

Deedee hit the brake and the front passenger fell forward. He lost control and tried to regain his position. There was an explosion and the shotgun suddenly felt a burning sensation in his stomach. Coco knocked the gun from the other thug's hand and grabbed it. Quickly Deedee pulled to a stop on a deserted corner.

"Get the fuck outta my car!"

The passenger didn't move and Deedee raised her gun to his face. He was staring in disbelief while holding his stomach.

"Bitch, you shot me?" he asked incredulously.

Coco was tussling with the back-seat thug as his partner was opening the door to get out. Deedee aimed her gun at him and he froze.

"Now if you don't take your stink ass outta my car, I'm gonna unload this shit on you!"

Under Deedee's steady gaze, the struggling thug relinquished Coco's arm and slowly opened the door. He joined his friend who was sitting on the sidewalk holding the gaping hole in his stomach. Fear and surprise registered on their faces when Coco stepped out of the car, and sauntered over to where they sat. She held the gun that previously had her captive. The preys had flipped the script and now held the gun in their hands. They looked armed and extremely dangerous.

"A'ight, who had that fat wad on them, yo...?" Coco asked, pointing the gun.

At first neither said anything and Deedee fired a shot. The two thugs cowered and seemed to be in fright as Deedee hair-trigger temper exploded.

"Okay, y'all think we fucking playing?" she asked aiming her weapon at the thugs.

"Him, him..." the one with the bullet already inside him said.

He was bleeding as he continued. "The bitch shot me."

Coco was about to reach into the pocket of the thug who was next to her, but he jumped up. Deedee fired twice in his legs, and he fell. Coco rifled through his pockets and lifted the money from him.

"Oh shit! The bitch shot me too!"

"What's wrong, yo?" Coco asked.

"I gotta get to the hospital. Give 'em the dough before I bleed to death!"

The girls took all the money and jumped into the car. Deedee aimed the gun at the two thugs and they dove into each other's arms, hiding.

"Yes, that's how I like to see y'all homo thugs," Deedee laughed.

"Let's get the fuck outta here—all them shots gonna attract po-po, yo!"

Both wounded thugs watched the black car disappeared into the still of the early morning mist, the sounds of music and laughter coming from the interior. Deedee stepped on the accelerator and they were gone.

"You are crazy, yo Dee!" Coco said laughing.

"No way another nigga taking shit away from my black ass again," Deedee said, sharing the humor. "You remember them niggas did that shit before. Uh-huh, that's not going down anymore."

"A'ight yo! I'm feeling you. They was soo fucking wrong, yo," Coco said, laughing. "I remember that shit, Dee. You were ready for the drama this time."

"Yes I was," Deedee laughed. "It wasn't going down like that. I was a scared vick that night and got my ass raped! I told myself that shit was never gonna happen to my ass again."

"That night created a monster, yo," Coco said.

In the dead of night, both girls remained silent for a few beats. The music of Michael Jackson rang out inside the car. Deedee stopped at a light and stared at Coco lighting two cigarettes.

"You are not alone
I'm here with you..."

She handed one of the lit cigarettes to Deedee, and they puffed silently in unison. They were two minds in a place common to only both of them. Over two years ago, Deedee first met Coco and the rest of Da Crew, Danielle and Josephine. It was a night marred by an event they would never forget.

The car idled at the light. Deedee's eyes were closed as she inhaled, and seemed to be in deep thought. Coco exhaled, staring at her and wondering.

"Are you okay, yo?"

"I was just thinking about that night those assholes raped me. And where were the cops?"

"They never around when you really need them, yo," Coco deadpanned. "That night was a fucking trip, yo. All I remember is getting clocked by a goon outside the club, yo."

"I remember it all..." Deedee inhaled then exhaled.

"That must've been some shit, yo. All I remember was the aftermath of getting off my ass outside the club after that nigga cold clocked me."

"I hear you and I'm telling you I wasn't going through that shit ever again," Deedee said.

"We were soo shook that night, yo. That was such a totally fucked-up night."

Outside the club, Coco gathered herself. She touched her nose. Blood appeared on her fingers, and her eyes stung.

"Those muthafuckas! Fucking bastards," Coco thought aloud, pulling off her headwear and dabbing at her nose.

The white do-rag was now stained red. She headed back inside the club. Her head was pounding from the blow. The music from the club only served to exacerbate the pain. She went straight to the ladies' room where she washed the cloth and stared back at her bloodshot reflection.

After she left the restroom, she went to the pay phone and paged her girls. They responded in a flash, and the three girls left the club without saying anything. Once outside, they walked a few feet away from the entrance. Coco held the headwear to her throbbing nose, hiding the bruise.

"Coco you're letting your dreads fly. What's up?" Josephine asked.

"This whazzup, yo!" Coco said, removing the blood-soaked wrap from her face. "Some niggas mush me and jacked da whip. They must've grabbed honey too, cuz I ain't seen her since. Y'all ain't seen her back in the club, yo?"

"No, we were all up in VIP. She wasn't back there," Danielle said.

"Yeah, Deedee was kidnapped!"

"Oh fucking shit! They didn't!" Coco yelled as Danielle and Josephine looked on in amazement.

"You know who could've done it?" Josephine asked. "Tell me so I can step to that muthafucka!"

"Ah Jo, you know you ain't gonna do a damn thing..." Danielle said.

"I didn't really see who they were, yo. But the voice sounded kind a familiar. It was like... Did any of y'all see Lil' Long leave...?"

"Coco, you know we were both all the way in da back booths. We couldn't see them. They could a left anytime," Josephine said.

"Word," Coco said, nodding her throbbing head in agreement.

"All she wanted to do was drop me at da rest, yo. That's it. And they jacked her. That shit is fucked up."

Coco searched for cigarettes. There were none. Her head throbbed. She wondered about Deedee. The thought made her whole body shudder. Then Josephine said it. Maybe Da Crew was thinking it, but nobody wanted to say it.

"We've got to call five-oh," Josephine said.

The words hung for a beat before the discussion began.

"Now, ya know them muthafuckas ain't gonna do shit," Coco said.

"I agree, we should call the cops," Danielle said.

"A'ight," Coco said.

The girls walked to the phone on the corner.

"Police, 911..." the operator said after Danielle dialed emergency.

"Yo, some guys just mugged some girls and stole a car. They kidnapped the girl. They had guns and they were shooting at everybody. It's crazy out here. Send your baddest peoples out here."

"Slow down, Miss. Where are you calling from?"

"We're at the corner of 116th and 1st. send the baddest cops."

Danielle hung up and the girls sauntered away from the payphone.

"I'm out. Y'all stay and talk with da cops. I gotta take care of my nose, yo."

"Yo, Coco, wait up. You know what happened. Come on, you gotta stay," Josephine pleaded.

"A'ight, I'll stay. But shit's not gonna be solved by talking all night with five-o. We don't even know if she stole da whip or if she had her license, yo," Coco said.

"Well, she said her uncle—" Danielle started saying, but Coco cut her off.

"Her damn uncle could've stolen that," Coco said.

The sirens sounded and the police arrived in a swarm. They came four cars deep, totaling nine officers. The cars moved slowly, red lights flashing as the dawn echoed an ominous air outside the club. Members of the baggy-clothes generation were still haunting their favorite hangout. The officers got out of their patrol cars and began to scrutinize the kids. What were they looking for? These kids didn't know. Each group gave a negative response to the police inquiries.

Quieted by the presence of the police, club-goers filed by the officers in a hasty urban exit, oblivious of whatever had taken place outside the club. Suddenly, the officers saw the three girls smoking while standing under a broken-down lamppost.

"Here they come, the city's finest tin badges," Danielle opined.

"Did any of you happen to hear any gunshots being fired? Or have you seen anything unusual?" an officer asked.

"I think it all happened over there," Josephine said, pointing to where they thought the Benz was parked. "Some kids jacked this girl and her car, and they took off, heading that way." Josephine pointed the officers to where the carjackers were last seen.

"Did you know the girl? Her name...?" another officer asked.

"Well, she—" Josephine started.

"Nah, not really, yo," Coco interjected. "That's all we know."

"Your nose looks bad. What happened?" the second officer asked, looking directly at Coco.

"A fight, yo. Someone messing 'round with my man, you know. Gotta defend what's mine," Coco said.

"It's a tough world, young lady. Did any of you happen to see any faces, or anything that may help to identify someone?" the officer asked.

"A black Benz... A bad car," Danielle said, her voice trailed off.

"That's it?" the officer asked. "Is that all you know?"

"Yeah, that's it. They jacked her right over there," Josephine said. "It was too dark to see much more."

"They...?" the first officer asked, focusing on Josephine.

"How many were there?" he questioned, excitement in his voice. "Two, three, four...? How many...?" he asked almost shouting.

"There were about two of them," Coco said sternly.

"And they kidnapped a girl," Josephine cried. "That's all we know."

"Stay here, I'm gonna get an ambulance," an officer commanded.

"Can you describe the girl? What was she wearing?"

"Black girl, black spandex and red sweater," Danielle replied.

"Anything else?" the officer mumbled, and proceeded to put in the call for an ambulance.

"Just a black girl in black with a black car... All black everything," Coco said sarcastically.

"That's all we know," Josephine said. The officers huddled. The senior guy returned.

"Stay out of fights," he said directly to Coco. "The rest of you best be getting home."

Sirens pierced the air. The ambulance arrived. Coco was given a bandage and treated by the EMTs. When she alighted from the ambulance, Da Crew ran to meet her.

"Well, it's not broken, is it?" Josephine asked.

"No. Takes more than a little punch from a sucker to break something here, kid," Coco bragged.

The girls embraced. This was the first time all three had shown any emotion, other than in their passion for singing. They hugged, and each thought about Deedee. Oneness enveloped the group, which came through in the tenderness of the moment. Coco, still a little woozy from *the alcohol and the blow to her nose, was now able to speak.*

"Wonder what's up with Dee. I hope she's a'ight," Josephine said.

"Yeah, I hope she's okay," Danielle added.

"She was only looking out for me. I owe her some kind a due, ya know?" Coco said, searching for corroboration.

The idea was still overwhelming to her. She had just met Deedee, didn't even know her last name, and was already feeling connected.

"Deedee was looking out, yo," she said, quickly summing up the moment.

"Y'all could stay at my place. My parents won't mind," Josephine said.

She did not look directly at her, but Coco felt the last part was meant for her. After all, had they gone to Coco's, her mother would probably be drunk and curse up a storm. Josephine understood. And besides, she had her own room, and her home was always clean.

"I got some loot. Let's catch a cab, yo," Coco said.

"Yeah, let's do, that," Danielle and Josephine agreed.

The girls hailed a cab, and it stopped. They looked at each other with surprise.

"Aw shit!" Danielle said. "This must be some kind a omen or something. Strange things happen in threes, and this taxi stopping for us makes two. No more car rides for the weekend, y'all."

The girls ran to the cab. The three girls huddled in the back seat of the taxi. The driver hesitated.

"A Hundred-and-Twelfth and Lenox," said Josephine. "What's the problem?" she asked repeating the address.

The driver glanced nervously at the rear-view mirror. His actions had the girls looking at each other then back at him.

"Aw c'mon...we ain't trying to jack your ass. See, we got loot, yo," Coco said, pulling out a couple of ten-dollar bills.

"See money. Now drive," Danielle ordered.

"Yeah let's go already," Josephine shouted.

"Alright," the cab driver said. *"Now I drive."*

"Think we gonna disrespect your livelihood, yo?"

"We should," Danielle said. *"Take his loot and all. Straight jacking..."*

"Will you cut that out Dani. Hello, we are trying to get somewhere here," Josephine said. *"She's sorry, Mr. Cabbie."*

Coco and Deedee were sitting in Deedee's new BMW, reflecting on the past. After a couple beats, they both shook their heads. The girls were recovering from the attempted carjacking. This time Coco was in the car. That night two years ago when they first met Deedee was forcefully taken, and she was by alone.

"Oh my God, I swore it would never go down again the way it did before," Deedee said.

"I'm telling you on the night it happened, I ain't know what had gone down 'til the cab driver told us, yo," Coco said. "We called po-po, and then we were out. Caught a cab to Josephine's home."

"As much as I try to forget that incident, I still remember that shit like it was yesterday," Deedee said.

"Dee, that type of incident stays with you until you die. You don't ever forget. And in my case, where I don't know the muthafucka who assaulted me, every man is a suspect, yo. That whole night was a trip."

"You said it Coco. It sure as hell was no joy ride."

"I hear you, yo. There was soo much shit going down that night, but I remember everything, yo."

"Everything...?" Deedee asked.

"Everything, yo."

The cab started moving, but the driver was still a bit uneasy. He kept glancing back as if he expected something. Nothing happened. The girls remained quiet.

"In my country people are poor, but not so disrespectful. They respect life and property. Americans, have no regard for either, especially Blacks and Latinos," the cab driver said.

"A'ight, a'ight be easy. Watch what you're saying or I'll have to let my girl Dani, jack your ass," Josephine said.

"I'm telling you, that is exactly what happened to a girl earlier. It's not your fault you've been brought up in a violent world..."

The cab driver's voice crackled through the tension in the air. The girls sat glowering in the back seat. Before they had playfully heeded what he was saying. Now he had their undivided attention.

"Uh, what did you say?" Coco asked with a annoyed tone.

"I said you've been raised in violence, and..." the cabbie said.

"Nah, nah, before all that, you mentioned something about a girl," Coco said.

"Oh yeah. I said that on the news someone call the police they saw a girl along Route 87? It was over the radio."

There was a deadly silence as the girls held their breath. Coco grabbed her bandaged nose as her heart sank. It had been on her mind since she had recovered from the punch in the face. Everything seemed to hurt a little more as the driver continued with the second-hand news.

"Apparently, she was raped," the cabbie informed his passengers.

"Wait up. What girl?"

"Found her where? Is she dead? Oh man. Damn!"

"They fucking did her, those muthafuckas," Danielle cried out in anguish.

Coco heard the other girls firing out questions, but was dry-mouthed. Things became a blur to Coco. She winced from the pain. Sitting erect, her back slightly arched, she put her hand to her nose. No sound came. She had just met Deedee, but the pain she felt was deep. Her head started to pound again. This was real bad. They had jacked her and the car. Why didn't they just take the car? Coco rewound the memory of the voices outside the club prior to her getting hit. She tried to mentally sketch the faces with the voices. Her head hurt. She stopped.

"Is ... the girl dead?" Josephine asked.

"No, no she's alive," the driver said.

The girls breathed a collective sigh of relief. "She was taken to a hospital," the driver continued.

Hope returned. The girls held one another's hands tighter. "She was badly beaten and raped. She's the niece of that famous music producer, Eric Ascot."

Eric Ascot! That's her uncle, thought Coco. The girls looked wide-eyed at each other. The mention of Eric Ascot's relationship to Deedee was a huge surprise. Eric Ascot was one of the most popular producers in the music industry.

"Those muthafuckas...! Ooh! I don't fucking believe..." Coco exclaimed.

"That shit is incredible. But that's city life for ya! Man," Josephine said, staring straight ahead. "That's why my dad wants to leave the city."

"Your dad's a player, Jo. That's why he wants to leave the city."

"They fucking did her."

The words were so final that they made the air go dead inside the taxi. The ride continued in virtual silence. Nothing more was said until they reached the building where Josephine and her parents lived. Coco paid the fare, and the girls walked to the entrance of the huge building.

"Dammit. I don't have any cigarettes," Coco said, searching her pockets.

"We could get some stogies off my parents," Josephine said.

She opened the door and the girls walked in. Coco gave an excuse for not calling home. She knew her mother would be asleep or drunk, probably both. Danielle called her mother. Josephine led the way to her room, and the girls followed in silence. Once inside the room, Josephine turned the television on. All three girls plopped down on the small bed. Josephine sprang up and tossed the remote to Coco, who began to scan the channels.

"Nothing but reruns," Danielle said.

Coco continued to channel surf. There were talk shows and religious programs.

"Misty and overcast..." the weatherman reported.

Josephine left the room then reappeared ten minutes later. She was carrying milk, soda, water, cookies and cigarettes. Coco helped herself to a cigarette and soda. She lit up and took a drag.

"This was a fucked-up evening, yo!" she proclaimed.

The girls remained silent and her thoughts disappeared in the cloud. They were reminiscing over the still-unsettling events. The girls sat around nodding their heads in agreement.

"Yep," Danielle finally said. "This was more a fright night than any Thriller could bring."

"Shit's foul," Coco said, and leaned back, closing her eyes.

The room seemed to grow smaller. Josephine had always liked to get away to this space. When she closed the door all the world's trouble stayed on the other side—except for today. The dawn had already dragged something sinister across the threshold of her room.

"Everything was fucking crazy that night, yo."

"It was. I don't think I ever can forget that night. And when those two muthafuckas tried that shit just now, you know I went right there, Coco."

"I hear you, yo. Madukes always say, 'what don't kill you, only makes you stronger'. You're an example of that, yo. They created a monster! I guess them two felt it for all the other goons trying a jooks."

"Yes, it was the wrong night, wrong time, wrong peeps, wrong everything."

Coco shook her head. She watched Deedee caught up in the moment, reminiscing. They had completely forgotten where they were. Then they heard the horns of motorists behind them. Both girls gave each other a knowing glance and smiled openly.

"...Though we're far apart
You're always in my heart..."

Scats from Michael Jackson were heard above the music blasting in the ride. Deedee drove across town to her uncle's place and pulled into the parking lot. They cautiously made their way inside the apartment building.

"True story, yo..."

The doorman held the door opened and watched the rear ends whisk by. His eyes followed them into the lobby of the Manhattan apartment owned by Eric Ascot. They stepped aboard the elevator, the door closed and, in seconds, the ride ended inside the hallway of Eric's apartment.

Deedee led the way to one of the six bedrooms. She opened the door, waved her hand against the wall, turning on the light. Coco stepped inside and glanced around the bedroom furnished with a queen size bed. There were matching dresser drawers along with nightstands on either side of the made bed. Lamps were sitting atop them.

"You should be good here. There's a bathroom over here," she said, walking to the other end of the room.

Coco's eyes followed her in wide-eyed amazement. She watched Deedee and knew they had formed a special bond since the first night they had met. They were survivors of bizarre episodes in seemingly parallel lives traveling so fast both Coco and Deedee thought they would have crashed. Though they were better friends now, as Coco looked around the room, she realized the difference still existed. Deedee was rich and could afford to extend her kindness in an extravagant manner. Coco was poor and had to struggle to make it. But because of their experiences the girls had forged a bond of friendship that was far more than either expected.

"Wow this shit is tight. Yeah I think I can crash here for a night or so, yo."

"You can stay as long as you want Coco."

"Don't tempt me, yo," Coco laughed.

"Oh, c'mon Coco, you know you can. We're besties like that."

Coco smiled and hugged Deedee. The girls broke away staring at each other, caught in the moment.

"We're always going through shit, yo. I mean look at tonight, Madukes wound up in the hospital again. And to top it off, we were chilling and those niggas tried to jack us—"

"Again," both Coco and Deedee chorused.

"But because of you and your little Annie," Coco said, pointing at Deedee's Hermes Birkin bag.

"I don't want to be a victim anymore, Coco. The old me wasn't working, so I had to do what I had to do to survive. I'm packing and if someone run up on me, this will back 'em up," Deedee said, reaching inside her pocketbook and pulling out the small handgun.

"Annie, go get your gun," Coco laughed. "Dee, put that shit away, you's a mess, yo."

"I'm being real. A lot of guys want to pimp smack you. I'm not taking that."

"You changed a lot from when we first met, yo."

"I know. I had to, Coco," Deedee said. "Remember when you told me about you being a victim?" she asked.

"Yeah, I remember telling you, cuz you could identify with that feeling, yo."

"Yes, that's right. That morning outside school, you told me that after you were assaulted, you felt like killing every muthafucka who looked at you," Deedee said.

"Yeah... And sometimes I still do. Once you been raped, you carry that scar around with you forever, yo."

"Well that's how I felt too," Deedee said with a wry smile.

Uncharacteristically, Coco walked about six miles to the school. Even so, she was early. Sitting on the bench just outside the school, she searched for cigarettes and found none. She stood and started the walk to the shop at the end of the block. Coco paused when a black Range Rover circled and stopped in front of her. Deedee hopped out. Both Eric Ascot and Sophia waved at Coco as Deedee approached.

"Whaz-zup?" Deedee shouted.

Her yelling shattered the morning air. Birds took refuge in nearby trees. Eric honked, and Deedee waved goodbye.

"What's poppin'? I'm goin' to da corner store, yo," Coco greeted, wondering if Deedee was feeling better.

"I'll walk with you, if you don't mind," Deedee chirped.

"That's cool, yo," Coco said, easing into a leisurely stroll.

"This seems like such a nice morning. I mean, the sunlight, the water on the grass. Damn, how could it be such a nice day?" Deedee pondered, lighting a cigarette. She puffed and passed it to Coco.

"Know what'cha mean, yo," Coco said.

They walked on to the store at the corner of the block. Coco bought cigarettes and a Coke. Deedee, got apple juice and chewing gum. The girls stood outside the store, sipping and smoking. They left as other students descended on the shop. Coco and Deedee walked back toward the school and sat down on a bench.

"It's still early," Deedee said.

"Yeah..." Coco said and her voice trailed off in sadness.

Was Coco's behavior just early-morning blues? Deedee wondered. Maybe she was tired. She knew Coco and the girls had been rehearsing for the talent-show finals.

"So, how's rehearsal?" Deedee asked.

Coco nodded and reached for her cigarettes. She lit one and stared upward, blowing the smoke out slowly. Deedee watched her, and Coco started to speak.

"Life's some fucked-up shit, yo," she said.

It occurred to Deedee that her own situation fitted the phrase better than Coco's.

"Yeah, I know just what you mean, Coco."

"But it could always be worse. No matter what, there's always gonna be worse," Coco continued, looking away. "I mean, yo...d'ya wanna take a walk?" Coco asked. She paused thoughtfully. "We best chill," she said. "Cuz I'll wind up not fucking bothering with this shit. I need da education, yo."

They remained seated on the bench. She lit another cigarette and Deedee joined her.

"You're alright, yo?" Coco asked.

Deedee thought about that. "Yeah," *she finally said, not fully understanding. It didn't seem to matter.*

Coco slumped back and said, "You're looking better, anyway. But I'm saying the feeling stays with you, yo," *Coco continued.*

Deedee stared at her, still unsure of exactly what was going on. Then Coco came up with the clarification.

"That feeling like a vick... That shit never leaves, yo. It becomes your fucking shadow, pops up in different situations. You be seeing faces, like it wuz that muthafucka, or this one."

Deedee listened, dangling her cigarette. She watched Coco's expression change from sad to anger.

"I know wha' da shit feels like, yo," *Coco said.* "See, I wuz fucking raped. Muthafucka got drunk wid my mom and when he wuz finished wid her, he came for me. My mutha, yo, she tried to fight him, and I did too. That muthafucka was big, yo. He kicked Madukes drunken ass and then took mine. Now every day I just be staring at muthafuckas, having flashbacks. I'm telling you, if I had a gun, that muthafucka would be straight spitting up lead. I'm telling you, shits fucked up when I be staring in muthafuckas' eyes, looking for him, yo. If I ever see his ass, I swear to God, he's dead, yo."

Students began entering the school. First they had to pass through the metal detectors. Some waved to Coco. She managed to ignore them and stared off, over the trees.

"I'll kill a muthafucka like what!"

Coco summed up a feeling that had haunted her for a long time. Deedee was surprised. She had no idea the morning would bring this revelation. She had planned on going to school, enduring as much of the stares as possible, and leaving early if they got her down. Now, she too would stare back at 'muthafuckas,' possibly locating the one who had caused her pain. It was a scary thought. Coco's grim expression made her realize that things really could be worse.

"Do they know about this, too?" Deedee asked when she saw Danielle and Josephine heading toward the bench.

"Nah," Coco sighed. "They wouldn't understand da half. You had to be there like a vick to fully get it, yo," she said, getting up to greet Danielle and Josephine.

They were standing close to each other, and Coco could see the look of determination on Deedee's face. She was still a very pretty girl. Being a survivor of abduction and rape changed Deedee's outlook on life. She had grown so much from her harshest experience. Looking at her, Coco wondered if anyone could be prepared enough for everything in life.

"You got heart, yo."

"I'm next door to the right. If anything happens just knock real loud. I'm a sound sleeper," Deedee said.

"A'ight Dee," Coco said. "Hopefully I could sleep this night off, yo."

"As soon as my head hit the pillow, I'll be out."

Deedee took her shoes off while speaking, and walked out the room. Coco put the headphones over her ears and reclined on the bed. She listened to beats that Eric Ascot had created for her. Nodding her head to the rhythm, Coco went into her flow.

"Yeah I like that, yeah I like this for club...Hmm, fire," she said aloud.

God bless the dearly departed,

here yesterday today and forever
your love lives in my heart
music makes you alive brings you closer
every day and I'm still a part of you
Spiritual healing lonely nights are through
Difference in a day spent making classics
Jo, Dani, Bebop I'm living for you
Listening to Miss Katie's voice
Missing you making me nicer
fills my soul lyrics coming tighter
I'm invincible truth be told
tougher than dice never shiesty
always calm and bold
Like your misses I don't creep
Oh my God look at the time...
Gotta catch some Z's, sleep...

The next morning, Coco heard the knock at the door. She was still in bed when Deedee walked in and energetically jumped on the bed.

"Hey sleepy head, you up?" she asked.

"I'm up now, if I wasn't, yo."

"You actually sleep with your headphones on, Coco?"

"It's the only way I sleep, yo."

"What? You were listening to music while you were sleeping?"

"What's wrong with that, yo?"

"Wow, I guess that's how you stay connected, huh?"

"Stay connected? Seriously yo... You woke up in a Dr. Doolittle mood yo?"

"Hmm, I think I'd like to plug into a vault of expensive jewelry and mentally slip them out. One piece at a time."

"A'ight Dee," Coco said. "I see you're sleepwalking."

"You're saying I'm daydreaming?'

"I'm saying you're delirious, yo."

Deedee watched Coco jump out of the bed and disappear into the bathroom. She emerged a few minutes later and smiled at Deedee.

"You did a number two, and stunk up the place, Coco?" Deedee asked with mock sarcasm.

"Why are you clocking me, yo?"

"I'm not clocking you, Coco. I was just saying—"

"I thought you were a heavy sleeper, and was soo tired, you'd be knocked out all day!" Coco asked.

"I was knocked out asleep, but Rightchus kept calling my damn cell, and woke me up. So I figured if I'm up you might as well be too." Deedee said.

"What he saying? Why didn't you say so, yo?"

"He spazzed on me, telling me I shouldn't be sending him money in his government name. Then he told me to lose all his info. He was gonna call me from another telephone and I should lose that number too."

"Why is he soo paranoid, yo?"

"I don't know. I just did what the hell he wanted me to do."

"He always trying a run game on everyone, yo. That's what's up with his paranoia."

Deedee laughed and eventually Coco joined in. Both had dealt with Rightchus' con game, and were aware of his mastery of the art of deception. His strategy relied on how much of what you heard, you believed. The girls burst out with laughter like schoolgirls with no worry.

"I guess you really do gotta laugh at yourself sometimes, yo," Coco sighed.

"Yes I agree, wholeheartedly," Deedee chuckled.

"So seriously, that's it? He didn't say anything about your uncle, yo?"

"He said he'd be calling me back and so far he hasn't."

Deedee pulled out her cell phone and checked it. She shook her head at Coco and seemed startled when the cell phone went off. Deedee stared in awe at the instrument loudly ringing in her hand. Regaining her composure, she answered the call and put the speaker on.

"Hello...?"

"This is Rightchus. You burned up everything with my name on it? Please do so. These peoples have eyes all over...and I don't wanna be involved. So lose my info and do not pass it on to anybody. Cuz y'all don't know them peoples."

"What people you talking 'bout, yo?"

"Oh no... Is that Coco again? I told you the less people know about this, is the—"

"Is the more money you're able to scam from my girl," Coco joined in. "We on to you, yo..."

"Coco, you don't have any idea. Don't even begin to think that way. Let's make one thing clear. Deedee called me. I never reach out to y'all. Matter of fact, I'm trying to get away from all that shit. What I'm about to say, y'all can take whichever way y'all want. But I know your uncle gotta buy out this case. And it's gonna cost him a lot. Or they gonna take his freedom."

"Really, are you trying to play me?"

"Why would I? You contacted me and asked me a question. And I gave you the answer. Maybe it's too much for you to handle but it is what it is... This case is gonna cost your uncle a lot of money. But I'm sure he got it. Poor people like myself would be getting the electric chair."

"How much is a lot of money, yo?" Coco asked.

"Oh, we talking anywhere in the two to three million range... Them peoples want that money—"

"What's your cut, yo?"

"Coco, just listen up and learn sump'n. I'm not getting none o' that. The lawyer probably keeping some for his self, like point five, but the rest goes to the other peoples involved. Not me."

"How do you know this for sure?" Deedee asked, sounding unsure.

"My name is Rightchus and I make it my business to know what's going on at all times on all fronts. They's been trying to setup your uncle for the longest behind those murders. Now that he's got that money, he's gonna have to pass it on. If he do what they tell him to do, he'll get that money back and more..."

"Who are 'they' that you're referring to?" Deedee asked.

"They is them. The peoples... I can't tell you too much more. They got eyes everywhere too just watching and waiting. All them killing that you supposedly know about... Those killings were nothing more than sacrifices that had to be made."

"Are you down south burning rocks in the church, Rightchus?" Coco asked. "You sound like you smoking, yo."

"Say what you want, Coco. I been told you that things ain't

always what they seem to be. It's whatever they want your eyes to see..."

"Why you going there like that? I'm just saying if you need to scam my girl come up with a better story than this science fiction, yo."

"I told you, I'm not trying to scam no one. It was your girl who contacted Rightchus. I did not reach out and touch anyone. Your girl called me."

"But all this B.S. conspiracy theory sounds like you made it up on the fly. You doing like you always do, yo—you scamming—"

"I'm a tell y'all, believe half of what you hear and nothing that you see. After we hang up, please lose my info. Please..." Rightchus said, interrupting.

"Oh, so that's how you gonna do us? You gonna take the money and run after trying to feed us this bullshit, yo?" Coco asked sounding angry.

"Okay, Rightchus, thanks and I don't think I need to talk to you anymore," Deedee said hanging up the call. "Hmm, alrighty then," she sighed.

"I hate for a muthafucka like that to be playing us like tricks, yo," Coco said in an agitated tone.

"Okay, anyone for breakfast?" Deedee smiled.

"I know you got dough to blow, but aren't you a little bit upset about being taken by this asshole, yo?"

"It cost me three hundred dollars to hear that the police led by these so-called 'peoples' are in conspiracy to get my uncle to pay two million for it all to go away. I just think it's a really expensive joke," Deedee laughed.

"It's great that you can take it easy like that, yo. I'd be on my way to South Carolina, or where ever his ass is, to get my money back."

"Let's forget about the little twerp for now and freshen up

then have some breakfast," Deedee suggested.

"I don't have any clothes. You didn't wanna go—"

"I gotcha my girl, you can select something you like from Deedee's closet. There's unworn stuff with tags still attached and there're—"

"Yeah, that's cool. But you only have them tight jeans and—"

"I got some dresses that you'll like. You know you may look good in that Versace or a Gucci... Hmm, I don't know. C'mon Coco let's go find you a dress."

"I don't want anything having me looking like a nerd or—"

"Coco, I told you I got you. You can be thugged-out wearing a nice dress you know...? It's just the mystique."

"Mystique my ass, niggas gonna think I'm a nerd and be hitting on me. I don't wanna slap a—"

"Today just chill out and don't slap anyone," Deedee said, cutting Coco off.

They walked down the hallway to one of Deedee's closets. She opened the door and Coco's eyes widened. It was a small room neatly packed and filled with clothes.

"A room for a closet, filled with nothing but expensive clothes and shoes... You been boosting or sump'n, yo?"

"Boosting...? No silly, shopping," Deedee laughed. "It's just that whenever I get bored or whatever, I go shopping for shoes or clothes," Deedee answered in a matter-of-fact tone.

"Lately, you must have been really bored, yo. It's like a store in here."

"Oh, I have about three or four more closets filled with nothing but clothes."

"What happened in your life that could've made you bored?"

"You went into the hospital. You were shot and I was scared. I did a lot of shopping with you in mind."

"Lemme find out...?"

"I just thought like if you'd like this dress or this pants or shoes and so on. I did it when my mother...ah...when she left..."

Coco heard Deedee's voice trailing. She smiled and hugged her friend. Deedee seemed lost in a thought for a beat.

"Easy with all this sadness, you might want to go on another round of shopping spree, yo," Coco joked.

"Hey, you read my mind. I was just thinking about that, Coco."

It was about midday when Coco and Deedee strutted out of the apartment building. The beguiled doorman held the door for a longer time and eyed the pair. He smiled and hugged his chest like he was having a heart attack. Coco was chewing, trying to get comfortable in her new attire. The simple Armani black dress and pumps made her seemed like a fashion intern, but her long, shapely legs made the doorman sigh. Deedee, outfitted in D&G skin-tight, black jeans and hoodie, seemed like a pro. Her backfield in motion had the doorman's eyes jumping to the rhythm of her steps. While walking down the block, the girls heard the whistles. Coco glanced at Deedee.

"I don't know how you handle all this attention, yo. How do you walk in those tight-ass jeans, yo?" Coco joked.

"Pay it no mind, Coco. Ignore it, that's how. Hey Coco, let's take the subway," Deedee smiled.

"The subway...? Dressed like this? Are you kidding me, yo? Let's catch a cab."

"Be daring and bold. Let's take the subway," Deedee laughed.

"I don't like the trains. Too many pervs ride that shit, yo."

"C'mon, Coco, don't be scared. It's a nice day and only one stop from here to the shopping district."

"I gotcha—you just want me to walk around in this dress and shoes, yo. It ain't that hard to figure your game out, yo."

"I just don't want to deal with parking," Deedee lied.

"How far is the nearest subway station, yo," Coco said, sounding annoyed.

"Only a couple blocks. I promise it's not that far."

"I'll pay for the cab, yo."

"C'mon Coco, you can pay for one later. After we're through shopping..."

Against Coco's wishes, they started out for the subway station. Each step Coco took was a learning experience, but before long she was mastering the art of walking in her new outfit. Beautiful and tall, both girls garnered enough attention. There were several times when Coco stop and glared at men lecherously staring at her.

On this sunny day in the city, they were a gorgeous pair. Eyes on the streets stared at Coco strutting in the windless sky, her Afro, a crown to the all-black Armani attire. Deedee's casual appearance was enhanced by Gucci shades, and her long black tresses flowed with her steps. Finally they walked down the stairs to the entrance of the subway station. Coco was still getting used to her shoes and moved cautiously. Deedee continued boldly downward to the world of straphangers.

Underground performers greeted them. A Mexican trio outfitted in cowboy boots, jeans and sombreros were singing Spanish lullabies. There was a soulful quartet, blowing vocally like the Four Tops of the Motown era. Deedee gave them five dollars apiece. Deeper underground in the subway station a group of B-Boys and girls were set trying to draw a crowd. Jugglers and hustlers were stationed inside the train station. So were players.

"Hey ma, you and your friend models...?"

"Ooh you got it going on. Lemme give you my number..."

Ignoring the unwanted soliciting and comments, the girls went through the turnstile. They walked casually along the platform. Some guys walked by the girls.

"Nice assets," one commented.

Coco glared at them while Deedee went poker-faced. She was used to the compliments whether they were genuine or fake. Coco was still trying not to smack anyone's face. Deedee turned and faced her.

"It's a daring and fun thing to do," Deedee said.

"What shopping?"

"No, to ride the subway..."

"Get your daring on, yo. Here comes one now."

The doors opened and the girls walked inside the car. It seemed all eyes were riveted on them. Coco tried to look away but only to be met by more inquiring eyes.

"It must be these heels, but it feels like everyone is staring my way, yo."

"The heels are hardly high. Mine are higher, but I never noticed how tall and in shape you are, Coco. The dress and pumps really bring that out."

"I tried on dresses with you before. Stop acting like a perv, yo."

"And you're very pretty—high cheekbones, and long shapely

legs, hmm..."

"Okay, you're beginning to get a little too personal, yo."

"I think it's the handbag that is most sexy about you," Deedee said giving Coco a quick once over.

"You're beginning to howl a lot like those wolves on the streets, yo."

"They were not howling like wolves. Some of these guys are genuinely from the heart." Deedee smiled. Coco glared.

She was about to open her mouth, suddenly the serenading of a soulful, classic ballad drifted through the car.

"Many a tears have to fall...
Doo...doo...doo
But it's all in the game..."

Both girls listened quietly while the quartet delivered the melody in superb Motown style. The train sped downtown and the next stop was theirs. Before the doors slid open, Deedee handed the quartet money. Coco and Deedee walked from the platform.

"I don't believe you just gave those guys a yard, yo. A twenty would have done 'em real good."

"I like that song," Deedee said as they walked up the stairs.

"You liked it that much, buy it for thirteen ninety-five, yo," Coco said when the girls hit Fifth Avenue and East 57th Street.

"Let's go to the Gucci store," Deedee laughed.

"Remember when you, I and Josephine came down here shopping for the first time?" Deedee asked.

"Yeah, I remember. It was on a day like today..." Coco said and her voice trailed.

"You were kinda rude to me, Coco," Deedee said.

"Damn, that was only like a couple years ago. I wasn't really feeling you too much back then. Why you gotta bring that up, yo?"

"Cause like you said, it was a day like today. And it just reminded me that's all..." Deedee's voice trailed, but she hadn't forgotten the time.

Early blossoms were appearing all around on this late April afternoon. Here in midtown, a busy pre-season summer sale raged down Madison and Fifth. In the hours that followed, the girls covered every fancy store on Madison, expertly combing through designer outfits that caught their every fancy. Occasionally, Coco and Josephine made faces of disbelief when they glanced at some of the price tags, which were displayed. Being a bit more privileged, Deedee didn't even bat an eye.

"Dior makes some nice evening joints but this shit is ridiculously expensive, yo," Coco said after going through a couple of stores.

"I ain't looking at price tags. I'm keeping my eyes peeled for something sexy from Donna Karan. Her boutique is close by," Josephine said.

"What, for the prom?" Coco asked.

"Not really but that could be a secondary motive," Josephine said, walking away and inspecting some dresses.

Coco lingered awhile and rubbed her cheek against the silky fabric of one particularly beautiful dress.

"Girls, there are no limits. Anything y'all see in here that y'all like?" Deedee asked.

"They a'ight," Josephine answered.

"Dior's style is the dopest, Coco," Deedee said, huddling next to

Coco. "I saw you had your eyes on that red outfit back there. That's cool. It would match your skin tone really well," Deedee continued.

Coco's brown eyes squinted in disbelief. She looked at Deedee for sometime without answering. When she spoke, she immediately regretted it.

"Why ya gotta be trying to make selections for me. I mean the dress is really nice, but how you know I wasn't just checking out the price"

"Coco—"

"I'm really not trying to get your opinion. The only reason I'm here playing your game is because Jo wanted to."

"I respect that, Coco. I mean I can't blame you for whatever you wanna hold against me."

"Hold against you? Do you remember that only a couple o' days ago you were calling me a hood rat?"

"Coco, I never called you that. I never did," Deedee said.

Coco stared at her with fierceness of a boxer facing his challenger. "I would never call you that," Deedee reiterated.

It came in a harmless whisper uttered without retreat. Deedee was in Coco's face. What is the plan if your opponent doesn't back out of the fight? Coco stared at Deedee's unshaken stare. All day long she had it in her mind to yell, 'To hell with Deedee because she's a phony bitch.' Now it seemed it was all just a big misunderstanding. Coco's mind was traveling at light speed. Was she deliberately trying to be mean to Deedee? There was no real need to be, Coco decided. Lost in her own thoughts, she could still hear Deedee's apologetic voice.

"I mean if I knew that's what you thought I would've called and really tried to apologize. I would not think that of you, Coco. You're far better..."

"So you wouldn't mind coming to visit me in da hood, then?"

"A visit is no problem. It's just that in light of what was going on at the time, I knew my uncle wouldn't let me go with you."

"Okay, maybe I was too quick to jump to conclusions. I'm sorry, Dee. How're your uncle and Sophia doing by the way?" Coco asked. She could be so cool, Deedee thought as she answered.

"They both good, I guess. Sophia went to work earlier and my uncle, he was in the studio all night doing his thing."

"That's good. I been home working on some rhymes too. Say whassup to them for me, a'ight?"

"A'ight, Coco. So, do you want to get that dress?"

"I really don't know. I'll take a look in some other stores, then I'll make a decision, okay?"

"That's all good, Coco."

"But Dee, how're you gonna pay for these outfits, yo?"

"I've got a card from my uncle," Deedee said with a shrug of her shoulder. "And I've never used it. It just seemed like a fun thing to do right now. Shopping with my girls," Deedee said as Josephine rejoined them.

"You got that right," Josephine said. "I've seen enough. Ladies, let's bounce up outta this piece."

"Oh, because you're through, we should?" Deedee said with a laugh.

"No! But I can't wait for Donna Karan," Josephine said, beaming, which left Coco and Deedee rolling their eyes.

They left the store and continued investigating all the sales. Crisscrossing from east to west, they left nothing but the pavement unturned. Their expedition went on, and the girls strolled down blocks and blocks of designer stores until they all had their complete outfit. Josephine claimed a black Donna Karan gown, which really complemented her now sexy physique and Deedee sparkled with a new Versace silver dress. Coco settled for the elegant red dress by Dior that Deedee had liked. It was an expensive but pleasurable time.

That was then but this was now. Life without the rest of the Crew for Coco. Despite missing her girls, Coco had to make the best of time. It would be her and Deedee. After a couple hours, they were through shopping. Coco hailed a cab and the girls climbed in. The cab driver put the many shopping bags inside the trunk. After Deedee gave the address, the driver smiled.

"Are you are fashion models or actresses?" the driver inquired, getting in the car.

"Are we...?" Deedee asked aloud.

"Did a lot of shopping today, huh?" he continued, while driving away.

"Did we...?"

"We did, yo."

Inside her uncle's apartment, Deedee sat on a sofa and checked her messages. Coco was rummaging through the bags trying to find something else to wear. She soon found a skirt that fit her looser. Checking the sarong skirt, Coco shimmied out of her dress. She stood in bra and panty looking for the matching scarf.

"You do have nicely toned legs Coco," Deedee said and continued to check her messages on her cell phone.

Coco slipped into the skirt and used the scarf to wrap her Afro. She glanced at herself in the hall mirror.

"That's why you're trying to get me to stock up on dresses and skirts, so you can see my legs, yo?"

"No silly. Summer's coming and it's gonna be hot. Plus

you might have an interview or two lined up. Acting as your fashion consultant, I wanted you to change up the look and feel of each interview."

"You sure that's your motive, yo?"

"Yes, for now maybe I'll be your manager or business partner in the future, but we'll take things one step at a time. But always know that I got your back, Coco."

Coco stared at her for a beat and thought of all the reasons she had tried to hate Deedee. But she couldn't ignore the growing connection between them. Coco clad in her bra and skirt, felt her heartbeat raced when she hugged Deedee. She tried to ignore it, but realized it was Deedee's heartbeat she felt.

The moment was intimate for both girls. Coco had let down her defense in more ways than one. Their bodies touched and Deedee's lips gently grazed Coco's. Coco didn't respond but felt the ignition in her brain and the spark in her lips.

"You're trying to kiss me, yo?" Coco laughed.

"I mean to kiss you on the cheek," Deedee smiled.

Coco felt Deedee heart thumping in her chest when her lips touched her cheek. They continued to hug and buried their heads on each other's shoulder. Sighing in relief, tears rolled down each other's cheeks. For the next few moments, nothing was heard except heavy breathing and two hearts beating as one. Deedee broke the sensually charged silence when she spoke. Coco nodded at her and they could see the tears rolling each other's cheek.

"I remember the first time I went back to school after the whole rape situation. And, man was I having the worst day of my life? I mean I wanted to just cry and then I bumped into you accidently and you saved the day."

"Word yo...?"

"Word up, yo. I really felt nothing but love for you since then. Because when I first met you, I thought you were just a cold person who needed to be loved. But that day I saw it in you, Coco."

"What you saw, yo?"

"I saw love in you. Real love..."

"What day was that yo?"

"Oh how could you forget? We were at school. I was walking outside Miss Martinez office and I was soo frustrated, I was about to light up a cigarette right there. And you were there in the hallway, by yourself. It was in the afternoon...?"

"Okay, I remember that, yo. I remember," Coco smiled.

Deedee slammed the door, heading toward the exit. This day had to end, she thought, reaching for her cigarettes.

The world is such a fucking wicked place, she almost said aloud as the tears sprung, filling her eyes with water and making her vision blurry. As she took out a cigarette, she bumped into Coco. Deedee's head rose. She wiped her eyes and turned to apologize.

"I'm sorry, I..."

"Need a light, yo?" Coco eyed the cigarette Deedee was trying to hide.

"No smoking in da hall, so we gotta take it to da toilet or da streets, yo."

"Cool. I was heading to the streets," Deedee said.

She was noticeably shaken. Coco saw the uneasiness immediately. Maybe this is the way all victims react, Coco thought as they walked to the exit together. As the two girls left the building, they paused. Coco gave Deedee a light. The smoke rushed to her lungs and Deedee immediately started to cough. Her eyes filled with tears.

"Let's get something to drink, yo." Coco said, patting Deedee's shoulder.

"Yeah, sounds good."

The girls walked to the corner store. Deedee chose apple juice and Coco bought soda. They moved to a bench in front of the school. Deedee felt better after a few sips. Coco lit a cigarette.

"How you feeling, yo...?"

"Oh, I'm better. All the initial tests were negative. That juice really hit the spot. Thanks Coco," Deedee said.

Coco watched Deedee inhaling easily now. Damn, did she forget already? Coco thought. The rape was only last week. Watching Deedee from the corner of her eye, Coco smoked freely but was confused as to how an experience like that could be so quickly forgotten.

"Yeah, true. Da soda is on time. But I'm saying how are you really feeling, you know?"

Coco gestured with her cigarette. She knew she was prying, but she felt suddenly that she was also a victim in the carjack. Deedee smiled. She had actually misunderstood Coco's question. It made her cheerful, even if she had to recall a bad ordeal. Coco marveled at Deedee's smile.

"You're funny," Deedee said through a chuckle. "I didn't mean to laugh, but I'm doing better, thanks. It's the first day back to school after about a week. It's kind a rough, you know. You know?" Deedee surprised herself with this burst of energy.

Coco nodded. They smoked and sipped and gazed lazily at passing pedestrians. Then they spotted Danielle and Josephine hurrying their way.

"Figured we'd find you here," Josephine said. Danielle and Deedee exchanged greetings.

"Hi, what's up? How you feeling...?" Danielle asked.

She passed Coco to kiss Deedee's cheek. Coco stood aside as Josephine did the same. Being with these girls again renewed the feeling of innocent camaraderie for her and brought a flood of emotions. Deedee cried as the girls hugged her. She motioned to Coco, who joined the group hug. Josephine and Danielle sniffled. Coco's eyes seemed damp. They huddled for a few more minutes then released one another.

Coco reached for a cigarette. Danielle and Josephine sat on the bench. Coco handed the lit cigarette to Deedee. She puffed smoothly and passed it back to Coco, who took a drag and passed it to Josephine. Josephine inhaled, and passed the cigarette to Danielle, who in turn puffed and passed it to Deedee. The cycle continued until the cigarette was finished. They all stood when the Black Range Rover pulled to a stop across the street. Eric waved.

"Oh, that's my uncle," Deedee said, motioning across the street. "Y'all wanna meet him? Maybe get a ride to somewhere?"

"We're gonna rehearse in da school auditorium, yo," Coco said.

"But thanks anyway for the offer," Danielle said, waving at Eric Ascot.

"Yeah, thanks. That's cool, you're always looking out," Josephine said.

She gave Coco a challenging look. Coco shook her head. Eric Ascot spun the vehicle around in front of the girls.

"Hello, young ladies," he greeted the girls from the driver's seat.

"Hi, Uncle E, I want you to meet Coco, Danielle and Josephine. They have a group called Coco and Da Crew."

"No...not anymore. We just Da Crew, yo," Coco said with a smile.

"Yep, Eric," Danielle said, sashaying toward Eric. "It's Coco, the crowd motivator, yo, Ms. Flamboyant Jo, and myself. We rep Da Crew."

"Love-lay Ms. Dani," Josephine said, rhythmically completing the

melody.

The girls laughed. Deedee opened the door and got in the van.

"Come check us this weekend. We gonna wreck shit at Busta's open-mike contest, yo," Coco said.

"I will, I definitely will," he said.

Deedee jumped inside, and the Range Rover pulled away. Deedee waved. The girls raised their hands.

"Peace," they shouted in unison.

"Okay, yeah, yeah. I remember that yo. I remember," Coco smiled.

Deedee's cell phone went off and she answered then hung up. She kissed Coco's cheek before untangling from their embrace.

"It's Uncle E. He wants you in the studio working with some new tech he hired. So let's get ready to bounce up."

"Okay, I'm ready to go right now. I want to stop at the hospital and give Madukes all these sleeping gears you got her, Dee."

"Okie dokie, we'll stop there first. Then go to the studio," Deedee said, throwing a T-shirt in Coco's direction. "Hey this may go well with your skirt."

Dressed in Chanel sandals, Donna Karan sarong skirt, and the white Cavalli T-shirt Deedee had thrown her, Coco stepped out the elevator. She walked with Deedee out of the building. The doorman stood holding the door open, gawking at the girls. They were headed to the garage and he watched their hips in full sway. Deedee was wearing a brown Dolce and Gabanna pantsuit that hugged her curves. The doorman had an eyeful. A few minutes later the BMW was pulling into traffic. Coco and Deedee pulled their Gucci shades down.

They pulled up near Harlem Hospital and took a tour around the block before finding parking. Accompanied by the stares of all the men in the immediate vicinity, the girls walked to the hospital's entrance. Coco and Deedee carried the shopping bags containing the clothing she had got for her mother. Coco went up to the information desk.

"I'm Ms. Rachel Harvey's daughter and..."

"One sec, please," the woman in thick glasses said. She quickly checked the log and turned back to Coco. "Your mother is still in intensive care on the eighth floor. You may go up and see her, but..."

The woman turned to see Coco and Deedee racing to the elevator. They got out on the eighth floor and walked toward the room where Coco's mother was. Coco and Deedee stood outside and looked at her mother. She was on a bed with tubes running in and out of her nose and mouth. Her eyes were closed and there was no way to tell if she was alive except for a tube floating up and down. A nurse walked over to the girls and spoke.

"Are you related to her?" she asked Deedee.

"Her daughter is right here," Deedee said, pointing at Coco.

"Coco..." Deedee said, gently tapping her friend, who was engrossed in looking at her mother.

"Huh?" Coco answered. She nodded when she saw the nurse.

"Okay, you were the one here yesterday, right?" the nurse asked and Coco nodded again. "You two could pass for sisters."

"Is she gonna be alright?" Coco asked. Her eyes were still on her mother inside intensive care.

"She's responding to the medication but it takes a little time. Your mother was also suffering some dehydration, and that didn't help. Her recovery will come along slowly, but she should come out alright," the nurse explained.

"We brought her some clothes and stuff," Deedee said.

"Okay, you can check the packages over here," the nurse said to Deedee. "If you like I could let you sit by her for a few minutes," she said to the distraught Coco.

Coco was stunned by the sight of her mother, and didn't hear or see when Deedee and the nurse took the shopping bags to another section of the hospital.

"You've done it again, mom. When will it end? Are you gonna stick around to tell me to stop saying 'yo'?" Coco asked aloud.

Staring at her mother's still body, Coco cringed as she silently counted the number of tubes connected to her emaciated body.

She found herself kissing her mother's exposed cheek and sitting at her bedside. Coco wrung her hands, shifting between anger, sympathy and love. Her emotions overflowed and Coco cried.

Deedee returned and watched Coco's hunched shoulders and could see that her friend was sobbing. She entered and stood behind Coco for a beat. Then Deedee placed her hands on Coco's shoulder. Teary-eyed, Coco stood, hugging Deedee. The girls embraced for a few beats in silence while the life-support machine made squelching sounds.

"She's gonna be alright," Deedee said.

"If you say so, yo," Coco sighed.

"Never give up on your mother, Coco," Deedee said with conviction. "I gave up on mine, and now I wish I never did."

"Yeah but—"

"I was six when I realized what was going on..." Deedee thought of the last time she saw her own mother. "And I should have done more to help..." Deedee's said, her voice trembling with emotion.

Then her voice suddenly trailed as she reminisced.

Her mother, Denise Ascot was heavy into drugs after her husband's death. Perhaps she couldn't handle his dying, or maybe it was the way he was killed. Whatever it was, Deedee remembered vividly that the last month or so before her mother was carried away. She was stealing to support a burgeoning crack habit. Her mother had lost a lot of weight. Her clothing no longer fit. Deedee remembered feeling real hatred toward her mother.

Her uncle had tried to explain, but Deedee couldn't understand, wouldn't listen. She changed her name on the school register by forging her mother's signature. Denise had been part of Deedee's name. She had been Denise D. Ascot, but changed it to Deedee. Deedee despised her mother, because of the drug use. During the period they lived together, Deedee would often wish death on her mother.

"I wish she would die," Deedee prayed daily. One day, eight years ago, the ambulance had carried her mother away on a stretcher. Denise had overdosed on crack-cocaine and heroin. Deedee felt some type of relief. She hoped her mother would never come back. After the overdose, Deedee never saw Denise again. She would miss her, but kept that a secret.

"How do you help someone who just keeps doing the same ol', yo? It's like she hasn't learned anything from her past," Coco said, walking out with Deedee. "Let's go to the studio, yo."

"You still shouldn't give up," Deedee said.

They walked in silence to the elevator. Deedee continued hugging Coco's sagging shoulder. Continuing beyond the boundaries of the Harlem hospital, Coco and Deedee put their shades on and walked to the car. The girls got in and Deedee steered the car into traffic.

While riding in the car, Coco seemed to be in a tranquil mood and Deedee remained silent. Outside the midtown studio, she parked and the girls walked inside the building. Upstairs, a young man sitting alone in the lobby took notice of them. Once they entered the studio office, they walked past the icy grills of Tina and Kim. Both looked surprised and did a clear double take at Coco. Deedee noticed and smiled as she went by.

"Hi," she greeted.

"Hello..." Tina and Kim said.

"Ah, here come my two stars now," Eric said, greeting them when the girls walked into his office. "You look real nice, Coco," Ascot smiled at Deedee. "I just wrapped up that movie deal. We got a two-and-half-million-dollar budget. Just now got off the phone," he said.

"That's great, Uncle E.," Deedee said, hugging her uncle.

"Congrats, Mr. Ascot," Coco said.

"How many times must I tell you that you can call me Eric or Uncle Eric like Deedee does," Eric smiled and hugged Coco.

"This is good news," Deedee said, looking directly at Coco.

"It certainly is, yo."

"Uncle E., I spoke to Rightchus and—"

The ringing of the telephone diverted Eric's attention.

"Forget it Mr. Ascot. I mean Uncle E.," Coco said, interrupting Deedee as Eric sat at his desk to answer the phone.

"Coco, I just wanted to—"

"Repeat the B.S. that the con man fed you...?"

Coco cut her off and drew her closer in a huddle. While the girls chitchatted, Eric got on the intercom and spoke to the receptionist. Soon the young man who was sitting in the reception area, walked into the office.

"Deedee, Coco this is Reggie Mills, our new studio engineer. Reggie, I'd like you to meet my niece Deedee and our new recording star, Coco," Eric said, smiling.

"Nice to meet you both," Reggie said.

Coco nodded, and Deedee said, "Welcome Reggie."

"Reggie comes with great credentials and recommendation and I expect a fruitful time here," Eric continued.

"Thank you for the opportunity. I look forward to working with one of the legends in the music field," Reggie said humbly.

"Alright, let's get it going then. Reggie you already know the lay of the land so why don't you load up that disc we heard earlier for Coco?" Ascot said.

"I heard a lot of great tracks, Mr. Ascot. Which one...?"

"*Tougher Than Dice*," Coco, Deedee and Eric chorused.

"Okay, let's get it going then," Eric said, hanging up a call.

Deedee, Coco and the new studio engineer, Reggie Mills engaged in small talk in Eric Ascot's office. Eric looked at the young man and gave him instructions. Reggie went to the sound room and was preparing the track for Coco's new single, when Coco and Deedee walked in. Coco reached for her notepad while Deedee sat watching Reggie. He was at the mixing board moving his long fingers around as if he was playing a keyboard.

"I really think that there were some nice tracks Mr. Ascot made," he said to Deedee.

"*Tougher Than Dice* will be the one," Deedee said.

"Without question...That's definitely gonna make a bangin'

single," Reggie said. "I heard some of her stuff on a street-mix CD. Coco definitely got it going on right now.

The music came up and he adjusted the midrange. Her head bobbing, Coco walked over to where Deedee and Reggie stood talking.

"You got polish on your nails, yo?" she asked.

Deedee and Reggie both glanced at her with quizzical looks. Coco pointed to Reggie.

"I'm talking 'bout you, yo," she said, pointing to Reggie.

Deedee glanced at the studio engineer's hand and laughed. Reggie was baffled and stood gaping at Coco's stare and Deedee's laughter. He finally went into the booth and adjusted the microphones.

"Sounds good to you?" he asked Coco.

"Yeah, yeah, leave it right there, yo," she said, stepping into the recording booth.

Reggie's fingers moved cautiously on the controls. His previously cool demeanor seemed a little rattled by Coco's remark and Deedee's fit of laughter. He was trying not to look at Deedee for fear she might resume laughing at him.

"I think it's cool when a person takes care of themselves," Deedee said in a matter of fact tone.

"So why were you laughing at me then?" Reggie asked, getting closer to Deedee.

He was close enough for her to smell his stench. Reggie was handsome and bold. He was in her face and Deedee backed up.

"Because I think Coco can be soo silly," she said and turned attention to the booth.

Coco reached up, grabbed the microphone and launched into a flow. Nodding her head to the heavy–bass-laden track, she sang.

My sisters always dreaming
about us being on top

forever our hopes will not die
through me you will always fly...

Suddenly her voice faded, and the beat played on without her lyrics. Deedee glanced at her through the glass separating the sound booth and the rest of the studio. Her best friend had turned her back toward her; Coco's shoulders were hunched, and she was shaking her head.

"Give her few and then we can start the track again," Deedee said.

"That sounded like a dedication song, huh?"

"Yes. I think the moment got to her though—she's been going through a lot," Deedee said.

"I heard about ah...her friends...ah, Da Crew—"

"Uncle E. told you about that?" Deedee asked hurriedly.

"Nah, that's old news in the music industry. I stays informed on industry news," Reggie said, smiling.

"I hope you don't get your info from Rightchus," Deedee, sounding sarcastic.

"Who...?"

"Never mind... It's an expensive inside joke."

Coco came out of the booth. She rejoined Deedee and Reggie sitting at the controls. The pair went silent when Coco sat down.

"Are you okay, Coco?" Deedee asked, moving closer.

"Yeah, I'm good, yo," Coco said after a beat. "Singing that song was stirring up all kinds of feelings inside me...I felt like I was off a little."

"Uncle E. will tell you if you're off and besides Reggie will fix it. Can't he?" Deedee said.

"I can adjust—" Reggie started to say but Coco interrupted.

"Oh yeah, let my voice go with the drums—" she started to speak and Reggie cut her off.

"You mean acappella style?" he hurriedly asked.

"If you let me finish then I'll let you know, yo," she said and smirked before continuing. "Like I was saying, let my voice ride with just the drums and percussions for the first stanza. I'll sing, then when I start rapping, you bring in the bass."

"Like this?" Reggie said, moving his finger across the controls.

"Yeah, then I'm gonna sing that first piece just with drums like, *Hmm yes. Y'all were my sisters now and always our dream was about us being on the top forever...Hmm, hmm...*"

"Okay, I feel you," Reggie said.

"How you gonna feel me and I ain't through yet, yo?" Coco testily asked. "Day-um, lemme finish what I gotta say first before you jump in, yo."

"Ah, Coco, let's take a smoke break," Deedee suggested.

"Sounds like a good idea, yo," Coco said, turning to look at her. "Yeah I ain't got no weed though, yo. And that's what I could go for right about now."

"I thought you had some from—"

"I did but I left that shit when I was changing clothes," Coco said.

"I got a little sump'n sump'n..." Reggie said.

Both girls glanced at him and smiled for different reasons. Deedee was happy that Coco's anxiety would be diffused. Reggie's helping hand in the situation didn't go unnoticed by Deedee. She watched him removing the bag of weed and a blunt from his pocket.

"A'ight, a man who comes to work prepared. You gotta respect that, yo."

"Priceless..." Deedee smiled, patting Reggie on the butt. "Let's go to the green room."

They walked out of the studio and into the small room with big, comfortable sofas. There was a small refrigerator in a corner. Graffiti art flossed on the walls. The place was also equipped with small tables. The three found a comfortable area and settled down. Reggie rolled the weed and gave it to Coco. She lit it and passed it to Deedee. The weed went around, circulating several times. Soon it was gone. All that remained was the high and the smell. Deedee got up to turn on the fan when Eric suddenly walked in.

"Now that everyone is high, let's get some work done. Dee, come with me," he said.

Coco lit a cigarette and got a bottle of water from the refrigerator. Reggie took a soda and they walked back inside the studio.

"I'm gonna arrange the track the way you want it. Then you can rock out," Reggie said.

"A'ight, I'll get my lyrics tighter. Good looking out on the smoke, yo."

"No problem, babes," Reggie said.

"Coco," Coco said, staring. "My name is not "Babes," it is Coco," she said.

"I hear you, Coco," Reggie said, taking his seat at the control board.

Coco sat down with her rhyme book and looked at the paper with words in front of her face. The lyrics she had composed should have been there, but she couldn't see anything. Coco didn't panic. She closed her eyes and waited for a few beats, knowing her vision would return. This always happens when I smoke, she thought.

A few minutes later, Coco heard the track ringing just the way she had wanted it. Her sight slowly returned and she threw a glance in Reggie's direction, her head nodding in rhythm to the music.

Coco waited until her sight was completely back before she tried to get out of her seat. She danced into the booth, and opened up with vocals on the microphone.

"Hmm..." Coco hummed. *"Hmm...My sisters always dreaming about us on being on the top forever, our hopes will not die. Through me you will always fly..."*

Later Deedee walked into the recording studio, and sat next to Reggie. They did a two-step to the rhythm while Coco laid down her vocals.

"Feeling like I'm losing my mind
calling out your names one at a time..."

Coco's flow paused then she said, "Just use the last part from 'My sister's always dreaming' Use that for the chorus, yo," she shouted over the microphone.

"I gotcha, Coco," Reggie answered.

"A'ight, yo..."

Deedee went into the sound booth and turned the microphone down. Reggie toyed with the controls watching the girls gathered in a tight huddle for a few beats.

"Yeah, I thought your uncle was about to get on your ass for smoking weed with us, yo."

"No it wasn't even anything like that, Coco. You know Uncle E. be getting his tokes on with his friends. He wanted me to be a witness on that movie contract. I'm part of the business you know, and Uncle E.

sometimes treats me like my father in some of the business deals. So he just wanted me to sign some papers for the movie deal."

"Okay sounds good, yo."

"We're in the movies officially, Coco. Pre-production starts right away. You're gonna be that star you were destined to be."

"That's the way it's going down, yo...? What about you, yo...?"

"I'm about my business so it's going down just like that."

In the recording studio, the beat played on. Reggie kept adjusting the equalizer until he had inserted all of Coco's takes at the right volume. He pumped it and it rang through. The girls nodded their head to the song and smiled.

Eric walked in the studio and listened for a while. He remained silent and sat at the controls with Reggie. The young studio engineer smiled proudly.

"I like it so far, but everything coming out of my studio gotta have ass on them," Eric said.

Reggie looked puzzled. He adjusted the volume and said, "I don't understand...?"

"Give me a little bit more bass," Eric whispered.

Reggie adjusted the bass and the music pumped through the speakers. Nodding his head to the rhythm of the beat, Eric said, "Yeah, that's what I'm talking 'bout."

"Sometimes when I feel I'm losing my mind
I call out your names... I hear y'all listening
Things don't always work the way we plan 'em
Your voices live through me just the same
Be my number one fan and I will succeed
I'll be felt the champion title I will claim
I'm making a stand feeling hard to defeat

We taking over just the way we planned
From the start doing it from our hearts...
Sisters always dreaming us on top forever
Reigning hopes never die you'll always remain
So fly.../Jo, Dani, Bebop living for you
Missing Miss Katie's voice y'all got her
Listening made me nicer music game sicker
Lyrics lock tighter feeling invincible Truth is
Her wisdom helped me survive all my fights
Made me stronger now I'm tougher than dice..."

The beat went on, Coco and Deedee danced out of the booth. They listened to the heavy sounds blasting from the speakers in the studio. They had been sounding playful—before the expert producer put his finishing touches on it. Now, the place was vibrating from the bass. The music took on a serious dance edge, transformed into a track that would move any wallflower.

"Hmm I like that, yo," Coco said, dancing to the beat.

"Yeah... That's it right there," Deedee said, joining her in a dance.

Even though it was incomplete, the first couple of verses, and the hook made it sound like a complete song.

"We got some more mixing down to do, but it's good right there," Eric said.

Deedee smiled when Kim and Tina walked inside and started dancing. Soon everyone was dancing around like the song was the hit of the party.

Feeling like a champion, Coco pulled out a cigarette and lit it. She took a drag and couldn't help but reminisce of the last time

Da Crew were together, and had won the talent contest. Danielle and Josephine were both there with her backstage.

"And the top three finalists are..."

The voice of the emcee boomed behind a thunderous drum roll. Da Crew heard the names of other finalists. Suddenly everyone was kissing and hugging them. The crowd converged on them, mobbing them. Coco spotted Deedee and Danielle hugging. She rushed through the crowd, and past the screaming Josephine, to Deedee.

"Lemme use your phone. I wanna call this old lady to let her know, yo," she said breathlessly. Deedee hugged her and handed over the instrument. Coco wanted to talk to Miss Katie and thank her, but the older lady was already asleep and Coco left her a message.

"We did it, Miss Katie. We won, yo."

Even though she was only reminiscing, Coco's thoughts brought goose bumps to the surface of her brown skin. The sound of Eric's booming voice brought her back to reality.

"Who's smoking a damn cigarette?" Eric asked.

The studio went silent when Eric's voice thundered. Reggie turned the music down, and all eyes went in Coco's direction. She was deep in thoughts and was the only one who didn't hear the question. Coco kept smoking until Deedee got closer to her.

"Uncle E. said you can't smoke in here," Deedee said.

"Coco, don't you know all the performers smoke in the green room? That's the only place where anyone can smoke," Eric said.

"I know that," Kim and Tina chorused.

"That rule applies to everyone, including the stars," Eric said, glancing at Coco.

She realized that all their eyes were focused on her. Pokerfaced, Coco snapped out of her trance and put out the cigarette.

"Okay, let's all take a break and let's get to Sardi's, dinner is on me," Eric said.

Coco and Deedee glanced at each other. Then Coco said, "I thought we'd be the only ones going, but I guess we gotta hang with riff raffs, yo."

"Don't worry, we'll sit away from them," Deedee said. "I'll drive Uncle E and Coco can ride with me," she said to her uncle.

"I'll see you guys there," Eric said.

Tina and Kim filed out behind Eric. Reggie turned off the music and secured all the programs. He efficiently stored the music along with Coco's lyrics. Coco and Deedee were watching him. He did take pride in his work.

"If I hear this on bootleg in the streets, I know where to come, yo," Coco said with a chuckle.

"I had to sign my life away to get this job. I'm not gonna mess that up," Reggie said.

When he was finished they all left together. Coco was in her usual bop while Deedee and Reggie walking behind her.

"Do you have a ride to the restaurant, Reggie?" Deedee asked.

"No," he answered.

"You can ride with us," Deedee smiled, getting in the elevator.

"So you guys just graduated, huh?" Reggie asked.

"Yes," Coco and Deedee chorused.

"I remember when I graduated. It was good times," he said.

"Oh don't try acting like it was that long ago. I read your resume," Deedee said and Coco smiled.

"No frontin' allowed, yo."

"I graduated three years ago. But it still seems like such a long time now," Reggie said. "You gotta grow up quick and be an adult. Get a job and all."

"Now you're sounding old," Deedee smiled and Coco chuckled.

They got off the elevator on the ground floor lobby and walked to the exit. The doorman held the door and smiled when he saw Coco in a skirt.

"Have a good evening," he said. "Thank you," Reggie said. "That's a nice ride," he continued when Deedee hit the remote starter.

"Thank you," Deedee said, getting into the BMW.

The girls sat up front and Reggie sat in the backseat. Music blasting, Deedee joined traffic flowing, heading cross-town to the restaurant. *Notorious Thugs* pumped heavy through the speakers in the ride, and the girls nodded their heads as Biggie Smalls rhymed.

Armed and dangerous,
ain't too many can bang with us
Straight up weed- no angel dust,
label us Notorious
Thug-ass niggaz that love to bust,
it's strange to us
Y'all niggaz be scramblin', gambling...

"Thank you," Deedee said to the doorman outside the restaurant.

The smell of burgers and steak filtered through the dining area greeting them. There was enough light in the place for Deedee to spot Eric. He was talking on his cell phone while Kim and Tina were working on their drinks. Walking ahead of Coco and Reggie, Deedee walked over and joined the group.

"Hey Uncle E," she said, and waved at Kim and Tina.

After ensuring that Reggie sat next to Kim and Tina, Deedee took up position beside Coco. A waiter came over and took their orders. Eric was constantly on his cell phone, Kim and Tina chatted, and Coco and Deedee engaged in small talk. Reggie kept his eyes on Deedee. And she glanced at him from time to time.

The waiter soon returned, placing orders of steak in front of Deedee and Eric respectively, then Coco, Kim and Tina. Reggie was last, and finally they all chomped down. The evening went on without any hiccups, everyone eating and drinking heartily. They all thanked Eric, who stayed on his cell phone throughout the meal.

After dinner, the group drifted outside. It was a cool summer evening. The city lights shone bright and Reggie invited the group to the nightclub.

"I'm spinning music at Amnesia tonight. It's really nice there. I'd like to invite you all to check it out, if you all want?" he said.

"Yeah that's a cool spot, yo," Coco said.

"Where's that?" Kim asked.

"Shut your face! You don't know that nightclub, girl? I heard it's hot," Tina said.

"The night is still young," Deedee said, looking at her uncle.

"Why not," Eric said, still on his cell phone.

"It won't cost you nothing and you all are gonna enjoy this spot," Reggie said.

The group split, heading toward their respective carriages. Eric escorted Kim and Tina to his ride. Coco had shotgun, Reggie rode in the back while Deedee started the engine.

Up in restaurants with mandolins,
and violins
We just sittin here tryin to win,
tryin not to sin
High off weed and lots of gin
So much smoke need oxygen,
steadily countin them Benjamins

As they pulled up outside the club, Deedee and Eric saw a long line around the exterior of the club. They parked and the group walked by patrons standing on line in designer clothes, their anxious heels cooled by the long wait.

Reggie led the group and they walked to the front of the line. Immediately security let the group through the velvet rope.

"Welcome to club Amnesia, Mr. Ascot," a bouncer greeted.

"This is Coco and Deedee," Eric said, taking a break from a conversation he was having on his cellphone.

"We're familiar with Coco. Are you performing?" someone asked.

"I'm performing," Reggie said, beating his chest.

"Oh, by the way, we here too," Kim and Tina chorused.

Chuckles filtered through the small gathering. The group was allowed to walk inside. Crowds of party people were on the dance floor of the popular nightspot. Reggie escorted the group to the VIP section behind the deejay's booth. Eric ordered a round of alcoholic drinks for Kim, Tina and himself. He ordered sodas for the girls. Reggie sat with the group for a few, then it was his turn to be deejay.

"Alright, dance and enjoy yourselves. I'm gonna spin the music for a while," Reggie stood and said, "Eric, thanks for dinner and I'll see you later," he continued, shaking Eric's hand.

"You're welcome," Eric said.

"Later y'all," Reggie said, walking away.

"Let's hear what you got, yo," Coco said.

Reggie went to the deejay's booth, and got in a groove, mixing some dance tracks. The party was jumping when Coco and Deedee hit the dance floor with the other revelers. The girls laughed and danced around with each other. A few minutes later, Eric posted up on the floor laughing with the two.

Then the deejay dropped *Wait* by Ying Yang Twins. Rumps were shaking to *The Whisper Song* when Kim and Tina invaded the dance floor. Coco shifted and Deedee moved away with her. Eric was left with Kim behind him and Tina in the front, both working him over.

Hey how ya doing lil momma

let me whisper in ya ear

Tell ya something that ya might like to hear

Got a sexy-ass body and yo ass look soft

Mind if I touch it and see if it's soft?

Naw I'm just playin less you say I can

And I'm known to be a real nasty man

From his perch in the deejay's booth, Reggie watched the action on the dance floor. While Coco's moves demanded attention, it was the sway of Deedee's hips that riveted his eyes in her direction. Adjusting the lights, the deejay followed her every move on the crowded dance floor. Tantalized by her dance, Reggie licked his lips. Deedee had clearly enticed him and had him fantasizing about being with her. She threw a glance up at him and he nodded his head in time with her rhythm.

Sandwiched between Kim's derrière, protruding from her tight jeans, and Tina's crotch humping, Eric was busy having fun. Remaining calm and cool, he smiled, enjoying himself.

I hear they say a closed mouth don't give in

And I don't mind askin for head

Ya heard what I said,

we need to make our way to the bed

You can start using your head

You like to fuck

Have your legs open all in the buck

Loud music continued pumping, hammering club heads with some heavy grooves. Prancing and jumping, they were all having a good time. The smile on Reggie's face broadened when he saw Deedee waved at him. He stood in the deejay's booth watching the dance floor.

"Wow I never seen you dance so much, yo," Coco laughed.

"I'm enjoying myself," Deedee said.

They saw Eric, Kim and Tina dancing toward them. Eric seemed happy and openly laughed. Coco made a face and did a spin move that would rival Michael Jackson. She danced away while Deedee and her uncle spoke.

"You seem like you're having a lot of fun, huh, Uncle E?" Deedee smiled, embracing Eric.

"Yeah, but I have to get out of here," Eric said, returning the embrace. "I got an early-morning meeting."

"Oh yeah, you have to meet with those executive producers, right?" Deedee asked.

"Yeah, at eight in the morning and it's after one," he said, glancing at his watch. "I'll take care of Kim and Tina. Make sure you and Coco get home safely," Eric said, waving at Coco.

Deedee kissed his cheek then waved at Kim and Tina. She walked over to where Coco was getting down with a group of club kids. It wasn't hard to tell that Coco was having a grand time throwing down. Slipping in and out of dance moves, she was in her zone. Then she spotted Deedee and laughed at the roar of the club kids. Coco slid over to where Deedee was two stepping, and the two girls chatted.

"The music is good, huh? The deejay isn't even running his mouth, right Coco?" Deedee said.

"Yeah, the deejay is doing his thing, yo."

"Oh yes. By the way, Uncle E. said he'll see you in the studio tomorrow," Deedee said.

"Okay, cool. Your uncle was illin'-out with them two skanky bitches, yo," Coco said, walking off the floor.

"Coco...? Don't say that about my uncle. He brings some class."

"They soo ghetto, they can't pay for class, yo. I hope that's all he's bringing. But..." Coco's voice trailed.

"Coco, don't be thinking that about my uncle. Those two...? Ooh..."

"I hope he's strapped up for them bitches, yo."

"Coco do not even imply—"

"Let's get a drink, yo."

Laughing, they walked to the bar. Coco immediately got two drinks. She took a sip and smiled. Deedee raised her glass, wondering what was behind Coco's wry smile. She played along with Coco, trying her best not to be nosey.

"But what...?" Deedee asked, after taking couple sips of her drink.

"I'm just kinda happy your uncle bounce, yo. I been needing a real drink."

"I hear you, Coco. Cheers," Deedee smiled. "Coco, I know you. Is that all?"

"I'm not the only one who's happy your uncle left either, yo," Coco said, gesturing.

They continued sipping while standing next to the bar. Deedee turned to see Reggie walking toward them. He walked to the bar and brought three drinks back. Reggie offered drinks to Deedee and Coco. Deedee took the drink and sipped.

"What kind a drink is this, yo?" Coco asked, looking at the glass.

"Vodka and cranberry," Reggie answered. "You don't like...?"

"It's all good, yo."

"Coco, would like to rock out on the mike?" Reggie asked after a beat.

Coco glanced around the crowded nightclub. She noted all the club heads jumping around before answering.

"Sure," she said.

Reggie led her and Deedee to the deejay's booth. The talented teen grabbed the microphone and was ready to throw down. Reggie and Deedee were on the floor dancing and cheering. Other club heads familiar with the talented teen, jumped when the announcement was made.

"Ladies and Gentleman, boys and girls, tonight we're gonna be entertained by none other than Coco the phenom..." the deejay announced.

The crowd roared, and reaching into her vault of rhymes, Coco started rhythmically spitting. The nightclub was ignited by Coco's flow. The teen let off her angst. Her raw energy ignited the speakers and sounds exploded.

I-I-I'm tougher than dice...
tough...tougher than dice
My name is Coco and
I'm tougher than dice...

Eric Ascot was driving uptown, music blaring in the black Maybach. He was smoking a cigarette when Tina touched him close to his crotch. Eric tried to ignore her and kept pushing the ride through the light traffic.

"Can I have one of your cigarettes, Eric?" Tina asked.

"Oh yeah sure," Eric answered, pointing to where the pack sat on the dashboard.

"You must be stressed from all that work and shyt," Kim said from the backseat.

Kim's fingers began slowly massaging Eric's shoulders and neck. He allowed her to continue moving her hands on him. Tina rolled up some cocaine with tobacco and weed. She smoked and passed it to

Kim. She pulled on it and put it between Eric's lips. The mixed of drugs and liquor had him going. Kim continued to massage his shoulder and passed the cigarette to Tina.

"If you keep that up we're gonna have to make a pit stop," Eric said.

"We 'bout that..." Kim said.

"Yeah, let's make that stop," Tina smiled.

Eric made a U-turn and got back on the West Side headed downtown. A few minutes later he parked inside a midtown hotel garage and was checking in. Walking to the elevator, Tina and Kim were on either side with their arms around him. They stayed sandwiched to him getting on the elevator. Inside the elevators, the hands of Kim and Tina did some exploring on Eric's body. Soon he was heating up and revving to have them both. Tina started out, massaging his head.

When her lips locked his in a deep kiss, Tina left no doubts about her intentions. While Kim rubbed his package from behind, Eric felt Tina's perky nipples piercing his chest. She turned around and jiggled her ass. Kim's assets were already making huge circles in Eric's mind. And Tina's bold actions were yielding huge results.

By the time the elevator doors opened, he was hard like a rock. They stayed close and stumbled into the room. Laughter followed the trio to the small bar. Kim and Tina followed closely. Soon the trio went back from drinking and back to more fondling.

"How'd you want it?" Tina whispered in Eric's ears.

"Nasty, but keep it safe," Eric answered.

"We have rubber," Kim announced, pulling out a pack of Trojans.

All three immediately went for it on the bed. After Kim quickly got undressed, showing her shapely ass, Eric was unable to resist the urge. Lunging forward, he grabbed the objects of his desire. His hands roamed all over her Kim's round derriere. Not to be left out, Tina pulled her top off, displaying a perfect set of melons. She tackled him, and straddling him, Tina closed her eyes as she kissed him.

Kim rubbed Eric's hard dick while they watched Tina slipping out of her tight jeans. When her ass finally popped out, Kim smiled. There was no competition. Tina jumped into the bed, pressing her buns against Eric's thighs. She reached around, undoing his zipper. Soon she was playing with his hardened dick while Tina kissed his lips, enjoying the ride. Kim was fondling his scrotum and loosening the belt to his trousers.

Eric's hands roamed over Tina's body, searching her hidden crevices. He was definitely ready and then his trouser fell to the floor. Eric lifted her legs in the air. Tina swung her arms around his neck and opened her mouth inviting his tongue deep into her throat.

His hands continued roaming her sexy body. Tina squirmed and ground her pussy against him. Eric picked up her hot body and flipped her. Her ass was wet and ready for his tongue licking. Kim had his dick in her mouth sucking while his tongue eased into Tina's exposed gushy pussy. She writhed in excitement when Eric buried his face into her moisture. Her legs dangling on his shoulders, Eric placed his tongue on her clitoris and launched her into ecstasy.

"Yes, yes. Oh, papi ahi, ahi papi..."

Kim was now sucking him to full hardness, licking his balls and asshole. Eric softly bit Tina's upper thighs and her voice trailed off. Eric resumed licking and tickling Tina's vaginal area bringing a river of moisture out of Tina. Her legs stiffened and shook. Tina arched her crotch. She maneuvered her body and her tongue joined Kim's mouth circling Eric's dick. The purple head was filled and pointing upward to the ceiling. Tina's mouth covered and swallowed the exposed, hard penis. Kim was sucking his balls.

Eric felt the sucking motion of Tina's mouth and Kim's tongue licking his balls. He struggled, holding their heads in place. His grip tightened and his head shook from side to side. Then his whole body heaved and bucked. Squirts of sperm oozed from his dick.

"Ugh, oh fucking yeah!" Eric yelled.

Tina sucked harder, continuing to provide deep throat. Eric's body stiffened again and he opened his legs wider for better support. Kim reached under his genitals and sent her tongue cruising along the rim of his asshole. Her tongue burrowed deeper and deeper, Eric held her head tighter and tighter. She continued letting her tongue burrow deeper into his asshole.

Eric felt Tina putting the rubber on him and then she got on top of him. He opened his eyes and watched her riding. Eric held her waistline. Her petite body was working on his dick while her big boobs bounced up and down.

"Te gusta... You like this?" Tina ground herself against his hardness. "Huh, tell me you're enjoying this?"

"Ah yes. I'm enjoying it, ah..." Eric grunted.

Kim brought her pussy and collapsed it in a heap on Eric's face. Eric groped her fat ass and stuck his tongue inside her pussy. Tina moved her body up and down, watching them for a few beats. Kim pulled Eric's dick from Tina's dripping pussy.

"Aye ma, whatcha doing?" Tina asked in a frustrated tone.

"Chill out," Kim said, licking on the hardened dick.

She pulled off the rubber. Twirling Eric's dick around, she sucked on it, and replaced it in Tina's ass.

"Ooh yeah, papi," Tina moaned.

Tina's hands were free and she inserted her finger in Kim's rectum, sending her into orbit. Kim's stomach muscles quickly contracted when she felt the buildup deep inside her loins.

"Ooh... Ah shyt! Ooh..." Kim moaned.

"Ugh... ugh, ahh... Oh yeah..."

Tina was on top, her eyes closed, riding. Kim raised her butt so that Tina's finger could easily penetrate her ass. Then she reinserted his dick into her hot pussy. Eric's pleasure system continued in both directions. Tina felt the throbbing of his huge dick in her pussy. Kim wiggled her big round ass, happily anticipating the pleasure of his tongue. She twisted her ass around putting all her pussy on Eric's face. He had never felt soo alive, Eric could feel his dick growing deep inside Tina's hot pussy. All of a sudden, Tina hopped off his erection and started to angrily shout.

"Get your big ass out my face, bitch!"

"Oh yes. Ah, ugh uh... Get you fucking finger out my brownie, ho!"

Eric grabbed Tina's head in an attempt to shove her gaping mouth onto his head. She wiggled free and her mouth exploded spitting venom at Kim. He sat with his hardened dick in his hand and watched Tina and Kim yapping at each other.

"He don't wanna eat none of that cootchie, bitch. He already tasted this," Tina said, slipping her fingers between her legs.

Sticky, white fluid spurted from her wet pussy lips. Kim sucked her teeth as Tina laughed, relishing the moment. Tina kept massaging her lips with the tip with her tongue. Eric was rubbing his shaft with his hand in an attempt to stay hard. Kim and Tina were both sexy women, but he was losing his battle to stay rigidly hard. Tina was about to climb on top, but Kim nudged her.

"It's my turn bitch," she said, patting Tina's ass.

"Damn bitch! Can't you wait? You fucking slut!" Tina cursed.

"No, you got yours already, bitch. Let me get some and shyt,"

Kim said.

She climbed over Eric and quickly straddled his dick. Tina had an annoyed look on her face when she saw Kim's fat, round ass making circular motion on Eric's dick. She saw the bored look on Eric's face. He sat up watching his dick sliding sideways out of Kim's extremely wet pussy. It was obvious Kim knew what she was doing, but Eric was clearly uninterested.

"He don't want none of that fat stink-ass bitch!"

"Hold up! Whose ass you calling stink? You ho! You...!"

"Lemme suck it for you, papi," Tina suggested when she saw Eric getting up.

He kissed her neck and breasts. Kim's ass rotated and shook, going buck wild against his dick. His dick could barely stay up. She spun around and gave him a view of her rotating ass.

"Ah-h... Yes-s-s! I love that dick!" she whispered.

Tina watched for a few minutes then she slowly pushed Eric's head back. Sucking on his lips, she slipped her tongue between his lips.

"Kiss me back, papi," she begged, rubbing Kim's breasts.

"Stop feeling on my shyts, you ho!" Kim shouted.

Eric finally came undone. Standing up he walked out of the bed and sat in a chair next to the bed. Kim eyed him longingly as he slipped on his boxers. She glanced at Tina, cupping her breasts, slowly grinding her body and pursing her lips in a kiss directed at Eric.

"Oh shyt, that dick would feel soo good right now," Kim moaned loudly.

"Yeah probably, but I need a timeout. Y'all are too much," Eric smiled, slapping both women's asses.

He turned to walk away, and saw both Kim and Tina's

expressions changing from confusion to sadness. Tina stopped moving around seductively then she slowly straightened up. Eric's mind wasn't in the moment and his body failed to respond.

"That's it? You no like me, papi?"

"He's not your papi, ho," Kim quickly said.

"I don't mean papi in that sense I mean... You know?'

"I don't know shyt, ho!"

"Look bitch if it wasn't for me all this wouldn't happen. Right papi...?" Tina added.

"You and this 'papi' shyt fucked up my whole program."

"You-ungrateful-big-ass-bitch...! How could you even..."

"Hey chill you two. Let's get some sanity here," Eric said, taking charge of the situation.

"Don't mind her stupid ass. What you want me to do for you, Eric?" Kim asked, grabbing her ass.

"You stinking, big-ass bitch! Now you wanna start running...?"

"Okay, hold up! Kim, why don't you go eat out Tina's pussy? And Tina you eat Kim ass, huh?"

The place went silent as both Kim and Tina paused to stare at Eric's face. There was a faint crease of a smile.

"Papi, are you serious? I don't wanna eat her big, stinking ass," Tina loudly objected.

"You'd be eating something tasty, ho. I wouldn't even think of putting my mouth on your rotten snatch. Cuz you a ho!"

Eric's mind seemed to be on a fast track. He thought for a minute. Then whimsically, he smiled and said, "A'ight, a'ight, I got a couple of G's a piece for you all."

Tina glanced at Eric then back at Kim. She saw Kim glancing at Eric and then back at her. Kim and Tina gave each other a big smile.

"How much is a couple?" Tina asked.

"Two, of course," Eric answered.

"Why didn't you say that before!" they chorused.

Eric released a chuckle. Before he could finish his laughter, he saw Kim closing her eyes as Tina positioned her face under Kim's ass. Before he could sit back comfortably, Kim was smiling jovially, riding up and down with so much frenzy that Tina appeared crushed under her ass. Eric eased back, smiled, and enjoyed their sex show. His mind was going faster than both girls' tongues.

He laughed loudly, thinking how money had changed everything. His thoughts fell under the spell of the sounds their sexual activities produced. Eric paused to catch his breath while puffing on his cigar and watch.

Tina's lips were locked on Kim's clit, while Kim made her ass move so fast that Eric's eyes had problems staying riveted on it. Kim's ass seemed as if it was detached from the rest of her body. With great effort, Tina's sweaty love box was being chewed on by Kim's mouth. All the while Kim was making a clapping noise with her ass.

Sitting there watching the girls eating each other, Eric's mind wandered to the rhythm of their orgy. The sound of their lips smacking and Kim's booty clap, transported him to a place where he composed music. He heard the sound of strands of hair being tugged from the back.

Kim was going wild on top of Tina, whipping her pussy into submission. She reached up and held on in an attempt to calm Kim, but there was no holding Kim back. Her lustful aura heightened when Tina pulled her hair. She seemed to move her ass even faster.

"Ah yes!" Eric yelled.

He felt the rush of creativity like it was an ejaculation seeping out of his brain. After watching for a while, Eric slipped on the rest of his clothing. He could hear Tina gagging as Kim continued her booty dance atop her face.

"Ugh...ugh...ugh..." Kim grunted.

"Eat me..." Tina screamed.

Kim responded by sticking her tongue deep inside her friend, and tasting the salt of Tina's pussy. Tina turned around and kissed Kim's neck. Kim nibbled on Tina's ears. Eric was dressed and smiled when he heard their moans growing louder. He paused, watching them changing position.

"Oh, oh it feels soo good! Oh Lord, I'm coming," Kim cried in salacious delight as Tina's mouth nursed her clit.

Kim sucked and toyed with her nipples. Tina's stiff tongue penetrated her moisture-laden pussy. Juices leaked and her legs bucked and kicked all the way. Tina slapped Kim's round ass. Kim repositioned herself and easily slipped her finger into Tina's asshole. The sensation brought Tina more pleasure.

Her legs trembled and Eric watched Kim gently spread Tina's ass. It was then that Eric saw the floral artwork tattooed on her lower back. His eyes widened when he recognized that words were also tattooed on her butt cheeks. 'NES' was written across one plump cheek and 'TO' on the other. The discovery made him leery, but Eric continued to stare at her butt cheeks.

Eric was thinking about leaving and decided to do just that. He pulled out some money and began to count it as Tina spread Kim's vagina lips apart. She started licking the pinkish insides. Kim wiggled her ass around as Tina's tongue darted in and out of her asshole and pussy.

Eric placed the money on the nightstand and his smile increased when he saw Tina gently applied pressure to Kim's quivering clit. Her pleasure was heightened when Tina put the index and middle finger into Kim's vagina and ass simultaneously. Two fingers fucking her caused Kim to shriek. Then Tina's skilled tongue moved in and ignited her passion. Tina's action launched Kim deep into ecstasy.

"Ooh..." She moaned.

Her body was writhing and her tanks were filled. Kim grew dangerously close to a fierce detonation and neither of them saw when Eric walked out and closed the door. Tina's tongue slipping into the wedge between Kim's brown round and her pussy. Tina's stiff tongue gnawed at Kim's love passage. This propelled Kim to grab a handful of hair and pulled.

"Ah...ah...ooh...ooh...oh, oh." Kim cried, her breath coming in gasps.

The eruption rocked her frame. Kim's big ass was rotating in the air and on Tina's face. Still smiling, Eric was already down the hallway and exiting the hotel turned on. The brief sexual tryst he had witnessed had him forgetting about all the legal problems he had been having. Gone for the time was the memory of his ex, Sophia. It was almost worth calling his lawyer to thank him for sending Kim and Tina. He decided that paying was worth the relief. Eric nodded his head to a song while contemplating. It was then that he decided that paying was not only easier, it was better.

Meanwhile in the hotel room, Kim's body arched and she let off a loud yelp as Tina's tongue started licking down her sugary walls. She reached down and grabbed Tina's ears pulling her face closer.

"Suck my clit, you bitch!" Kim screamed, getting totally vulgar.

Tina shook her head, rubbing her tongue against Kim's ass

while Kim sucked her pussy. She smiled when Kim slowly crammed two fingers in her pussy again and again. This drove Tina crazy and she put her fingers in Kim's pussy.

"Oh, ah, yeah, oh yeah," Kim cried.

She was on the brink of bliss when Tina spread her butt cheeks wide. Tina's tongue was darting on every inch of her ass, increasing her carnal delight.

"Oh yes, yes...!"

Rhapsody engulfed her and forced Kim to squeal loudly. She raked her nails on the bed and her torso collapsed against the soft pillows. Kim was massaging her breasts while Tina spurted juice from her pussy. Then they lay tangled, drenched in each other's sweat. Tina's body slowly jerked. It was an explosive end to an alcohol-infested and drug-ravished torture their minds had been through.

A tingling sensation between them was all that was left to their climax. They looked around then smoked in silence. Their heavy sighing was the only sound coming from minds slowly recovering from sexual euphoria.

Later Kim and Tina walked out to the parking lot and signaled for a car. Eric had already paid a cabdriver, and he picked them up the moment they walked outside. Kim and Tina each counted two thousand dollars apiece. Both girls remained silent. They held each other close, and smiled, enjoying the ride uptown.

"See you in the morning," the driver said when they reached their destination.

"Okay, goodnight," Kim and Tina chorused. Arms interlocked they disappeared inside the building.

Coco walked off the small stage of the club. She had performed and wanted to smoke a cigarette. Coco pulled a cigarette and lit it. She took a couple of drags and chilled, watching Deedee and Reggie dancing.

"There's no smoking in the club. You've gotta leave..." a voice said.

Coco turned to see couple of burly club security guards walking toward her. She smirked and took another drag. If they were kicking her out, she might as well keep smoking, Coco was thinking as the bouncers descended on her.

"Oh, it's Coco..." a bouncer said.

"Okay, follow us Coco, we'll show you where you can relax and smoke," the other said.

"A'ight, cool," Coco said.

She followed the bouncers to an upstairs passage that led to a balcony. They opened the windows and she could feel the cool, summer night's air. The bouncers allowed Coco to smoke while looking at the stars in the sky. She puffed, thinking that she had arrived.

Meanwhile on the dance floor, Reggie was working his way into Deedee's mind. They danced close and Deedee smiled. She didn't mind when Reggie touched her. Pirouetting, he saw her ass and Deedee shook her derriere even more. Reggie played along with her teasing, his body moving along with her rump shaking. It was on up in the club, Deedee leaned and Reggie was on her ass, grinding.

"Wow Deedee!"

"Wow what...?" Deedee said turning around to face him.

Reggie was sorry he had disturbed the groove she was. Now Deedee appeared annoyed. Trying to make light of the situation, Reggie looked her up and down. Then he smiled.

"I didn't know you could dance like that," he said, still smiling.

"Like what?"

"Well, you know...?"

"No I don't," she said.

Her dance movements came to an abrupt end. Deedee's hands were on her hips and in the dim of the light, Reggie looked baffled. Her demeanor had changed and he wasn't sure how to correct it. The pace of the music slowed and club heads were onto booty calls. Reggie glanced around and saw that there were still a few couples slow grinding on the floor.

"Tell me," Deedee urged, getting his attention. "Do I dance like a stripper, a skanky ho', a ghetto girl, a slut a—"

"No, no it's not like that. I was just saying that you can dance period..."

He paused, trying not to say too much. Reggie was being real careful, he didn't want to draw her ire and felt he had already. Deedee in the meantime looked at him from head to toe, her eyes smiling. Reggie stared at her speechless. Getting closer, he caressed her hips and tried to kiss her lips. Deedee moved away, easily avoiding his attempt.

"Not so fast, mister," she said, kissing him on the cheek. "Thanks for the dance."

"My pleasure," he smiled. "So can I at least have the digits?"

"Sure," Deedee said.

They exchanged numbers and went on dancing until closing. The lights were turned on and the music was turned down. They saw Coco staggering toward them.

"Y'all ain't gotta go home but y'all got to get the fuck up out," Coco chuckled.

Deedee stared at her. The twisted smile and drawl were clear indicators. Deedee slowly realized that Coco was inebriated. Reggie also saw that Coco definitely had too much to drink. He reached out to help steady her sway.

"I don't need no muthafuckin' help from no nigga, yo!"

"My bad," Reggie said, raising his hands.

"I got my girl, Dee, right here," Coco said. "I'm good, yo," she continued.

Deedee put her arms around Coco and they walked out of the club. Reggie walked behind them. He helped to get Coco in the back seat and Deedee drove off with Reggie in the passenger seat.

"Where should I drop you?" she asked.

"Maybe you should get Coco home first," he answered.

"Don't worry about Coco. Where do you want to go?" she asked.

"Uptown, One-Forty-Fifth and Edgecombe," he said.

"Wasn't that easy?" Deedee asked, driving off.

The BMW dashed through the light traffic of a city that never sleeps. Dawn was golden and the sun was about to peek through the blue skies. Deedee steered the Beemer to Reggie's destination. Getting out of the car, he leaned over in an attempt to kiss her. She shifted, easily thwarting his advance.

"See you Reggie," Deedee smiled.

"Drive safely," Reggie said, returning the smile and waving.

"Are we there yet, yo?" Coco asked from the backseat.

"No, not yet, Coco," Deedee answered and drove away.

Early morning drizzle of rain caught Deedee helping Coco from the backseat of the car. They struggled from the garage to the lobby. The doorman was trying to help Deedee, who was having a difficult time keeping Coco's wobbly legs from buckling.

"I don't think that's a good idea," she said, waving him off.

The doorman stared at the two teen girls and licked his lips. Deedee tugged at her top, which had risen exposing her midriff.

"Good night," the doorman said, staring at both of Coco's middle fingers.

With Coco's arm locked around her shoulder, Deedee struggled off the elevator. She quietly helped Coco to her room and helped her out of her clothes. Clad in T-shirt and panties, Coco was off in La-La land as soon as her head hit the pillow. Deedee took off her pants and got in the bed. She cuddled next to Coco. While the sun pushed its head over dark clouds, both girls slept.

It was after midday when Deedee awoke to the ringing of her cell phone. After disregarding it for a few rings, she picked it up and checked the caller ID. It was Reggie. She closed her eyes, ignoring the call. A few minutes later she heard it ringing again.

"You better answer that, yo. It's been ringing nonstop."

Deedee looked around and saw Coco coming out of the bathroom. This time Deedee picked up the phone and without checking, she launched in a tirade.

"Reggie, I didn't give you my number so you can annoy me!"

Then Deedee made a surprise face and an embarrassing laugh escaped before she said, "I'm sorry Sophia. I thought it was this guy... Yeah I can meet you at your office. You mind telling me what it's about?"

Coco curiously eyed Deedee's changed demeanor. She waited for her to hang the call before speaking.

"That was Sophia?"

"Yeah, she wants me to meet her at her office."

"She ain't said what it's about, yo?"

"No... But it certainly didn't sound too positive," Deedee said, sitting up.

"When are you gonna meet her?"

"Now... I'll drop you at the studio and—"

"Can you drop me at the hospital?"

"Sure—"

"I'll catch a cab from there to the studio, yo."

"Okay," Deedee said.

Seemingly in deep thought, she got out of bed and walked out the door. Coco showered and later met Deedee sitting alone at a huge dining table.

"You a'ight, yo?" Coco asked.

"I'm just a little puzzled by Sophia's call that's all," Deedee answered, getting up.

Later, they were out the door and into the lobby. Deedee drove all the way in silence, and Coco pulled her Gucci shades in front of her eyes.

"This bright sunlight is killing my eyes, yo."

They drove in silence the rest of the way. Behind her shades, Coco closed her eyes and remained quiet. She heard Deedee speaking and thought she was dreaming.

"Why didn't she just tell me on the phone...?" Deedee asked.

Coco glanced at her without saying anything. Deedee seemed to be thinking aloud so Coco couldn't give an answer. She looked on with interest.

"I'd think the phones are safe enough. Or maybe they're bugged... I mean," Deedee continued. Pulling to a stop, she glanced at Coco. "I'm sorry I got caught up with this phone call from Sophia. It's pretty baffling..."

"Do you want me to go with you?"

"No, you go visit your mother. I'll be back to get you later."

"Drive safely yo," Coco said, getting out the car.

Deedee watched Coco ease into her bop down the street. Driving away, thoughts of the phone conversation earlier with Sophia steered her toward the attorney's office.

Moments later, Deedee parked in a garage and walked to Sophia's office in the heart of downtown. She walked upstairs and was immediately greeted by Sophia.

"Hi Dee, come with me."

Deedee followed behind Sophia. Her heart was thumping in her chest, and she didn't know why. This caused her some irritation as she felt pushed into a corner by her anxiety. Her defense mechanism kicked in.

"Sophia, I thought you said you're not going be involved in the case?" she asked.

"Things have developed and—"

"What things, Sophia? All this mumbo jumbo does not make sense to me. First you said you're not gonna be involved because of your job and now you're calling me about—"

"Dee, in fairness to you, I wanted you to hear this from me. I didn't want you to hear it through the media," Sophia said.

They walked into her office and Sophia closed the door. She ushered Deedee to a chair and kept standing while she continued speaking.

"I was asked to be a witness for the prosecutor," Sophia said, staring at an aggravated Deedee. "Your uncle was implicated in murder and I have knowledge about several events that took place because of a deal he made with Busta."

"So you wanted to see me because you're going to help these people send my uncle to jail?" Deedee sarcastically asked.

"No, I wanted you to hear something and maybe you can see a different side of your uncle."

Deedee watched her put a disk in her computer and pressed play. Through the static of the recording, she could hear the voices of her father and her uncle mumbling. Then Dennis Ascot's clearly said something about her mother to Eric.

"Denise smokin' crills, E... That shit is an embarrassment. I gotta get rid of her ass... That drug got her tainted..."

"How you gonna do that? You married to her Dennis!"

"Murk her if I have to. Eric I gotta prevent that bitch from poisoning everything."

"There's no other way...?"

"Nah, she ain't worthy to be alive..."

Crackling with static, the recording came to an abrupt end. Deedee had listened carefully and Sophia said nothing. For a couple of beats, the tension in the air crackled like the sounds over her father and uncle's conversation. Deedee's stare suggested that she needed more answers. Sophia tried to clear any doubt about the reason for letting Deedee hear the taped conversation.

"Your mother's body has been found. She was killed and buried. We... the authorities received information and dug her body out of a ditch. She had been shot. Since your father is no longer around, Eric has to answer for her murder," Sophia said.

There was a long pause and Deedee looked around in confusion. She couldn't believe what she was hearing. Tears ran down her cheeks and she covered her face with her hands. Sophia watched for a few minutes. Bending over, Sophia held Deedee's heaving shoulders.

"It's gonna be alright..." she said, holding shaken the teen.

"How's that gonna happen? My mother is dead and my uncle's gonna be charged for it...? What's gonna be alright about that situation, Sophia?"

"Well I'm doing all I can to help—"

"Yes, you're helping to send my uncle to prison. Why Sophia? What did my uncle do to you where you feel it necessary to personally go after him the way you have?"

"Personally gone after your uncle? I have done no such thing," Sophia said, sounding agitated. "Eric has gone foul of the law. And because of my job, I have to cooperate with the investigation. I could go to jail, Deedee. It would be guilt by association. I know what he's done and it's wrong," she said with conviction.

Deedee looked at her and frowned in contempt. Sophia sat

back feeling defeated. It was obvious that Deedee loved her uncle too much to let him go down for murder. She tried to convince Deedee.

"I'm helping and what you're doing is hindering. It's because of the love—the passion you feel for your uncle is clouding your judgment. Take your time and think about it. I'm sure you'll see that your uncle needs help. He's done a bad thing, Deedee."

"How could you?" Deedee asked after a beat. "You were engaged to my uncle and now you treat him like a villain. Sophia, he paid for your law school and I'm sure he never once asked for any of the money back," Deedee said with disdain.

Sophia could hear the bitterness in Deedee's voice. She slipped quietly into her office chair, wishing she didn't have to bring the teen bad news, but she felt she had to do it.

"Even though you're not connected to the murders, you can still be implicated and tried as a conspirator," Sophia said.

"What're you saying, Sophia Lawrence?" Deedee asked.

"I'm just making you aware of one of the courses the law could take," Sophia said.

"But that's not what you want me to know. You want to tell me that if I don't cooperate with you and your cronies in sending my uncle to jail, you're going to have to send me to jail too," Deedee said, standing and pointing at Sophia.

Deedee was annoyed and her voice was raised, but she wasn't backing down. Poised and confident she walked closer to where Sophia sat behind the desk.

"What kind of person are you, Sophia? Deedee asked, and without waiting for an answer she continued. "You pretended to be an Ascot, and got everything you wanted from my uncle. But I'm an Ascot by birth, honey. And you'll never get me to sell out my family.

Take your deal and shove it!"

Slipping on her Gucci shades, Deedee turned and walked out the office. She slammed the office door, closing the relationship she had with Sophia. Their affiliation had been like mother and daughter, yet it had run its course. Deedee kept walking and was out of the office building before erupting into tears.

Sitting in her BMW thinking about riding uptown to see Coco, Deedee's mind wouldn't let her shake the thoughts. It was futile, but she tried not to remember that Sophia had been such a close family member. Deedee always loved her. Sometimes she had even felt closer to Sophia than to her uncle. The conversation she had just endured had severed all the good memories. She was left with a feeling of disgust and resentment deep in her guts.

Deedee started the engine, and tried to remember the good times they had. Instead, the first time she truly became connected to Sophia replayed in her head. It was after Deedee had come out of the hospital. She had been raped and her uncle didn't know what to do with her. Alone in her room, Deedee was hating herself when Sophia knocked on her door.

"Dee? May I come in?" Sophia asked knocking gently.

"Hold on. Just a second Sophia," Deedee said, opening the door.

Sophia walked in and Deedee immediately went back to her bed. She wrapped herself under the covers.

"Hey, girlfriend," Sophia said, trying to sound upbeat.

Deedee mumbled but Sophia ignored the inaudible response.

Sophia's presence made her feel safer.

"I brought some water. Cold water, with a few ice cubes... I thought you could use a little. I know I could."

"Well no, but—Sophia, have," Deedee began, looking down on the beige carpeted floor. She continued. "Have you ever been raped?"

The blunt question caught Sophia off guard. For just an instant, she wished she could say she had been so she could offer that support, but that type of tragedy had never happened to her.

"No," she replied. "I have never been raped. I can imagine that it's a most terrible thing." A brief pause followed. "Do you want water now?"

"Thanks," she said, reaching for the glass. She sipped and spoke. "It's bad. It's really, really awful," Deedee cried.

Deedee gulped the rest of the water and felt it roll down her dry throat. A surprise burp caused her to look at Sophia, who had been standing in the middle of the room. They smiled. Deedee walked over and hugged Sophia.

"Thanks," she said. "I'm sleepy, but could you stay with me until I go to sleep?"

Deedee was at Harlem hospital in a matter of minutes. Combing the block, she slowed down, searching to find parking space. On this clear day, Deedee's mind was still smarting from Sophia's revelation. She tried to tune the words out, but the mind-worm was stuck on nonstop auto-replay. Deedee felt like a cruel joke had just been played on her by someone she loved and cared about. She had just been had. The hurt was deeper because Sophia was someone she trusted. She finally found an available spot. Still confused and angry, Deedee lowered the volume of the car radio and slowly backed in.

After paying at the meter, she was about to walk across the street to the hospital entrance when she spotted Coco standing outside and smoking a cigarette. The hunch of her shoulder warned Deedee of Coco's pensive mood. They nodded, and Deedee acknowledged Coco's signal. Waiting by the car, she lit a cigarette and took a long drag. Coco was wearing a YSL denim jumpsuit, and her familiar bop. Her Gucci shades did nothing to hide the disgust on her face.

"What's the matter with you?" Deedee asked.

"Madukes going back and forth, that whole shit is soo fuckin irritating!" Coco answered, clearly frustrated.

"How's she doing?"

"Not too good, yo..." Coco's voice trailed.

She puffed on her cigarette for a beat. Coco let out a sigh as smoke came out her mouth and nostrils. Deedee calmly eyed her, deep in thoughts. Coco was so frustrated with her own situation she didn't seem cognizant of Deedee's demeanor. They stood smoking without speaking then Coco flipped the cigarette away and spoke.

"So what happened with Sophia, yo?"

"Ah well, it wasn't good..." Deedee started then her voice trailed.

"Yoo-hooh, yoo-hooh, Coco! Oh, is that Deedee with you?"

The girls heard the familiar voice of the guidance counselor from High School. Both had counseling sessions with the older woman while they were attending school. The girls stared blankly at each other before speaking.

"Mrs. Martinez...?" the girls chorused while reflexively tossing their cigarettes.

"Ah, ah what're you doing here, Mrs. Martinez?" Deedee asked.

"Well since you asked my husband's a doctor here and—"

"A doctor...?" both girls echoed.

"Yes, a medical doctor and he told me about..." Mrs. Martinez's voice trailed.

"And he told you what?" Deedee asked.

"Well, this has to do with Coco. I wanted you to know that I'm really sorry to hear about your mother and I can arrange a place for you to stay just in case—"

"We got it all figured out Mrs. Martinez. You didn't have to come all the way out here to tell us that, but thanks anyway," Deedee said, stepping forward.

"That's good, that's good that you have it all figured out. But how about college?" the guidance counselor asked. "Now that your mother is in this condition then you should be thinking... God forbid—if she doesn't make it. You'll be without any support Coco."

"We've got college figured also," Deedee said.

"Well in either case, my husband has a foundation that offers scholarships to disadvantaged minority students,like yourself, who are talented, and skilled in academics such as you are, Coco. And are struggling econically. Coco, I know you're into music, and will probably do well, but this is just in case that plan doesn't work out. Then you can always resort to plan B."

"Plan A is education and so too is plan B, Mrs. Martinez," Coco said confidently.

"Okay then, this should help shine some light on your plans," Mrs. Martinez said, handing Coco a folder filled with papers. Then she continued. "All you have to do is promise me you'll fill out the forms, and mail the package back to me with the envelope inside. I can retrieve all your records from the school."

A gush of wind sent air whipping around the trio. Coco paused and looked at the folder Mrs. Martinez offered. It was labeled Minority Scholarship. After what seemed like an eternity, Coco took the folder.

"Maybe you should be giving it to someone who really needs it," Deedee said assertively.

"Denise, you're well-off and—"

"Mrs. Martinez my name is Deedee. All my friends call me

that so—"

"Well Deedee, you're from a rich family. Your uncle—"

"My uncle's biz is his own, Mrs. Martinez!" Deedee said, sounding irritated.

"Good looking out, Mrs. Martinez. I'll fill it out and mail it back to you," Coco said, stepping in between Deedee Mrs. Martinez.

Coco's reaction eased the rising tension. Mrs. Martinez smiled at Coco.

"You're welcome, Coco. Deedee, I'm glad to see that you're once again outgoing. And you girls can go back to your cigarette smoking now," she said.

"Well thank you, Mrs. Martinez," Deedee said with sarcasm.

Deedee smirked as the girls waved and the overly friendly guidance counselor walked away. Deedee shook her head while Coco silently looked on. Coco stared at her best friend and slowly realized how emotional Deedee appeared.

"Damn girl, you were kind a went in on poor Mrs. Martinez. Be easy, yo."

"Coco, that nosey woman put me through soo much after that rape incident. I didn't know whether to thank her or beat her down!"

"Okay chill, yo. She's just trying to help."

"Help...? She just wanna find out things so she could go gossip," Deedee deadpanned.

Dressed in Chloe sandals and Donna Karan dress, Deedee seemed to mentally shift gears. Coco saw tears streaming from beneath her Gucci shades. By the time Coco reached out to hug her, Deedee was bawling loudly. They hugged and Coco guided her inside the car.

"We ain't gotta go nowhere, yo," Coco said, helping Deedee. "I just don't want anyone to think I'm jacking you."

"Jacking me...?" Deedee asked. Then she laughed. "You're soo silly," she continued, laughing while drying her tears.

"Let's get out of here, yo. This place's getting me emotional too."

Coco walked to the passenger side and got inside. She sat staring at Deedee who continued chuckling. Reaching for a tissue, she blew her nose and chuckled some more.

"Damn yo, that shit wasn't that funny. I guess you needed a joke."

"Yes, I did," Deedee said and paused.

"I mean that incident was not too long ago and Mrs. Martinez is helpful and she might not have realized that you're still a little jaded by—"

"Are you talking about what Mrs. Martinez said?"

"Yes, but I don't think she meant it—"

"I mean she counseled me after the rape incident went down, yada-yada, but that's not what's bothering me. It's what happened when I saw Sophia."

"So what happened when you saw Sophia, yo?" Coco asked after a beat.

"You don't want to know."

"I guess that's why I'm asking," Coco deadpanned.

"Well besides her being a bitch-"

"A bitch, yo...?"

"A bitch. I found out from her that my mother is officially dead. Shot dead. And my father and uncle might be responsible for killing her," Deedee deadpanned.

Coco stared at Deedee in surprise and heard her voice echoing. There was an incredible look on Deedee's face.

"Hold da fuck up? What yo?"

"If I decide to do so, I may cooperate with the DA and they will not implicate poor little old me."

"What da fuck? I thought I had problems. Damn yo!"

"I was a rape victim, so they won't implicate me. As for Ms. Sophia Lawrence, she'll be cooperating. She told me an unknown source told the DA all about the conspiracy and will testify to it."

"Get da fuck outta here! That's some crazy shit, yo."

"Tell me about it."

"Oh that's all fucked up. So what are you gonna do now, yo?"

"I don't know. I know I'm gonna tell Uncle E what took place between me and Sophia. I'll let him decide. He brought her into his life and paid for her education, and this is the way she goes about thanking him—by testifying against him."

"That's soo fucking wrong, yo. So are you gonna testify or get implicated?"

"I'm getting implicated," Deedee said, starting the car.

Coco stared at her and said, "Then I should be implicated too. I was there when everything went down, including the shootings, yo."

"So you already know how it went down, Coco."

"Dee, say no more. I remember, yo."

Lil' Long rang Eric Ascot's doorbell. Sophia promptly answered the door, barely opening it. Lil' Long kicked the door completely open and smacked Sophia with the butt of his gun. He stuck the nozzle in Eric Ascot's chest, while standing over Sophia's unconscious body. The taxi with Coco, Deedee and Kamilla, Vulcha's girlfriend in it had long arrived at Eric's house. They had witnessed Lil' Long's dramatic entry.

"Is there another way in?" Kamilla asked.

"Yes," Deedee said.

"That's probably where Vulcha went," Kamilla said. "He gave me a twenty-two. I'm gonna go back there and surprise him."

"Let me go with you, yo."

"No, Coco, come with me," Deedee said. "Let's go through the other entrance and get the guns. Uncle E keeps them in his bedroom."

"A'ight, yo," Coco said.

She helped Deedee climb through the window. Meanwhile Kamilla entered the rear door. She heard Lil' Long yelling loudly.

"They killed my man! For what...? You muthafuckas has got to pay!"

Kamilla, not knowing what she was up against, entered the room and pointed her gun at Lil' Long. Before she could pull the trigger, Lil' Long's gun blasted twice. Kamilla fell in a heap. Her made-up face splattered on the wall like some grotesque artwork. Lil' Long turned the gun back to Eric. Eric's mouth was agape. He held his hands high.

"Put your mo-muthafuckin' h-hands d-down, nigga, this ain't no fucking stick-up. See, it's like this; in order for me to be immortal, all weak niggas must die," Lil' Long said.

Then, without warning, an explosion filled the room. Lil' Long wobbled and staggered. He turned to see Coco holding a smoking shotgun, and Deedee, pointing a forty-five at him. Another outburst hit him and he slumped on his knees.

"Take that, Mr. Immortality," Deedee said, holding the weapon.

"Hello!" Coco said. "What you know bout that, huh?"

The Desert Eagle remained in Lil' Long's grip as the blood oozed profusely from his slumping body. Deedee took aim and squeezed off one *more round. Lil' Long fell forward, his body twitching.*

"I know all about the killings before and after that, yo. That Lil' Long nigga didn't die right there. The police killed him and tried to pin it on Eric," Coco solemnly announced.

"You're a true friend," Deedee said, hugging Coco. "Are you ready to go to the studio?"

"Yes I am."

The BMW joined traffic heading downtown. The light traffic made the cruise downtown much easier. A few minutes later, they arrived at the garage below the studio building. Coco watched Deedee hurrying inside. She knew Deedee was on a mission and walked behind her, giving her support.

"However this goes down, Dee... I got your back, yo."

With a determined silence, Deedee nodded and the elevator arrived. They rode in silence and Deedee strutted to her uncle's office. He was there on both his cell phone and office phone. Deedee turned to Coco.

"I'd rather do this by myself," she said.

"Cool, I'll be inside the booth, yo."

Coco strolled to the other side of the studio, already thinking about the recording session. She entered the booth and saw Reggie with headphones on, listening to a track. The music was so loud and he was into it. Reggie never saw Coco until she was close to him.

"What up, yo?" Coco greeted.

"Hey Coco, how're ya? You ready?"

"Let's get this thing done, yo."

"Let's do it," Reggie said, removing his headphones.

"Let that beat flow through the speakers, yo."

"A'ight, I was about to do that," Reggie said, walking to the main console.

Sitting down, he moved his fingers across the controls. Soon the music came blasting out of the speakers. Reggie bounced his head off the heavy bass-laden beat. Coco was already rocking out. Entering the booth, no longer thinking about her mother or Deedee, Coco started singing a hook.

Deedee heard her uncle on the phone and sat quietly waiting for him to be finished. Eric Ascot glanced at the troubled expression on his niece's face. His cell phone was at one ear and he wondered for a beat while listening to his office phone.

"Are you in rush, Dee? Or do you wanna see me later?" Eric asked Deedee. "This may take a few minutes."

"I'll wait," Deedee said.

Her eyes sadly wandered around the office, and she saw all the platinum plaques lining the wall. Then she took a good look at the collection of books and statuettes that decorated the place. Deedee's stare lingered on the picture of her father in close embrace with his brother. She got up and was about to walk closer when she heard her uncle's voice.

"What's bothering you, Dee?"

"Oh uncle, I went and saw Sophia earlier and..." Deedee's voice trailed.

"And what...?" Eric asked in a matter-of-fact tone.

The expression on his face betrayed his thoughts. Deedee saw the agitated twitch of his eyebrow and decided to be as honest as she possibly could.

"She said you're being charged for the murder of my mother and the district attorney office has a tape of you and my father plotting to kill her before he died—"

"Before he was killed by the police, Dee," Eric interrupted.

"Sophia played the tape... She let me hear you, and I did. Uncle you gotta tell me. Did you have anything to do with my mother's death?"

"This is grown folks' biz, but since you let yourself in, let me hip you to certain things. Ten years ago, your mother became hooked on crack cocaine. She stole from my brother and compromised his security and your future. She needed help. After your father was killed I got her placed in rehab. She stayed for a month then she ran away. I haven't seen or heard from her since then. Now how am I gonna be involved in her death when I didn't even know she was alive for the past seven years?"

"I—"

"As for Sophia feeding you all that bullshit..."

"She wants me to testify against you and if I don't they can charge me," Deedee said.

"No, no honey. You don't have to do a damn thing. First of all you're a minor and—"

"Uncle, I graduated. You treat me like I'm seven, not seventeen," Deedee said. "I'm going on eighteen. Give me some credit here."

"You're legally a minor and you have nothing to do with this. What else did Sophia say?"

"She basically wants to keep her job. She doesn't want to testify against you but she said because of her job she has to or she could be disbarred. I mean she got into a lot of detail but it was mainly that I should cooperate with the investigation or face being indicted."

"I'm about to put a stop to all her B.S."

Eric walked to his desk and picked up the phone. He quickly dialed the number, and Deedee waited in silence as the phone rang on the other end.

"Max Roose please," Eric said.

Deedee listened as her uncle waved her off and said, "This really is adult biz. You stay out of it. I'll handle it." Eric picked up his ringing cell phone. "They have no right in getting you involved and as for Sophia, I'll handle her," Eric continued as he checked the caller ID on his cell phone. He answered it. "Silky Black, congrats on that new track. Yeah I got a beat for you... Hold on a minute, Silk... Yeah Max we have to meet..."

Eric Ascot moved from one phone to the next. Deedee watched him for a few beats then she walked to the wall decorated with a collage of snapshots. The picture was worth a thousand words. Memories of her father shot through camera lens helped Deedee to see how close Eric Ascot was to his older brother, her father. The photos on the wall showed them together surviving and building a musical empire. Deedee wanted to believe in her uncle. He was always forthright with her. And Eric Ascot was all about building the family business. She had watched him for seven years.

She felt like she was part of it now. It was a connection she could not resist. He helped Sophia and she had turned on him. Deedee felt bonded and couldn't turn on her family. Her mind drifted through her past and brought her to meeting Coco. She and Da' Crew were really excited to know Deedee's connection to Ascot Music. Now she was in the studio recording. Deedee shook her head, this couldn't be bad, she thought.

Whatever I live I write
Even when times are warming

The rhymes I'm writing are
tougher than dice and...
I'm balling ain't got to go so far
Deserving all the millions I'll collect
Even though I ain't hit that high note yet...

Coco was in the recording booth spitting lyrics on a new track. Kim and Tina heard the sound banging and walked into the recording studio. Watching in awe, they were moved by the song Coco was blowing. Then she would spit a rhyme and sing some more. Clad in tight jeans, their bodies swayed to the beat. Reggie spotted them standing at the door and waved them inside.

"You've been working all morning on that one track. It really sounds good even with her voice on it," Kim noted.

"Shut da front door! You can say that again," Tina said. "I can rap a little so maybe one day me and you can work together," she flirted.

"Aw thanks, but stop hatin'. Coco sounds good on it. Her spitting is on point," Reggie said.

"Who's hatin'...? Shyt, I ain't," Kim said. "Before I had my son, I used to be the lead singer in the church choir, back in the days."

"You go, girl," Tina exclaimed, high-fiving Kim.

"No, but seriously, Coco is methadone dope. I mean she give you shit to lean on," Reggie said.

"Well, I may not be methadone and shyt, but I can really sing," Kim said.

"Yes you can. I hear you singing and I know you up there with Mariah or one of them," Tina said.

"I sound more like a younger Mary J. Blige," Kim said.

"Don't go there, girl. Uh-uh—not Mary J. No, no girl, you ain't no Mary J."

"What you try'na say?"

"I'm sayin' you a good singer, and all. But you ain't no Mary J. Mary really got it going on. Plus those some big shoes to fill," Tina said.

"Coco is really good though," Reggie said.

"She got her style and the kids, they like that rap and singing together. She got that going on," Kim said.

"Ain't nobody said she ain't got something. I'm certainly not," Tina smiled.

"This shit's gonna bang in the clubs!" Reggie said, taking his eyes off Kim's ass and passing his fingers over the controls.

"You should take a break before you bust a blood vessel with all that excitement," Kim suggested.

"Can't right now... Coco's going in on this track," Reggie said, keeping his fingers on the control.

"I thought we could go to lunch," Kim said.

"I can't," Reggie said.

"Then we're gonna order lunch. Can we get you anything?" Tina asked.

"Yes, a chocolate shake and cheeseburger with fries," Reggie responded, reaching into his pocket.

"Don't worry about it, baby. It's on us," Tina said.

"Thank you," Reggie smiled.

"I'm feeling that young bwoy and shyt," Kim laughed.

"Shut your face, bitch! But he got sump'n going on," Tina smiled, looking back at Reggie seductively.

He smiled at Tina and sat down at the controls. Reggie watched Coco then his fingers moved across the knobs. Sounds blasted louder out the speakers. Reggie bounced his head off the heavy bass. Coco was rocking out, singing a hook. Kim and Tina were about to walk out, but paused at the door. Their eyes were transfixed by at the prodigious teen performing in her world. All heads were nodding to the rhythm of the song.

How big you want it they ask
When they serving me checks
Dreaming how I started out on shoestring diet
Wing and a prayer got me a musical connect
Getting ready to rumble championship fights...
Rocketing nonstop to the top I'll never drop...
This ball still here shooting at starlights
Out during day and night running my laps
Rhymes I write are tougher than dice...

Coco was still in her zone when Tina brought Reggie's orders. Reggie, caught up in the process of his work, didn't acknowledge her. She gave him a kiss on his lips and pat on his head. Then she pointed to the food next to him and slowly walked out. She continued watching Reggie who was captivated by Coco.

Her face appeared sad when Deedee strutted through the soundproof door of the recording studio. His chocolate shake was complete liquid and his burger had gone cold. Reggie saw Coco walking out of the recording booth. Finally he turned and looked at his food. Coco wore a smile of satisfaction, as Reggie stared in dismay at his lunch.

"I guess you'll have to get something else for lunch," Deedee deadpanned.

Reggie looked at his lunch then back at Deedee and laughed. Deedee frowned but soon joined him and they were both cracking up.

Coco stared at them both in quizzical silence.

"Okay, really... Lunch that funny, yo?"

"You should've seen Reggie's face when he first saw his lunch. That was soo funny," Deedee said, chuckling.

"I was all into the music and I just forgot all about—what's her name...? Well, she was ordering lunch and..."

"I really don't wanna discuss losers, yo."

"Yes, let's go out and eat if you guys are finished, Coco," Deedee said.

"Yeah let's do that, yo."

"I guess you're gonna need lunch also," Deedee said, laughing at Reggie.

"You're going to lunch, now? I mean it's after two," Reggie said.

Deedee and Coco were already walking to the exit. Reggie watched them and turned down the music.

"You're upgrading with one of the owners," Deedee said.

"Is that a yes?" Reggie asked.

"What do you think?" Deedee asked.

Fried chicken on tray, burgers on the grill and the smell of steak wafted through the diner. Entering the restaurant, Coco saw the contours of trouble on Deedee's pretty face. They were seated quickly despite the afternoon crowd. Coco sat opposite Deedee and Reggie. Her mother's condition began to weigh heavily on Coco's mind again. The time in the studio had provided great relief, but now the sudden rush of thoughts returned, triggering pensive silence in Coco.

Wordlessly she watched Deedee and Reggie. They seemed to be hitting it off alright. He was chatting, and brought up Coco's exploits in the studio.

"Coco has got that crazy dope flow. This package is gonna be tight. That joint we were working on is slamming," Reggie gushed.

Coco stared at him and the waiter showed up. He took their orders and walked away. Deedee saw Coco's demeanor changing and smiled at her.

"Coco, I guess he's not received the memo... *Vibe* article said Coco's what's next," Deedee said.

"Yeah, I hear you. I seen that piece on her and now I've heard her close up. She's crazy nice," Reggie said.

Coco acknowledged the compliments with a nod of her head. She was still thinking about her mother but had not fully heeded the conversation. Deedee and Reggie engaged in small talk until the waiter arrived with their orders.

They went through bowls of salad. Reggie had his fresh chocolate shake and cheeseburger. Deedee ate the same but Coco's turkey burger remained untouched. Fifteen minutes later, Reggie was finished, and with her burger half gone, Deedee glanced at Coco. She motioned for the waiter, he returned and Deedee requested the check. Outside, Coco lit a cigarette and smoked. Deedee and Reggie joined her.

"I guess you weren't feeling your burger?" Deedee asked Coco.

"I wasn't feeling hungry after all the greens, yo."

"Yes, that was a lot of salad. But the food was really good," Reggie said.

They smoked for a few and walked slowly back to the building. Coco appeared to be in her own world and Deedee let her be. Instead of badgering Coco, Deedee and Reggie kicked it as they walked. Outside the building, Coco was still quiet and Deedee moved closed to her.

"You know what I'm thinking...?" Deedee asked.

"It's that time...?" Coco said, raising her eyebrow in mock

surprise.

"We're gonna roll something?" Reggie asked.

"You're sharp, but it's strictly a girl thing, yo."

"You got it, Coco. Reggie we'll see you later," Deedee said, waving her hand.

"Thank you for lunch," he smiled.

"We'll continue the recording session later, yo."

"Cool, I'm gonna mix that down and let you hear it later. What should I tell your Eric if he asks for y'all?" Reggie asked.

"Tell him we went to do some girlish things," Deedee smiled.

Reggie walked inside the building and turned to see the two girls disappear in the garage. Coco and Deedee got into the BMW. The car rolled out of the garage and joined traffic.

"Let's go shop until we drop," Deedee said.

"Oh, you must be going through deep depression, yo."

"Exactly..."

The sunrays bounced off the asphalt while the girls high-fived. Deedee slipped her Gucci shades back over eyes. She calmly watched traffic while handling her whip game proper. Coco turned up the volume of the music, and leaned in the passenger's seat. The BMW purred through the busy afternoon traffic. Coco and Deedee shared a cigarette while quietly nurturing their emotions.

"Dee, you know what?"

"What?"

"Shits always gonna work out in the end, yo."

"I know Coco, but it stings when you first find out the truth about certain things."

"Yeah, I hear you."

"I mean right now I don't even know who to trust, Coco."

"I guess you've gotta trust yourself on that, yo."

"You know when I told Uncle E about everything with Sophia, he didn't confirm or deny. He just told me to stay out of grown folks' biz. And even though I've graduated from high school and ready for life, I'm still a child."

"It seems like your uncle is trying to protect you, yo."

"You can say that again, Coco. The discussion started out good until Uncle Eric said he was gonna take care of Sophia. Then things didn't go too well after I asked how."

"No you didn't yo. You did what...?"

Deedee pushed the BMW into a parking lot in the heart of the shopping district of Manhattan. The sky was clear and blue, and clouds gathered softly when they walked out. Coco turned to Deedee and smiled.

"I guess you asked the wrong question, yo."

"He got really angry, Coco. He kicked me out of his office. He said I needed to take five, Coco. My uncle has always shown me nothing but love."

"Yeah, but you were insinuating—"

"I didn't realize that until the words were already out my mouth. And then it was just too late," Deedee said, shaking her head. "Coco, I wasn't wrong to ask the question—"

"Yeah, but you practically told him you didn't believe him or have faith in him, yo," Coco said, interrupting Deedee.

They joined the lines of pedestrians crowding the sidewalk. After stopping to get matchng shoes on their feet, the two girls walked and Deedee glanced warily at a busy Fifth Avenue shopping district. They walked closely and Deedee looped her arms through Coco's.

"I want you to complete this sentence, Coco," Deedee said. Coco glanced at her quizzically and Deedee continued. "Believe only half of what you hear and none of what you see..." Deedee's voice trailed.

"That goes double for TV. Cause the joke's on you me."

"That's exactly what Uncle Eric said when I told him about Sophia. He also said it was grown folks' biz. I went into his office and you know how I was hot about how everything was going, you know? Finding about my mother's situation was pretty troubling especially coming from Sophia. Uncle Eric just dismissed it all. But it still bothers me, Coco."

"Maybe he's right, yo. You should just let it go."

Deedee looked at Coco then silently turned her focus all around on the late June afternoon. Midtown was in full summer swing, crowded sidewalks with shoppers moving swiftly along Madison and Fifth. Before dusk arrived, the girls had covered most of the stores on Madison. Silently combing through designer outfits that caught their every fancy, Coco and Deedee's eyes met occasionally. Coco would wear a look of disbelief looking at some of the price tags displayed. Deedee didn't even blink an eye.

"Tell him we went to do some girlish things," Deedee laughed, recalling what she had said earlier said to Reggie.

"Exactly..." Coco said, joining her best friend in the joke.

They went on an exciting and expensive shopping expedition. Deedee shopped until they were about to pass out in exhaustion. Coco had multiple shopping bags from Dior and Coach. She quietly looked at Deedee struggling with the bags from Polo, Chanel, Gucci, and Fendi. They had a pleasurable time, but it was beginning to wear thin. Coco made a recommendation.

"I think we could chill now, yo," she said.

"I'm glad you called it because I'll keep going."

"I mean we alrady copped plenty stuff. What would you do with all the bags?"

"I'll carry them back and forth to car," Deedee answered, showing her expertise.

"Okay I feel you, yo," Coco smiled.

They continued down Fifth heading to the parking garage. Then the smell of steak caught their smell and the girls made their way inside Mr. Chow restaurant.

No sooner had they been seated when they saw Eric and his attorney Max Roose, shadowed by bodyguards, walking inside the popular eatery. Deedee waved at Eric. He quickly spotted her, and walked over to the girls' table.

"Hey, you guys sure are racking up on clothing," Eric smiled.

"Yes, well you did say leave grown folks' biz to grown folks. So that's what Coco and I were doing. Girls' stuff like shopping," Deedee said with a cheerful smile.

"Well don't spend all your money on only one thing," Eric said.

"I didn't, we got shoes from Dior and Manolo Blahnik. Jeans and skirt outfits from Donna Karan... Underwear from Victoria's—"

"Okay Deedee, I got the picture," Eric said, hastily interrupting her. Turning to Coco, he said, "Coco, I heard some of the tracks. Reggie was back in the lab mixing down. They're coming along fine. But that song, *Tougher Than Dice*—I wanna feel more of your pain in it... The blood and guts of it," Eric said, looking at Coco. "Good work so far."

"Thank you, sir," Coco blurted.

Deedee glanced at her then back at her uncle. Coco stared at her and for a beat there was an uncomfortable silence.

"I don't have much time to sit and chat," Eric said, standing up. "Listen if you'd like I'll get one the security guys to help with the bags. You guys need help or what?"

"No Uncle, we'll be fine. See you later," Deedee said.

She stood and gave him a kiss on his cheek. Eric smiled and patted her cheek. Then he embraced her.

"I got you a nice suit, Uncle E. I hope it fits," Deedee said.

"Thanks, Deedee. What color is it?" Eric asked. Deedee glanced at Coco.

"Black," Coco and Deedee chorused.

"I'm sure it's nice. I'll see it later," Eric said, walking away.

The girls ordered and ate while Eric Ascot and Max Roose discuss his case over a couple of martinis.

"I don't recall you buying your uncle a suit, yo."

"I know," Deedee smiled. "So that means after we put these bags away in the car, we can go back start shopping all over again."

"That's so devious."

"Why? You wanna go back to the studio or shop?"

"Well you know I wanna make it in the music game. But today I'll skip the afternoon studio session and do the girls' stuff," Coco said.

"You've already made it, Coco," Deedee said. "We'll stop by the studio later and hear what Uncle E was raving about."

"Sounds like a bet, yo."

"Let's go shopping."

They did as Deedee suggested. Coco sensed that shopping

and getting dressed up offered a cure for Deedee's illness. It gave her a sense of power. And Coco was a cornerstone, someone strong to lean on. Soon they had put the bags in the car and the girls set off shopping.

Reggie was inside the studio his head bouncing to the beat. His mind and talent were driving him to come up with the hottest mix down. It had to be one that would impress Eric Ascot. Reggie knew it would lead to bigger and better things even his own studio. Fingers gliding across the keyboard, he made subtle adjustments, changing the sounds to his keen ears.

He didn't realize that eyes were on him. Reggie kept making changes, biting his lips and pausing here, turning there. His athletic physique intrigued her mind. Tina smiled when she studied the total package. The sound charged through the speakers devouring the air, the thump of the base measured in heartbeats. Reggie didn't see Tina walking up behind him.

"Reggie, Reggie, Reggie," she shouted.

Spinning around, Reggie knocked Tina over. She fell back and was on her derriere before Reggie realized what had happened. Luckily the soundproof recording area of the studio was lined with thick, carpeted floor. The music was still pumping loudly when Reggie rushed to help Tina to her feet. Reggie held her arm and pulled, and slipped. They both landed in a heap. Finally, Reggie was able to help the giggling Tina to her feet.

"Thanks," she said, kissing him.

He was still holding her close and she moved her body even closer to his. Reggie felt the heat of Tina's flesh and kissed her again. He left the music pumping in the background when Tina held his hand. Licking her lips, she dragged him back to the green room.

The door closed and in a flash she was on her knees, unzipping his jeans. Tina smiled and bit her lips when she saw Reggie's package. Parting her soft lips, she took the head of Reggie's hardening dick into her mouth. Her tongue snaked around his dick. Soon it was fully ready and pointing to the ceiling. Flicking her tongue around his growing head, Tina continued sucking him off. The music pumped loudly while she sucked his balls. Her tongue dancing up and down his shaft excited Reggie.

"Damn, ma," he hissed loudly.

"You got any condoms?" Tina asked, rubbing her fingers over his shaft. "You have a big helluva dick and we can't do nothing without no rubbers," Tina said, teasing Reggie's hardened dick with her stiffened tongue.

Suddenly he grabbed her, lifting her up and pinning a surprised Tina against the wall. Her knees were wobbly and Reggie easily raised her skirt up. His hands were massaging her panties and his fingers invading her crotch. In one motion, his hands were ripping her panties off.

"No, no Reggie!" Tina begged. "Papi, go get a condom or sump'n!"

Her pleading came too late. Reggie didn't heed. His dick was hard and his mind was out of control. He grabbed her and pinned her against the wall. She struggled but his six-foot muscular body was too much for Tina. She gave in and straddled his muscular waist with her legs. Reggie was kissing her neck and hoisted her body. Soon he was entering her hard and ramming his dick into her.

"Oh yes, papi!" Tina moaned.

Reggie continued thrusting into her. Tina was trapped in ecstasy and blissfully clinging to his strong shoulders. She hoisted her legs and felt him go deeper. Tina gripped her nails into his sweat-soaked skin. The music was still pumping and Reggie's dick was sliding in and out of her moist, sweaty frame. She bit his neck and looked up to see Kim walking away shaking her head. Reggie was in throes of lovemaking and never even heard when the door closed.

"Are you coming soon, papi?" Tina asked.

There was no answer from Reggie, but his hips were moving faster, swinging like a sledgehammer burying deep inside her.

"Papi, papi, bust-off in my mouth. Please, papi!" Tina screamed when she felt his breathing growing rapid.

Lowering her legs, she managed to squeeze him out of her. She was on her knees and Reggie was fighting to give it to her doggie-style. Tina slipped out of his sweaty grip and immediately slid his pulsing dick inside her mouth. Tina sucked and Reggie's exploded. He grabbed her head on his dick while shooting sperm down the back of Tina's throat. She swallowed it, licking her lips and smiling up at him.

"You're loco, papi," Tina said.

"Lemme show you how crazy I can get," Reggie said, coming at her and flexing.

"Nah papi, save that for next time. Don't get too greedy now," Tina said in mock seriousness.

She kissed his dick and was off her knees. Patting him on the butt she smiled and kissed him.

"Run along and finish what you were doing," Tina smiled.

"Gimme some more a that gushy stuff," Reggie said.

"Shut your face and be a good boy, Reggie," Tina said, chuckling. "I'll bring you some food. That's why I first came to get you."

"But you get got," Reggie laughed, fixing his clothes.

He was walking away when Tina shouted, "What do you want?"

"Same thing," Reggie answered and without looking back, he continued out the door.

Tina fixed her clothes, sighed, and made the sign of the cross across her chest. She walked uneasily to the bathroom to fix her makeup. Kim walked in and Tina's nose twitched uncomfortably when she sniffed her friend's attitude.

"What's wrong with your fat ass, bitch?" Tina asked.

Kim turned the handle of the tap and let the water run for a while. Then she glared at the mirror's reflection of Tina, who was trying not to look directly at her. Kim watched Tina applying lip-gloss for a few beats. Then she said, "You're such a fucking slut!"

"Who you calling a fucking slut, bitch...?"

"You, I'm talking to Tina Martinez," Kim said, boldly stepping into Tina's space.

The music played on loudly and they were arguing inside the bathroom. Coco and Deedee walked into the lobby.

"I gotta hear the song that your uncle was talking about, yo."

"You couldn't wait, huh? Let me see if he came back. Maybe he could try on his new suit."

Deedee walked quickly to her uncle's office and Coco went toward the recording studio. She could hear the loud yapping form inside the ladies room as she strolled by. Recognizing the voices, Coco paused, stood outside, and listened.

"Oh you gonna be the big bad bitch, huh?"

"Yes cuz every time I say I like a guy, you always fuck him and shyt," Kim said, sounding annoyed.

"Shut your face, Kim. It ain't what it seemed. That lil' episode with me and Reggie... That just got out of hand, that's all. You can have him. I promise I won't bother him again."

"And what about Eric Ascot...? I said I liked him and boom you all up in his face, kissing him and all that shyt."

"Well I can't help if niggas want me, bitch."

"Yeah, first you set them up and then you fuck them. You're nothing but a cheap-ass ho'!"

"I ain't no studio ho, bitch! I just do me! You're always with me when I'm doing my thing. So I guess that makes you one too, bitch!"

"Nah, I'm not like you, Tina. You just a crotch-grabbing-cum-filled-bag-of-nothing...!"

"Don't hate cuz I'm beautiful," Tina said, waving her arm.

"Nah, that ain't all the way right. As a friend you're dirty, rotten and shyt," Kim said.

She allowed a handful of water to collect, and splashed it on a wide-eyed Tina then Kim walked out. Tina looked at herself in the mirror and stomped her heels.

"Shut da front door! No, no, no you didn't bitch!" Tina shrieked and went back to fixing her makeup. "Hatin' ass bitch!" she mumbled.

The tap was still running when Coco slowly walked to the sink. Checking herself in the mirror, she threw sideway glances at Tina.

"I wasn't talking to you. So don't be feeling like I was," Tina said.

"I know, yo," Coco sarcastically said while turning off the tap.

Tina glanced awkwardly at Coco for a beat. Clearing her throat, Coco checked her reflection in the mirror. The smirk on her face was all Tina needed to see. She felt compelled to speak.

"I don't know what the fuck you heard. But I ain't fucking with anyone up in here," she said defensively.

"I didn't accuse you of anything, yo. So I don't see why—"

"Nah, nah, because you came on the tail end of what that bitch was saying. And I just wanted you to know that my man is a lawyer," Tina said, turning to walk away.

"Whatever," Coco said.

Scowling, Tina glanced back at Coco. The look on the teen's face was enough warning to make Tina continue walking out the door. Coco walked to the recording studio. Deedee and Reggie were sitting closely and talking.

"Coco, the song sounds really cool. Reggie let me hear it," Deedee said.

"Oh word, yo. He let you hear it, huh? I wonder who else heard it, yo?"

"Uncle E and I guess me, why Coco?"

"I'm just asking, yo. You gotta be careful of folks around here. Haters are all around."

"Oh I know what you mean, Coco. They both just left, but they don't matter," Deedee said, looking at Coco.

"Hmm, anyway play that shit, yo."

Reggie set the track up and the beat came blasting though the speakers. It vibrated the air, but Deedee could feel the tension in Coco. She watched while Coco held her head down and nodded in rhythm. Then all heads were nodding to the music, but Deedee sensed there was something wrong. They heard Coco's voice take off, crescendo soaring above the beat. Her vocals rang through the speakers, but she sat in pensive silence.

She was still seemingly in a trance after the music stopped. Coco was preoccupied with her thoughts and didn't hear Deedee's question.

"Earth to Coco, come in Coco. Well, what do you think?" Deedee asked.

"Huh...? Oh it was good. I like it but I think it needs a better hook, yo."

"As an artist, I'd say that it's not completely finished. But as a lover of hip-hop music, I'd say it's perfect for today's market," Reggie said. "Heads gonna be bouncing to this," he continued and turned up the beat. "This gonna be pumpin' in da clubs."

"A'ight, a'ight, I heard it all, yo."

"Coco, let's go to the club with Reggie," Deedee suggested.

"Nah, I think I'm a chill and write some rhymes. I should try to come up with a better hook, yo."

"Coco you don't wanna hangout? That's a first. Next thing you're gonna tell me you don't wanna smoke some weed with us," Deedee said. "Reggie got some—"

"I don't give a fuck what Reggie's got, yo!"

Her tone was worse than she intended, but Coco didn't care. She was already out of the studio and hurrying to the lobby. Deedee looked at Reggie and he stared at the door.

"Her mother is not well," Deedee said, rushing out the door.

Deedee returned alone a few minutes and sighed. Reggie walked over and embraced her. She let him hold her body against his for a few beats.

"I'm alright," she said, moving away. "Luckily when we went shopping today, I bought her a phone."

Reggie turned off the control and powered down all the equipment. Then he closed the door and met Deedee in the lobby.

"Did you call her?" he asked.

"Yes I did. She's not picking up," Deedee said. "Let's go to the spot. I'll chill there for a minute. Maybe by then she'll call."

Coco had disappeared into the night's air. Deedee was left wondering why, while putting pedal to the metal, and racing to the club's location downtown. Quickly they found parking and were walking inside the crowded nightspot. Reggie grabbed two drinks for them, and they chilled at the bar sipping.

"I don't know what got under her skin. Earlier we were soo cool. I mean we went shopping and everything was all good between..." Deedee's voice trailed. "I'm sorry," she said, downing her drink.

"Let me get another drink," she said to Reggie.

He smiled and ordered another round. The bartender served the drinks to Reggie with a wink of approval. Reggie put his arms around Deedee's waist.

"Let's dance," she whispered.

They entered the crowded dance floor, grooving to the sound of Tribe Called Quest. Q-Tip's voice was humming. *Vivrant Thing* was rocking and Deedee was buzzing from the drink. Reggie smiled as she turned and shook her thing. They laughed and he pranced around enjoying every shake of her hip.

Special girl, real good girl
Biggest thing in my itty-bitty world
Called her up and she made me feel right
Wish the bliss could never take flight
Sittin' back with this mike in my hand
Spittin' hot shit tryin to see grand
Imprinted on my mind every minute
Make my plans and you always in it, yo
You're such a vivrant thing,
Vivrant thing, a vivrant thing

After paying the fare, Coco jumped out of the cab and walked into the hospital. Visiting hours were coming to an end for the day. As the last remaining visitors filed through the doors of the elevators, Coco slipped past security. Soon she was sitting alone staring at her mother, who was sleeping quietly with tubes and machinery monitoring her every breath. A nurse saw her and walked over to where she was.

"You can't stay up here all night," the nurse said. "You should go home and get some rest."

Coco stared at her as if she was speaking a foreign language. The distraught teen said nothing.

"Did you eat?" the nurse asked.

Coco nodded. She glanced up at the older woman and could see the look of sympathy written all over her face. Her expression revealed an inner conflict, shaded by having knowledge of something grave displayed when she opened her mouth. Dressed in white, her frown of affluence was betrayed by the uniform she wore.

"Your mother has to stay for a lot more tests," she said in a tone of sympathy.

"Is she gonna be a'ight?"

"After all the test results come back, you'll have clearer answers to all your questions. I'll give you another half hour and then you'll have to clear out," she said, walking away.

Coco was left with optimism and held on to it for dear life. She stared at her mother, wishing for the best, but also feeling the whole situation was hopeless. There was a gnawing in the pit of her stomach. No matter how positively she tried to spin the situation, it remained the same. She couldn't rid her mind of what she had heard coming out of the bathroom back at the studio.

Shoulders sagging, Coco walked to the lobby and got on the elevator. She wanted to tell Deedee what she knew. Then she struggled with the thought, walking outside the hospital. The night's air felt good and she decided to walk home. All of Coco's brainpower seemed to push her toward telling Deedee what she heard about Reggie. She needed time to think about it and decided not to tell Deedee right away. Things will work out, Coco silently thought. She was thinking of a master plan and a way to bring it up when she saw her cell phone ringing. It was Deedee. Coco pressed the ignore button.

"She's still not answering?" Reggie asked.

"No she isn't," Deedee answered.

They had started dancing to *Vivrant Thing* then grooved to the music of Slick Rick the Ruler. Deedee let herself go, having fun booty shaking. Moving her body, she pranced to the beat on the dance floor. As time flew by, Reggie and Deedee became friendlier and soon they were slow dragging. His arms were all over and she didn't mind when their lips momentarily touched. Floating in Reggie's embrace, he was guiding her every move of her hips grinding against him. She felt his lips on her neck and chills rushed through her body.

Deedee was offering no resistance to Reggie's advances and flirtingly gazed into Reggie's curious eyes. His six-foot frame collapsed on her and their lips locked. Deedee felt his tongue probing inside her mouth. Clumsily she tried kissing him back. Their bodies stayed glued together until the lights came on. Still in his embrace, Deedee exited the nightspot.

They walked out together, holding hands and laughing. It had been a good night despite Coco's behavior. Deedee got inside the car with Reggie trying to kiss her. Ducking under his arms, she opened the car door and jumped inside.

"Thank you, Reggie," Deedee said. "But I'm afraid that's all the kissing we'll be doing for the rest—"

Reggie reached across, silencing Deedee with a kiss. Lips puckered together, they stayed that way for a few beats.

"Okay, okay, you proved your point. I get it. You like kissing," Deedee said, pushing Reggie away from her.

"I don't like kissing, I like smooching with you," Reggie laughed.

"Yeah right, nice line, I bet you tell all the girls that."

"Nah, my lips are something I share only with you."

She drove slowly, navigating the city's early morning traffic. Reggie was sitting close but Deedee's thoughts turned to Coco again. She dialed the number and listened as it rang. Deedee heard the same outgoing message, informing her that the subscriber had not setup her voicemail.

"It's three in the morning, Dee. Coco's probably asleep or getting some," Reggie said.

"No, something's up. I know it," Deedee said, glancing at Reggie.

The ride ended and Reggie again tried to kiss Deedee's lips. Her mouth remained closed and Deedee puckered her lips.

"Good night," she said.

"Good morning," Reggie said. "You can come upstairs if you wanna chill for a minute or so."

"No, I'll take a rain check on that one," Deedee smiled.

He got out of the car and walked away. Deedee rejoined traffic and moments later she was parking outside Coco's apartment. She saw the same group of people milling outside the building. Checking her Louis Vuitton handbag, Deedee made sure she was strapped. Then she stepped out of the car and strutted across the street.

Their eyes were focused on Deedee, coming toward them. Dressed, in black jeans and matching denim top, Deedee's Louis Vuitton, six-inch heels clicked. She recognized the guys standing around were the same group she beefed with before.

"Hey, girl," a kid said.

Deedee said nothing and kept her handbag close. She remembered Coco telling her always, "Be yourself around them. They can smell fake asses, yo." Following that rule she tried to ignore him.

"Hey you Coco's friend, that model chick," he continued.

"Hi," Deedee said, without staring at him.

"Yeah, you fine girl," the kid said and walked away when she reached the entrance.

Their eyes were still following her when she walked inside the building and ran up the stairs. Deedee reached the third floor and was banging hard on Coco's door. She could hear the rustling coming from inside.

"Who da fuck is it?" Coco barked.

"It's Dee."

"Dee who?"

"Deedee, dammit Coco!"

"Don't be acting up or your ass will be yelling at me from outside the door."

The locks were clicking and Deedee saw the door opened. Coco was standing in the doorway in T-shirt and boxers, looking at her suspiciously.

"Why don't you answer your phones?"

"My phones...?"

"Yes, your cell phone and house phone."

"I didn't hear them ringing, yo."

"Aren't you gonna invite me in?" Deedee asked, brushing by Coco.

"You already in... He with you...?" Coco asked, looking up and down the hallway.

"Who...?"

"You know, your new boyfriend, yo."

"Oh, you must be talking about Reggie. I mean he's kind a cute and all, but we just like checking each other out for now."

"You and everybody else, yo," Coco said, closing the door.

She put the locks back on and walked toward the living room. Deedee followed her and sat down when they got there.

"What are you talking about, Coco?"

"I ain't talking 'bout nothing.

They sat in an uncomfortable silence for a couple beats. Sitting in the living room Deedee stared quizzically at Coco trying to figure out exactly what was going on. Coco walked to the kitchen with Deedee following closely behind her.

"So you gonna keep following me around, yo?"

"Yes, why don't you tell me what you want to…?"

"How'd you know I'd be here, yo?"

"I know you, Coco, and I know how you think."

"Well you should know I ain't no snitch. But I overheard some shit about your new boyfriend, yo."

"Like what…?"

"Like he might be getting it on with Tina, yo," Coco said with conviction.

"You mean Tina and Reggie…?" Deedee asked, leveling her eyes at Coco.

Her response was in such a blasé tone that Coco thought for a moment that Deedee didn't really care. Coco's expression revealed her doubt about the situation, but when she spoke it was clear.

"Yes, or that bitch Kim. He all up in one of them ghetto girls' ass, yo," Coco said.

"And you know that for sure or…?" Deedee laughed.

"I don't know anything for sure. I just caught the tail end of the convo between them two skanky, ghetto-ass bitches at the studio."

"Don't let your emotions run away.

"He probably in them tight jeans, and wack sneakers doing them right now, yo," Coco said. "So keep laughing, everything is funny now."

"Coco, you are bugging. Me and Reggie were at the club until a few minutes ago," Deedee said, still laughing. "And those sneakers are Asics. They are nice."

"It's whatever then…! Keep doing you, yo. I don't even care about his wack sneaks. Them shit's never match his tops. You're caught-up in his game and I'm really celibate and don't give a fuck, yo."

"Stop shouting before you blow a blood vessel."

"That's the same shit madukes tell me. Her ass in the hospital laid up right now."

"Is that really what's bothering you? Because as far as me and Reggie are concerned, there's nothing serious. I haven't done anything, but if you know something for sure then—"

"Nah, I don't! I'm sorry I even mentioned that shit, yo. Just forget it, yo."

"Coco, we cool and all but you cannot let your fears rule you."

"My fears?"

"Yes, your problems with Kim and Tina lead to certain fears. Then these fears are translated in your behavior toward them. If Reggie wants any of them, he's grown. But why would he mess with two zeros when he could hang with dimes..." Deedee smiled at Coco.

"I'm glad you see it that way. I gotta get some rest, yo. You wanna sleep in my room. I'll sleep in madukes's room."

"My fears, huh...?"

The girls had awakened the next morning and the topic was still the same. They had chitchatted about the day's activities and Coco had just finished with the bathroom. Deedee was sitting in the living room waiting on her.

"Coco, let it go already," Deedee said. "What's the matter? You woke up with a stick up your ass or sump'n?" Deedee laughed.

"Yes, I did. This nigga ain't no good. I'm saying, yo."

"No you're sounding like your madukes," Deedee laughed. "This guy is twenty-two. He's a senior at City College. He plays chess and runs track and field," Deedee continued.

"Oh, I see you read his resume? I'm glad. But he's all about running alright... Up in all them asses..."

"Coco stop spazzin' on me. Let's go so I can shower and change—"

"Oh, so you can't shower here? My place is not good enough, yo?"

"No, it's not that, Coco. It's because I have no clothes here, and I wanna change my clothes. That's why I take a shower."

"Oh, so you only take showers when you wanna change clothes, yo? Not because you wanna wash your ass?"

"Coco...!"

"It's only a question. You don't have to burst a blood vessel screaming at me, yo."

Later Coco locked the door, and they walked out together. Coco and Deedee strutted across the street to where the car was parked. There was a ticket on the window and all four tires were missing. The girls stared at each other for a beat then looked around at the people standing in front of the building.

"Shit!" Deedee shouted.

"Oh shit! This fucked up, yo..." Coco's voice trailed. She turned around and walked back across the street. Then she shouted at the people in front of the building. "Ain't nobody know shit, right?"

The people milling in front of the building immediately turned their attention to Coco. They said nothing, but stared at her as if she was speaking a foreign language. She heard them mumbling to themselves before one of them spoke.

"I just got out here and thought it was an abandoned car," one said.

"Yeah, I seen some bum took 'em wheels off," another person said.

Coco hissed then walked back to where Deedee stood,

gathering her wits. She watched in abated silence while Deedee dialed her uncle's number. They spoke for a beat. Then Deedee went into the dash and pulled out a card. Shaking her head, she dialed for roadside assistance. The girls shared a cigarette while waiting for the tow truck. They saw the same man who had fixed the flat tire. He was now pushing a supermarket-shopping cart containing four tires.

"Y'all wanna buy some tires. What up? I know you could use some wheels," he greeted.

Both Coco and Deedee glanced at him then back at each other. Coco flicked the cigarette and examined what was in the shopping cart. She saw Deedee's brows furrowed in a scowl of anger. Coco raised her hand to stem the emotional outburst she coming from Deedee, but it was too late.

"You can't be serious! Your ass must be bugging!" Deedee said.

"Easy yo," Coco said.

"But Coco, he can't be serious. Those look like the damn tires that were on my car."

"They may look like yours, but these are mine," the man said.

"Really...? You cannot be serious," Deedee said, sounding angrier.

"They's mine," the man said.

"I'm calling the police," Deedee said, eyeballing the man.

She saw his disheveled aura. His jeans were old and dirty, his shoes and shirt were equally torn. Life seemed to have knocked him into a dark corner, from where there was no return. Deedee continued looking the man up and down. Then she heard Coco's interference.

"How much are the tires, yo?"

"They regularly go for fifty dollars apiece, but I could let you have them for one-fifty," the man said.

"Are you for real, a hundred and fifty dollars...? They look like the tires that were on my car."

"A'ight, take it or leave it," the man said, walking away.

"I'm calling the police," Deedee said, pulling out her cell phone.

"We'll take them for forty and give you ten bucks to put them on, yo."

The man paused and seemed to be pondering Coco's offer. Deedee was at wit's end and was about to let off screaming on the shabbily dressed man. Coco put her hand over Deedee's mouth, restraining the irate teen.

"A'ight, I gotta go somewhere so let's be quick," he said and started unloading the wheels.

The tires were a perfect fit. In no time, the man had the tires back on the car and Deedee reluctantly paid.

"Throw another twenty in and I hook you up with some wheel locks. If you gonna park in this neighborhood you gon' need 'em," the man said.

Deedee was steaming, throwing daggers at him through an icy, evil stare. Coco shook her head, looked the man up and down then said, "We'll take it, yo."

"You can spare a cigarette? I'll pay you back once your friend pay me."

"No, that's all good, yo."

The girls got in the car and drove away. Deedee waited and joined traffic. Her wrinkled forehead made it clear that something was bothering her. She wanted to say it but didn't. Coco did it for her.

"I know what you're thinking, yo." There was a long pause before Coco continued. "You're thinking that those tires were yours and you just got sold your own tires."

"By a damn tire thief," Deedee added, guiding the car through the midday traffic of the busy city streets. "You should've charged him for that damn cigarette."

Eric sat in his studio listening to the new songs Coco had done. His eyes were closed and his ears perked up at her rhymes. He smiled at Coco's metaphors and the hard-edged rhymes about her life. Her soothing voice was thrilling, but compassionate, delicately offsetting the reality of her hip-hop opera. Eric was enjoying the music when his cell phone went off. He would not normally allow any disturbance when he was in the listening room, but this time he made an exception.

"Hello, Sophia. I been trying my damndest to reach you..." he said, answering the call.

After agreeing to meet with her later that evening, Eric returned to listening to the talented teen. He took mental notes of the areas in the song that needed stronger lyrics, his head nodded to the rhythm of the bass-heavy beat. Eric felt his heartbeat rising, he slowly realized that wanting to see Sophia became urgency. His pulse raced with precision tempo of the pounding drum and bass.

Later, he was walking back to his office and he saw Coco and Deedee strutting into the studio. He was smiling when the girls approached him.

"Uncle E," Deedee shouted, hugging him.

"Hi Deedee, what happened?"

"You're not going to believe this but I..." Deedee's voice trailed as she glanced at Coco.

"Hi, Mr. Ascot—"

"Something must really be wrong because I've told you a thousand times already that it's cool to call me Uncle E. Uncle Eric. Coco's still calling me, Mr. Ascot and you've got that look. Tell me what's up."

"Oh, it's really nothing to be concerned about, Uncle," Deedee quickly said.

Eric smiled at his niece and addressed the artist whose music he had just heard.

Deedee wandered out of the office, Reggie, racing out of the recording studio, bumped into her.

"Hey Dee," he said, holding her to prevent her from falling.

"Oh my..." Deedee said, shaking her head and maintaining her balance. "Are you in a hurry or what?"

"Yes, sorry I gotta get the disc from ah... The boss, he was listening to some of the tracks Coco did. Sorry to almost run you over, Dee. I mean I never meant to," Reggie said, guiding Deedee away from the studio's entrance.

They walked away, heading in the direction of Eric's office. Inside the recording studio, Tina adjusted her lipstick and fixed her tight skirt about her. Then she peeked from behind the door, and seeing no one, she walked out. Tina was chatting on her cell phone while toting a small breakfast tray, sashaying through the office.

"Uh huh, it's going down, I tell you..." Tina loudly continued on her cell phone.

Meanwhile, Eric glanced up when he saw Deedee and Reggie laughing and walking into his office. He was still giving Coco his review of her work. The talented teen listened intently to Eric's advice and smiled.

"Good looking, Uncle E," she smiled confidently.

"That's what we do... Polish it, and we'll make it shine," Eric said before acknowledging his niece. "Hey Dee, lemme get at you," he said to her.

"Okay Uncle E," Deedee smiled.

"Good job, Reggie. Take that disc and make it mo' better," Eric said. He glanced at Coco before continuing. "Coco knows exactly what to do."

"No doubt, yo."

They walked out of Eric's office, leaving Deedee standing at her uncle's desk. Eric waited until the door was closed before speaking.

"I'm meeting Sophia later and... Well I don't know what she has to tell me but it's probably not good. How d'you feel? She told me about meeting with you."

"Just watch out for whatever it is she's trying to pull. I don't know if she's a friend or an enemy."

"Everyone's got an opinion. No matter what, it belongs to them. And neither of us cannot change it. They have to be willing to reconsider or..."

"Uncle E. She's the one who needs the lecture not me. She's hiding behind the fact that she's working at a law firm and her business associates are asking her to cooperate in a personal matter and she's chosen the side of business over a friend and former..."

"Former partner she was engaged to."

Eric smiled at Deedee. He realized that she was cornered by her concerns, and he tried to set her free with a disarming gesture. It didn't seem to work and Deedee's mind was still brooding when she heard her uncle's voice.

"We'll work that out. I also want you to ease back on spending.

Matter of fact, spending is a wrap for the month with your last spree, or I'll be forced to take your card."

"Okay Uncle, I understand," Deedee said in a steady tone of voice.

She stared at her uncle's face searching for answers to ease the discontent she felt. Then she heard another jolt to her senses.

"You're really chummy with Reggie...?"

"Yes we've hung out a few times. Nothing serious though—"

"Let's keep it like that. He's just a schoolboy trying to be the man. He's not in your—"

"I can think and make decision about boys, Uncle!"

The words had jumped out quicker than Deedee could control the thought. She stared at her uncle's silent reaction and realized the shock was deeper than anticipated.

"Really Uncle...? I have it under control. I know all about sex," she said deliberately.

They looked at each other, and were both concerned about the statement in different ways. Deedee saw it one way and Eric saw it totally differently. Standing at her uncle's desk, Deedee continued searching for answers. She wanted to ask him about her mother's disappearance, but that would just be opening old wounds that she was trying to keep closed. And now, she could no longer shop when she was feeling depressed.

His desk was framed with papers and pads of notes. It was as disorganized as her thoughts. She boldly fought back the tears of despair. Her mind was being dragged to a place where she was not willing to go.

"I'll be responsible," Deedee sighed.

"Okay, I guess. I mean what more can I say," Eric said.

It was times like this one that made him miss Sophie's

wisdom. He didn't want to lose his niece. But he had to respect her wishes. Respect begets respect, Eric thought, sitting at his desk and watching Deedee.

She waved and walked out of the office. Prancing, she disappeared into an elevator and quickly walked to her car. Then tires screeched as Deedee drove away. She was still thinking about the conversation she had with her uncle. Before she realized what was happening, Deedee found herself on the Long Island Expressway. Speeding, she was pulled over and escaped with only a warning from a friendly officer. She quietly made her way to Eric's summer home and parked.

Deedee walked into the huge home and sat in the kitchen. The place was recently renovated and cleaned up. Fresh paint and marble couldn't cover up the pain Deedee was feeling. She wandered to her room and changed into her bathing suit. Then she walked out to the poolside and dove into the fresh water. Deedee's shapely legs kicked while she did several laps. Her thoughts drifted and soon she had left her uncle and Sophia behind.

He was probably going to stay in the city overnight, Deedee surmised. She sat poolside thinking of throwing a party. She started dialing on her cell phone, but Coco's number just rang through to her voicemail. It dawned on her that she was dialing Coco's number for the sixth time. Coco was the only friend she had. The call rang through to Coco's voicemail.

Deedee hung up without leaving a message. She stared at the huge mansion. A lot had happened here after she was raped. Deedee felt herself going down in the dumps of her thoughts to the place where she had hid the horrid experience. It was then that her cell phone rang and she jumped to answer. Checking the caller ID, she answered in disappointment.

"You don't sound too happy to hear from me..."

"Hey Reggie... Are you and Coco in the studio still recording...?"

"Coco was here and left. Your uncle bounced too and I was just finishing up..."

Deedee heard chuckling in the background. Her ears perked but she was unable to tell if it was music playing.

"Hmm, hmm... Hey, so ah... Reggie. If you want, bring some friends, stop by it's gonna be a pool party. I'm out in the Hamptons. I'll text you the address."

"So you want me to bring some bottles or...?"

"You can bring whatever..."

Again Deedee heard noise in the background. She strained trying to identify the sounds, but Reggie's voice was too loud.

"Okay, text me the address and we there..."

Deedee heard what Reggie was saying, but she was too busy listening to the noise in the background. The humming caused by the dial tone jolted her back to reality. She sent the text with address and directions.

Neither of them saw the unmarked cars covering the eatery where they met. The small restaurant downtown was his choice. It was supposed to be a clandestine meeting between exes, but it was wired for more. Eric had already swallowed two shots before Sophia walked into the quiet eatery. He watched the room light up as if it were smiling to meet her acquaintance. Sophia walked to where he sat and greeted him first with a handshake then they hugged. Their embrace ended abruptly when she shrugged.

"You smell really lovely," Eric said, breaking an awkward silence.

"You certainly look more dapper than ever," Sophia smiled

sarcastically. "You've been busy huh, Eric?" she nonchalantly replied.

Her glance at the two shot glasses had been a misleading clue. Eric's expression remained unshaken. He still loved Sophia and was studying her. She remained silent and her body bent seductively as she sat down under his glare. A dull silence fell on them and for a few moments. Eric chuckled and broke the tense silence.

"Oh, you're talking 'bout these glasses...?" he asked, looking down at the table.

A waiter brought garlic bread and a bottle of red wine. Sophia's sarcastic smile turned into a full-sized pitiful chuckle by the time she spoke.

"If it was just drinking, you'd be fine. But it's all this other stuff..." she let her voice fade when she saw the waiter coming back.

He showed Eric the bottle and popped the cork after Eric's approval. The waiter poured two glasses.

"Are you ready to order?"

"The steak is great..."

Sophia raised her hand. Eric paused and waved at the waiter. He nodded then walked away. They waited until he had completely disappeared before lifting their wine glasses in silence, and barely looking at each other. Eric and Sophia sipped the wine. The red liquid disappeared down their throats like the good times they had. The after taste left their minds reeling.

"You've been very bad, Eric," Sophia scolded. She took another sip, carefully metering her words. "I wish there was another way I could say this but I have to be honest. I know you did a lot of things under the guise of helping your niece. But some of those things were about Eric being selfish."

Sophia picked up her glass and this time she was staring at Eric's face. She drank the rest of the wine then poured herself another glass.

"What are you talking about?"

"You did a lot of things because it was about Eric Ascot!"

"Such as...?" he asked, tugging at his collar.

"Such as ... Your Armani suits are not gonna cover up all the shit you been up to."

"What have I been up to, Sophia. Since you know all this shit about me. Spill it!"

"Well let's see where should I begin?" Sophia gulped her wine. "Hmm let's start with... Ah... Killing, I should say, being involved in the alleged murder of your niece's mother. You were involved in Busta's murder. He was your best friend. Your name and gun came up in the murder of a police officer that was investigating you. Do you want me to continue...?"

"Go ahead. Be my guest."

"After having an affair with a minor, Danielle, your niece's best friend, she was murdered and somehow is probably connected to this murder-for-hire organization that I know you have used."

"First of all she wasn't a minor. She was nineteen..."

"Oh wow, I guess that makes you look good. You are nearly twice her age."

"It was something that happened. And those murder charges are all based on circumstantial evidence."

"Well, here's something else that happened. Not only do they have you on tape planning to cover up some type of killing, but they have a witness that can put you at the scene of at least two of the murders..."

"What? That's bullshit! That idiot Rightchus, he's a fucking liar!" Eric snarled too loudly.

His reaction caused the restaurant to stir when his fist

collided with the table's California oak top. Other diners in the eatery shot looks of concern at Eric and Sophia. He angrily gulped his wine while returning their stares.

"I remember when you used to be such a decent guy. Now I really don't know who you are, Eric."

"You know me Sophia. We been together for seven damn years. I'm the guy you were gonna marry..."

"Okay what about your nemesis, huh? He carved his name on my back with his cigarette lighter, Eric."

"I offered to pay for the surgery—"

"What about the mental scar. It still burns, Eric."

"I'll heal all that—we were in love—"

"Yes, *were*... But that guy I loved has since left the building. Now what's left is someone that not even I know."

The fourth glass of wine slipped down easier, soothing Sophia's parched throat. Eric watched her pour another glass, emptying the bottle. She drank her wine and drained the glass. Then she got up and walked away from the table taking her handbag with her.

"Where are you going?"

"I'm leaving. I want to get far away from you Eric!" she spat.

Sophia kept walking while other diners peeked at the couple's lives heading to disarray. Eric dropped a few bills on the table.

"Sophia, wait up," he said.

"It's too late. It's over, Eric."

She walked away to the exit. Eric jumped up and was about to start after her, but the waiter intervened. Checking the money on table, he pointed to his hand. Eric was about to walk outside after Sophia, but collapsed in his seat.

"Not enough," the waiter said.

Eric fished inside his pockets and nothing came out. He

ditched his jacket and pulled out his credit card. The waiter took it then walked away. By the time he came out of the restaurant, any trace of Sophia's whereabouts was gone. One of the unmarked cars remained. The occupants watched Eric pacing left then right before walking to his Jaguar and slipping inside. He drove off with them tailing him.

Seemingly agitated, Eric glanced at the Rolex on his wrist. It was after twelve in the morning, too late to call Deedee. He guided the luxury auto toward the Long Island Expressway. He saw the headlights in his rearview mirror. The sea salt in the air always cleared his head, Eric thought. Dropping the top, he let the Jag's engine roar. The headlights that had been following quickly disappeared from his rearview.

Music was blaring from the poolside of the mansion. He must sell this place he thought and froze in his tracks. There was a full-fledge party by the pool. Eric looked around and saw his neighbors dancing and getting low. He waved at Deedee and her friends, celebrating, drinking and smoking. Disappearing inside the mansion, he grabbed the mail and browsed. Eric was about to leave when he heard a familiar voice.

"Mr. Ascot, you're just getting here?"

Eric turned to see Kim and Tina coming toward him. He smiled acknowledging them, but he was surprised to see them here.

"Reggie told us about the place. We were with him cleaning up at the studio. And then Deedee called him... Next thing, we here and shyt," Kim said.

"I just got here myself but I'm gonna leave..." Eric's voice trailed.

"Ah, don't leave Eric. We could have some fun and shyt," Kim urged.

"Yes, we don't have to hang with these teens..."

"Well y'all aren't that much older."

"But we likes us some older, confident men," Kim smiled, rubbing her ass against his crotch.

Tina got closer and soon the girls had Eric in a sandwich. His body fell in rhythm with theirs and they were grooving to the beat. Kim was working her ass, and Eric's mind seemed to be changing when Deedee walked into the room. With arms folded, she watched for a few beats before saying, "Hey, Uncle. I thought I saw you come inside here. Took me a minute to find you but I didn't know—"

"I was just leaving," Eric said and saw that Tina was playing with his remote starter.

"What's this for...? A video game or sump'n like that?"

"It's the key to the Maybach," Deedee deadpanned.

"I'll take that," Eric said, hugging Deedee and walking out. "I trust that you'll be responsible..." Eric let his voice trail, and hugged his niece.

The party was still jumping when he drove out. He looked back thinking about leaving the key in the Jaguar. Deedee would probably stay there for the night. Seeing Kim and Tina there was enough. Eric wanted to relax at his city digs and planned on returning to the Hamptons the following day. He never turned back. While the party continued, the Maybach sped toward the city.

Deedee wanted her uncle to stay, but after witnessing the physical assault Kim and Tina delivered, she was feeling relieved that he had left. The party was popping and then slowly it went to an extreme slow grind. Deedee smiled when she saw everyone having a good time.

By six in the morning the music was off and just a few couples were left drinking and making out by the pool. Deedee checked the area and saw no one else.

"Good no one drowned," she said.

"That's very good," Reggie smiled.

He was picking bottles off the floor and saw Deedee checking her cell phone. His arms encircled her skinny waistline. They were both wearing swimwear. His shorts and her two-piece bikini suit did nothing to hide their emerging feelings. Deedee tried to wiggle free as Reggie held her in a tight embrace. She could feel him swelling and fended him off with a quick, deep kiss. It seemed to curb his appetite long enough for her to wiggle free. Deedee ran off but Reggie was quick to catch up to her. Their lips collided with the fury of hot passion and they shared each other's breath.

"I love your eyes," Reggie smiled.

"Why Reggie...?"

"They just feel like they touch your insides."

"Is that what your fingers are trying to do?'

Reggie laughed loudly. Deedee's question had caught him off guard. He boldly fought off the embarrassment.

"My bad," he said.

Kim and Tina stared at him with derision. When they heard his weak apology they both hissed their teeth in unison and walked away.

"Like he don't wanna fuck the bitch," Tina said.

"I don't know what you see in his ho ass anyways..." Kim said. "He's a male version of a chicken head."

"Shut your face, Kim. It's just like you all into Eric, but that nigga been running from you like you got dragon breath, ever since we had him up in the telly," Tina said. "No difference. We both chasing these niggas—"

"Bitch I don't chase Mr. Ascot. And I sure ain't got no dragon breath. Seriously I just ain't no ho like your ass, hounding that punk-ass nigga. You know he wanna fuck Deedee but you still up in him, giving him ass and brains for lunch and breakfast."

"Oh you gettin' all personal now, bitch?"

"Whatever bitch, I ain't got no dragon breath. You cock-blocking bitch! Go hound Reggie."

"Shut-da-fuck-up! Now you hatin'. I don't hound him. He hounds my ass. I put that kitty on him and he can't get enough."

"You're such a show-off bitch."

"You know that if Eric wasn't gonna have the both of our asses that night, he wouldn't have gone to the telly with just you alone bitch. He had his GPS on this ass, and he was like bring your friend along."

"Oh, go fuck yourself. I could a had Eric all to myself, but your ass just greedy that's all!"

"Really bitch...? You think so...? A'ight let me see him on your fat ass just one time without me, and my kitty help, bitch."

"Bitch, you just concentrate on cock blocking that fake-ass wanna be deejay. I will concentrate on a real millionaire ass having nigga."

Glasses clinked and both girls gulped. Kim was clearly offended, as she immediately poured another glass. Tina wandered off. She was following Reggie and Deedee around the mansion; but in arguing with Kim, she had lost track of them. Her eyes drifted through a maze of possibilities. Doors were everywhere.

"Damn, it's huge in this bitch! There could be like a hundred doors or so up in here," Tina said.

"Players' choice," Kim laughed.

"You the one who stop to drink and chat... Now I lost the two of them. You gonna have to help me find their asses. I don't want her to get that dick. Plus he took us here—he gotta take us back. Fuck it, we ain't got no ride back if we don't find his ass."

"That's real talk! Let's find their asses and shyt. I gotta go home and take care of Roshawn."

With different purposes, they set off checking doors, one at a time. The process was exhausting but Kim and Tina kept at the grind.

"When we find their asses I'm gonna run up behind Reggie and flat-line that nigga."

"I wanna see that one. Bitch you just talking. Soon as you see that nigga you just wanna drop your panties."

"You's a lying ass bitch. That nigga just be open and—"

"Shush... Shut da fuck up. I think I hear sump'n," Tina said, quietly opening the door.

They were inside. Their lips locked and Deedee held Reggie's shoulders. His eyes were closed and his tongue wandered through the chambers of her mind. The sexual sensation was fulfilling, causing her breath to come in gasps. Deedee's soft brown eyes were filled with lust. She felt his penis throbbing and her legs were weak. Reggie swept her off her feet and gently placed her on the bed. Her body twisted against his, Deedee was writhing in delight.

"Let's wait 'til tomorrow," Deedee moaned.

Her panic sounds made her appear fragile. Power swelled both Reggie's heads. His manhood rose as his hands roved over her body, raking Deedee's breasts. Hungry pants escaped from her lips, bringing pleasure to onlookers and participants.

Deedee smiled when she felt her feelings awakened by his probing hands. Reggie kissed her neck and her body relaxed against his muscular frame. His jaw worked tirelessly to satisfy her. Sucking her pussy until Deedee screamed, Reggie's head kept bopping up and down, eating her out. Her legs shaking, Deedee's moans grew louder.

"Oh, ah ooh yes!" she pulled his face deep inside her thighs.

"Shut da front door! That nigga never eat me out that long," Tina whispered, her fingers rubbing her clitoris.

Both Kim and Tina found a position out of sight, where they could see Reggie and Deedee's bodies. The couple was too engaged to noticed them. Kim's hand freely stroked her pussy while watching.

"Maybe he likes how her pussy tastes and shyt," Kim smiled.

"Shut your face," Tina seethed.

Wearing a frown, she watched Deedee's head rocking back and forth. Tina looked at Kim openly turned on. Then both watched the sexual interlude while rubbing on themselves.

Deedee held on dearly to Reggie's head. Panting loudly, she felt the release causing her body to shudder. Her flesh was tingling and she could feel his penis poking her. Her whole body trembled and she felt a rush of energy. Deedee panicked and closed her legs. The head of his penis had made contact with her exposed soft flesh. Wet and dripping, Deedee opened her legs and let him inside her.

"Just for a minute, Reggie," she moaned. "Oh yes," Deedee said when she felt his head entering her.

Her body twisted in delicious delight. Writhing, she held onto his shoulders while he took her from the side. He was holding her stomach while sliding his dick in and out of her pussy. Deedee gushed and felt her juices rushing out. Her hands reached back and grabbed his dick when she felt pain. Holding his dick and massaging it, Deedee guided him in and out of her moistness.

"Please don't come inside me. Spray it all over my breasts," Deedee ordered.

"Yes baby," Reggie whispered.

His body was rocking back and forth. He slammed his waist into Deedee's midsection. She tried to hold on to his dick but it was a losing task. She felt pleasure and slowly raised her legs, Deedee took him all inside and the pain subsided as his flaming hot dick burned through her wet flesh. He would not be controlled. She could feel him swell inside her and his short breaths came faster.

"Oh shit! Oh God! Ugh!" Reggie shouted and exploded at the same time.

Deedee pulled him out of her but some had already hit her legs, her pussy and her chest. He let off all over her breasts. His body jerked while his dick kept spraying.

"Damn nigga!" Deedee said, pushing him away. "You must've been hard up."

Reggie moved closer and hugged her. He was about to open his mouth when there was a loud knock on the door. Both Reggie and Deedee looked quizzically at each other as the banging continued.

"Reggie I know you're in there. But we need to go home," Tina shouted.

"Oh yes, I totally forgot about Kim and Tina!" Reggie said, jumping out of the bed.

"Reggie, open up the damn door. We already know you're in there doing your thing. You ain't nothing but a ho'!"

"You better open the door before she breaks it down," Deedee laughed, shaking her head.

Reggie opened the door, and Kim and Tina stormed inside the room. They both were sniffing around without saying anything.

"We know y'all doing your thing up in here. I can't hate you player, but your game is weak, nigga. Get your shit on and take our asses home now!"

"Hold on now. Neither of you drive?" Deedee asked.

"She's a good driver," Tina said, pointing at Kim. "But his ass brought us out here."

"Yes but your asses wanted to come right?"

"Yeah, but you still gonna take us home. After all this, me and Kim ain't got no other way to get home. And we gotta be at the J.O.B.

We got things to be cleaning up and all that. Right Kim?"

"You were the one who wanted to come out here. You should've figured how you were gonna get home and shyt," Kim said.

"You weren't complaining earlier, bitch. Don't forget that you still gotta go to your mother's to get Roshawn," Tina said.

"Don't be tellin' me shyt! I always do for my son, ho! It's you that need to—"

"Alright already...! Enough of you two...!" Deedee shouted, getting out of bed.

Kim and Tina watched her sexy naked body glide to her clothes. She pulled her car keys out. They were all still staring when Deedee reached in front of Kim. She handed the car keys to Kim.

"Now you know how you're gonna get home," Deedee said. "Just bring it to work with you alright?"

"Okay cool. But how I'm gonna find my way?"

"Just set the GPS system," Deedee answered.

"I got you. You coming Tina?"

Tina was staring at Deedee's sexy naked body crawling back into the bed with Reggie. Her mouth dropped open.

"Fuck that fool! I'm riding with you, girl!"

The door slammed shut and Deedee was back into the bed with Reggie. They were cuddling.

"Wow you must be really feeling me. You did that for me?" he asked.

"Don't flatter yourself, player. Your game is weak. I just hate Tina's nosey ass."

Meanwhile outside, Kim adjusted the GPS and pulled off. She glanced around, enjoying the smooth ride of the car. Tina sulked in the passenger seat next to her.

"Deedee's a nice girl and shyt," Kim said.

Tina did not respond. She stared out the window into the early morn. After a while she glanced at the car's interior.

"This shit's a dope car," Tina said. "And she's nice."

"That Deedee... Wow! She's got a dope body and shyt," Kim blurted. "If I was into girls like that, I'd definitely try to bag her and shyt," Kim continued.

"Shut your face, Kim! Okay yeah, her body is nice, but that's because she ain't got no kids," Tina admitted after a couple beats. "I mean not that my body ain't nice too. Since I had my Angel my body... Yes I can stand to lose a few here or there but on a whole, but my body is kinda there."

"Bitch, your body is neither here or there. It's gotta do with your overall assets—that's the shyt," Kim said.

"Look Oprah, just because you got that nice juicy ass, you think you can be an expert huh? I still ain't seen that phatty working any magic on Mr. Ascot, ho," Tina said and the car swerved wildly.

Kim was shooting daggers at Tina. If that didn't produce the desired effect, the look on Kim's face made it clear to Tina that she was determined to get her point across. Kim regained control of the car, but her reckless action scared Tina.

"Oh shit! Look the fuck where you going and stop staring my way, bitch. Keep your eyes on the road crazy bitch! Shit... Hiss... Oh dear Holy Mary, mother of Jesus Christ, pray for us to get home safe," Tina continued, waving her hand across her chest in the sign of a cross.

"That one was for talking all that shyt! You just don't wanna admit that Deedee is smarter and more attractive than your ass."

"Okay! I admit it. But that doesn't mean you have to kill us trying to prove it," Tina screamed.

"Never mind that... I just had to get your attention. You know, put some reality in your life... You gonna have to either share Reggie with Deedee or leave them the fuck alone."

"Reggie's cohones is big enough, and his dick way long enough for the both of us. She could keep him. I'll have my fun," Tina chuckled.

"So that means you gonna share that young-ass nigga, huh?"

"Somebody gotta show him how to dig out honey dip back," Tina laughed. "Well you saw him, right? That nigga barely got up in that ass when he just busted off."

"She probably have a nice gushy, tight pussy to go with that... Hmm body. Oh shyt! You in trouble bitch. Go back to fucking that attorney. At least he got money and his own place... What Reggie got besides dick, huh? Leave him for Dee. That's my girl," Kim smiled.

"Fuck you smiling like that for? I may not be in the same class of bitch she is with all that money and all, but I'm still there," Tina said, looking at her reflection in the rearview mirror. Again the car swerved.

"You're not even in the same school. She's going to college and you're gonna work for her."

"Okay, I mean, she all that...I'll give her that," Tina shouted. "You ain't gotta kill my ass, bitch."

"Thank you... Say it like you lost him."

"Wait lemme tell you sump'n. Reggie, that nigga got a big-ass dick. He bust a nut in that bitch, all that nice body shit will swell all out of proportion," Tina said.

"You open on that nigga's dick, huh? You slut," Kim said.

"Shut da front door, bitch. I don't be lettin' that nigga nut in my ass. I don't want no more kids."

"We don't want another baby-daddy unless he giving up a dick full of Benjamin's!"

Kim and Tina slapped high-five. Both laughed, and Kim guided the car on the Long Island Expressway heading for the city.

He woke up and wandered through the mansion, checking the interior. Reggie walked so far. He totally forgot the direction he had traveled in. Checking each door in one direction, he finally found the room where Deedee was in bed. She was naked, curled up, quietly asleep and Reggie moved closer to her and heard her breathing. He bent over and kissed her. She stirred and locked her lips with Reggie's.

His hands wasted no time in searching her supple body. She sucked his lower lip into her mouth while they made out. A smile suddenly spread across Reggie's face when his fingers made contact with her treasured spot. She was juicy with anticipation. Her legs wiggled free and he tried to enter her, but Deedee was ready and slipped her leg around his, blocking his entry.

"You've gotta use a condom. This time it's for real," Deedee firmly said.

"Babe, it's early I'll get it later," Reggie said, kissing her softly. "But I don't need a condom to do this," he continued and immediately flipped her over.

Before Deedee could protest she felt his tongue on her clit. Reggie sucked at her pussy lips and Deedee's muscles relaxed, and her juices flowed.

"Oh no..." she moaned. Her sounds faded to unintelligibly uttering as Reggie's tongue penetrated deep inside her. "Uh... Oh ugh..."

She felt her legs kicking involuntary and Deedee grabbed his head. She pulled at his hair and a scream gurgled in her throat.

"Oh please oh please stop...Oh no..."

Reggie kept munching and sucking. His fingers tickled the entrance to her asshole sending shivers all through Deedee's spine. Her body wiggled and she held on tightly to Reggie's head and exploded in his face.

"Ooh... Ooh... Ah... Ah... Oh yes!"

Deedee's naked body opened like a flower and Reggie hovered over her, kissing and sucking her nectar. He licked his lips heartily a combination of his sweat mixing with her juices filled his palate. Reggie wanted more and tried to shove his hard dick into her, but again she moved her legs and blocked him.

"You did that shit last night, and that was on me. You're not gonna get anymore unless you get a condom."

"Your uncle don't got any stashed—"

"What? Reggie go to the store and get a pack. Or you'll be going home without getting anymore. I swear!"

"A'ight cool, I'll do what you say. But babe, how am I gonna get to the store? I don't have a car, and you gave what's-her-name your ride."

"I gave Kim my car to get home. Also to take your shit-talking friend, Tina outta my head," Deedee said and hopped out of the bed.

Reggie's eyes closely followed her nude body to the window, and back between the sheets. Deedee smiled at him and said, "Uncle Eric's Jag's there. If you promise not to wreck it. Then Reggie you may use it to go to the store."

"Do you have the directions to one that's open this early?"

"It's seven in the morning. It's not that early. Stay on this road, and you can't miss the small shopping district with a service station."

"In a Jag that should be about five minutes," Reggie playfully smiled.

"Boy, just go to the store and don't you wreck my uncle's car."

"Where are the keys...?"

Deedee got out of the bed and went outside. A few minutes later, she returned to the room and said, "Check inside the car. Uncle E more than likely left them there."

"Damn, ain't he scared that someone breaks into the garage and steals it...? I mean, that ride probably worth some dough."

"Yeah, but that's my uncle for you. He believes in playing it like that. So far all the cars have been safe. There's always someone here working or whatever."

"I hear you. But sometimes it's better to be safe than sorry," Reggie said, and quickly stole a kiss. Before walking out, he turned around and asked, "Dee, do you need anything...?"

Deedee smiled before responding. She grinned as she said, "You're thoughtful, huh? Cool... Surprise me with some candy."

"I will do that," he smiled.

He kissed her again before walking out. This time he stared deep into Deedee's soft brown eyes and gently touched her lips with his. She pulled him close to her breasts and kissed him hungrily, moving her tongue against his. The ferocity of her passion consumed him causing Reggie to fall on top of her. He held her close, until his breath came in gasps. Mustering enough strength, Reggie managed to push away from Deedee's captivating presence.

"Hold onto that for now. I'll be back soon," he smiled.

"Be back soon," she smiled, blowing him a kiss.

He ran out the room and was heading down the stairs. Reggie saw that there was someone in the mansion cleaning and he kept it moving. Pushing the door open, Reggie was off running through a long driveway and ended up close to the garage on the far side.

Deedee chuckled from her window watching him run. He opened the door and gave her the thumbs up. She smiled that he had spotted her watching him. Deedee was about to walk away from the window when the loud explosion rocked the entire mansion.

The morning sky had erupted into golden flames as soon as Reggie closed the door and turned on the ignition. Deedee's eyes widened and her mouth dropped opened but no sound came. The car had exploded. She found herself pointing and staring at the fire and pieces of the car that had blown off in the explosion. The fire raged and alarms went off. Neighbors were running from their homes. Deedee lost control and started screaming.

Eric awoke from a very deep slumber. After stretching for a few minutes, he lazily hobbled to the bathroom. He turned on a television screen, and stared blankly at the morning's stock report. A few minutes later, he emerged wearing Polo bathrobe, and walked to the kitchen. Eric turned on the coffee pot and listened silently to the radio.

The fusion sound of Guru and Donald Byrd played. The evocative mixture of Hip Hop and Jazz rang out from his stereo. Eric had toast and coffee while the music played on. He was soon dressed, and remembering what Sophia had said last night, Eric dialed his attorney. The man answered immediately.

"Good morning, Eric."

"Good morning, how's it going?"

"Well, we have another two weeks before the court date. So we should be seeking to find out exactly how much a settlement will cost you..."

"Sophia mentioned that they have someone who could place me at one of the murders... probably this con man they called Rightchus."

"I don't know... I know they have police following you at all times. So be real careful..."

"Tell me something else," Eric said, smiling.

"Turn on your television... I think they're talking about your place in the Hamptons..."

"Ok but I gotta take this!" Eric said, tossing the cell phone from his hand.

He picked up another. Then another cell phone started ringing. Eric threw the other on his bed.

"Yes..." he answered and listened intently. Then he added, "Deedee's alright? Okay. I'm on my way there right now."

He raced out the front of the building and jogged to his car. Eric jumped inside and paused for a beat. He slowly got out and placed a call on his cell phone. A few minutes later a tow truck pulled up and the Maybach left on the back of a flatbed. A black limousine pulled up and Eric hopped inside.

Police along with fire and other emergency vehicles were everywhere. A complete hour had elapsed by the time Eric arrived at his East Hampton mansion. His heart raced when he saw the burnt car, and the stench of barbecued flesh lingered. An officer lumbered over to him.

"Are you Ascot?" the officer asked.

"Yes I am," Eric answered.

"Follow me, sir."

Eric walked behind the officer, checking out the burnt Jaguar. There were pieces all over the front of the house.

"Do you know the young man who was driving?" Without pausing for an answer, the officer continued. "From the tidbits we got from your niece, we were able to determine that his name was Reggie and he worked with you in your studio."

"Yes," Eric somberly answered.

He scoped the area again and again. Glass windows were shattered and parts of the garage were burnt. There were minimal structural damages, but a human life had been lost. Again Eric vowed to sell the place.

"I guess we'll talk some more," the officer said, handing Eric his card.

"May I go and see my niece?"

"Yes, sure. She's inside with a doctor. We'll be here investigating and will find you if we have further questions. By the way, do you have any idea who might want to kill you?"

Eric stared at the officer for a few beats. He scratched his head as if searching for the right answer. Shaking his head, Eric Ascot continued inside the house. An older man greeted him.

"It was me who called you Mr. Ascot."

"Thanks, what happened?"

"We covered the party like you asked us to and Deedee had a young man and two other women here after everyone left. This morning, we checked the grounds and everything seemed okay. I came inside just as the young man was running out. I told him I work here, and he told me he was a friend of Deedee's. He continued on his way and then he got inside the Jaguar. And boom—the car exploded as soon as he turned the ignition on."

"It was meant for me. I took the Maybach, but I had had the Jag for a few days now."

"Somebody set an explosive device, maybe from the city..."

"How's Deedee?"

"Shaken, but she's doing better. The doctor gave her a sedative. She's in her room recuperating. We're going to clean up and make sure everything is restored."

"Thanks," Eric said, nodding and walking away.

He went to Deedee's room and found her resting in her bed. Eric moved closer and sat next to the bed. He watched his sleeping niece for a few minutes. Eric walked to the window and stared out to where the explosion had taken place. His brows furrowed into a deep trench of concerns. He glanced at Deedee when she spoke.

"Uncle E, it was awful," she said.

Eric went back over to her, and held her tightly in a loving embrace. He was happy that she was alive and wanted to hear what happened, but what mattered was that she was all right. Squeezing her tighter, Eric said, "I'm soo happy you're alright. I can't afford to lose you, Dee."

Coco fixed her backpack and plugged her headphones into her ears. She closed the door and locked it. Then motoring down the stairs in rapid fashion, she walked out. It was a squally, humid day and they were outside. The early worms from her building were all over the front of the place. Some were carrying coffee cups, others eating food, and drinking bottled water. Nearly all were smoking and escaping the cramped confines of their apartments.

"Hey Coco, your friend was on TV this morning," someone said. He was standing over the fire hydrant with a large wrench.

"Oh word?"

"Word up..." he said, too busy opening the hydrant.

"I'll call her and see what's up," Coco said, easing into her bop. She couldn't wait to get to the studio and wasn't waiting around for the hydrant to be fully opened.

She was into her bop and disappearing into rush of the subway station. It was time for the studio, and she had been yearning to get there since visiting her mother in the hospital. The train came and she sat listening to her headphones, but her mind stayed on her mother's condition. Coco was soon walking out of the subway, and rolling up to the doors of the studio. She saw Deedee's black BMW parked outside, suggesting that Deedee could be already upstairs. Coco rode the elevator upstairs and as soon as she got off, her jaw dropped.

"Good morning. Who are you here to see?" A police officer asked, greeting Coco.

"I'm an artist and I'm here to record a—"

"Stand over there, Miss," the officer said, rudely interrupting Coco. "The recording studio is closed until further notice," he continued.

"Huh...? What? You for real, yo?"

The agent walked away without responding. Coco glanced around and saw that there were agents everywhere, and they were removing everything out Eric's office. She was placed in an area next to Kim and Tina. Coco looked suspiciously at them.

"We got here like you and found the feds here taking shyt!" Kim said, throwing up her hands.

"Where's Deedee?"

"She damn sure ain't here," Tina chuckled. "Karma is a bitch—last night she taking my shit, and today feds taking her shit," Tina said dryly.

Coco saw Tina smoking and standing behind Kim. Tina's frown of resentment left Coco guessing. There was a pause and the girls sized each other up. Tina staring at Coco's furrowed brow, and Kim looking the teen up and down.

"I like your outfit," Kim said. "Them Gucci sneaks is happenin', right Tina?"

"They a'ight," Tina said after a beat.

"They the same ones I thought you said you wanted when you had some money and shyt," Kim said.

"They a'ight, but too many people wearing 'em now and I don't particularly have a shoe fetish like some peeps I know."

"Hmm, hmm, anyways... Dee was home in the Hamptons last night. Reggie took me and Kim and some other peoples over there to her pool party and shyt," Kim said.

"You never got the memo, Coco? Maybe, she didn't invite any ghetto girls," Tina laughed.

Coco stopped looking around for Deedee, and directed her attention at Tina. Smirking, she pulled out her cell phone. She flipped through the directory and dialed. Coco turned her back to the Kim and Tina before speaking into her cell phone.

"What da fuck is up, yo?"

"What? You just heard about the shit that happened this morning?"

"What shit that happened? When this morning?"

"Coco, I'm your friend and if something goes wrong with you I wanna know immediately and vice versa."

"That's why I'm calling, yo. The police are at the studio and they are taking papers, pens, computers—"

"What? Coco, are you sure?"

"I'm here at the studio right now. Me and them two, uh, chicks... Oh they were driving your car? I thought you were here in the studio... You out in L.I., and *what* happened? Get da fuck outta here. Dee, you better tell your uncle they just removing shit and they ain't saying shit to nobody... They just taking shit and writing receipts."

"Shit Coco! I'm with my uncle now... Sit tight. We're on our way."

"Okay, yo. I'll see you in a few."

They stood around watching the officers tagging and removing every piece of equipment, from Ascot's office. The officers routinely glanced at them while binging out equipment, including computers, telephones and fax machines. Coco lit a cigarette and started humming the lyrics to a song playing on her headphones. An officer soon cautioned her.

"I think this is a no-smoking area, Miss. So please put it out."

Coco glanced at him as if in protest, and slowly took her headphones off. She took a drag, and crushed the cigarette with her Pradas. Both Kim and Tina, standing next to her, scrutinized the rebellious nature of Coco. They also appreciated the fact that the officer had spoken to Coco and not them. In that one moment, they shared that certain insolence in Coco. She never mentioned Tina had been smoking.

"You too, Miss," he said, pointing at Tina.

"I like your shoes," Tina said to Coco. "They're nice."

Coco stared at her then at Kim and said nothing. She nodded at both and went back to singing along with the music playing in her headphones.

> "...Said it to you once show it to you twice
> Life of a ghetto girl's tougher than dice..."

The teen turned and saw a smile on Kim's lips. She was also singing the lyrics. Coco returned the smile.

"You know this song, already yo?"

"Yeah, you and Reggie been working on it so much and you know the hook is catchy and shyt."

"You've got a cool voice. You sing?"

"Blow her away with a song!" Tina immediately shouted.

"No, I'm 'a sing the hook from her song..." Kim said and let her voice trail. Then she launched into the song with so much gusto that even Coco was amazed.

Dreaming how I started out on shoestring diet
Wing and a prayer got me a musical connect
Getting ready to rumble championship fights...
Rocketing nonstop to the top I'll never drop...
This ball still here shooting at starlights
Out during day and night running my laps
Rhymes I write are tougher than dice...

Eric and Deedee got off the elevator with great haste. Eric headed directly to an officer.

"Who's in charge here?" he asked one of the officers, who pointed to another person.

"He's over there."

"You've gotta speak with my lawyer first!" Eric shouted, approaching the man.

Then Deedee noticed Coco standing between Kim and Tina, and she raced toward them.

"Really...? This is soo hood for y'all to be standing around and fussing with each other when this shit is going down!" Deedee shouted. "How could y'all be so inconsiderate," she said, glancing at the look of bewilderment on the faces of Coco, Kim and Tina.

"Soo hood...? What'cha talking 'bout, yo...?"

"Yeah, that was soo yesterday. What the hell is eating you...?" Tina asked.

"Ain't nobody fussing up in here but them feds and shyt," Kim added. "We're on to *Tougher Than Dice*."

"Coco's new song is a banger!" Tina said. "I like what Kim did to it. She sang that to death."

Deedee lowered her voice and stared in disbelief at Coco, Kim and Tina. Then she said, "You guys weren't about to throw down then...?" Deedee's voice trailed and her eyes narrowed. "It's just that I saw y'all, and I know about the beef between y'all..."

"No, Kim was singing my song and she was killing it, yo."

"Yeah, she definitely bodied that song!" Tina said, and high-fived Kim.

"Ok, my bad... So y'all haven't heard then?"

"No, we haven't heard nada 'cept from the feds, yo."

"Heard what...?" Kim asked.

"Yeah, what...?" Tina echoed.

"Someone set a bomb underneath my uncle's Jaguar..."

"The Jaguar's blown up? That's an expensive ass ride," Tina said, shaking her head. "Whole lotta money went up in flames."

"Shyt, at least your uncle's good."

"Yeah, my uncle's good."

"Hmm, hmm, he's over there right now arguing with them feds, so thank God he didn't get hurt," Kim said, staring in Eric's direction. She turned back and looked at Deedee.

"But Reggie..."

"Wha' happened to Reg?" Tina asked.

"It's bad... It's real bad..."

Coco, Kim and Tina all listened intently to Deedee, but her voice trailed. This time she couldn't choke back her tears and Deedee started crying. Coco moved closer and hugged her then Kim and Tina joined in.

"You'll be a'ight, yo."

"Reggie was in the car when it exploded," Deedee blurted, crying.

"Shyt no!" Kim said.

"He's dead? You sure?" Tina asked.

"I'm sure," Deedee answered with a nod.

"Why would anyone wanna kill my Reg?" Tina shrieked.

"I don't think it was ever meant for Reggie," Deedee said, her voice cracking with emotion.

Without concealing her feelings, Deedee's tears freely flowed. Then her eyes seemed to drift. Glancing around, it looked like her whole world was crumbling, and everything was falling apart in slow-mo.

"Oh my God! Not my Reggie!" Tina shouted.

Tina made the sign of the cross and staggered as if she had been hit by a blow. Kim grabbed her, but not in time. Tina collasped on the floor. Deedee turned around, and saw her uncle in a heated argument with two officers.

They kept shoving papers after papers at him. Deedee saw her uncle slap the search warrant from the officer's hand. Two other officers rushed over. Quickly they restrained Eric then placed him in handcuffs.

Coco was scowling at the officers. She suddenly raced over to aid her music producer. Another officer grabbed Coco, and restrained her from behind. Coco struggled with the officer who was trying to put her in handcuffs. She was coughing from his chokehold. Kim was on her knees next to Tina's limp body. Deedee heard the cry, and did not mask her fury as she watched officers put Coco in handcuffs and led her along with Eric toward the elevators.

"What the fuck is happening? What're you doing?" Deedee shouted.

"Stand back! This is an official U.S. government investigation," the officer shouted at Deedee.

After shaking the unconscious Tina without getting any kind of response, Kim quickly realized she was not having much success reviving her friend, who remained lying motionless.

"Shyt...! Tina needs water...!" Kim hysterically shouted while glancing around. No one responded to her cry for help. "Shyt, y'all best cut out all da fuckeries and someone get my girl some water before she dies. Dammit!"

Our titles interlace action, crime, and the urban lifestyle depicting the harsh realities of life on the streets. Call it street literature, urban drama, we call it hip-hop literature. This exciting genre features fast-paced action, gritty ghetto realism, and social messages about the high price of the street life style.

DEAD AND STINKIN'
STEPHEN HEWETT

A GOOD DAY TO DIE
JAMES HENDRICKS

WHEN LOVE TURNS TO HATE
SHARRON DOYLE

IF IT AIN'T ONE THING IT'S ANOTHER
SHARRON DOYLE

WOMAN'S CRY
VANESSA MARTIR

BLACKOUT
JERRY LaMOTHE
ANTHONY WHYTE

HUSTLE HARD
BLAINE MARTIN

A BOOGIE DOWN STORY
KEISHA SEIGNIOUS

CRAVE ALL LOSE ALL
ERICK S GRAY

LOVE AND A GANGSTA
ERICK S GRAY

AMERICA'S SOUL
ERICK S GRAY

Mail us a List of the titles you would like include $14.95 per Title + shipping charges $3.95 for one book & $1.00 for each additional book. Make all checks payable to: Augustus Publishing 33 Indian Rd. NY, NY 10034

▲
HARD WHITE
SHANNON HOLMES
ANTHONY WHYTE

▲
STREET CHIC
ANTHONY WHYTE

▲
BOOTY CALL *69
ERICK S GRAY

▲
POWER OF THE P
JAMES HENDRICKS

▲
STREETS OF NEW YORK VOL. 1
ERICK S GRAY, ANTHONY WHYTE
MARK ANTHONY, SHANNON HOLMES

▲
STREETS OF NEW YORK VOL. 2
ERICK S GRAY, ANTHONY WHYTE
MARK ANTHONY, K'WAN

▲
STREETS OF NEW YORK VOL. 3
ERICK S GRAY, ANTHONY WHYTE
MARK ANTHONY, TREASURE BLUE

▲
SMUT CENTRAL
BRANDON McCALLA

▲
GHETTO GIRLS
ANTHONY WHYTE

▲
GHETTO GIRLS TOO
ANTHONY WHYTE

▲
**GHETTO GIRLS 3:
SOO HOOD**
ANTHONY WHYTE

▲
**GHETTO GIRLS IV:
YOUNG LUV**
ANTHONY WHYTE

▲
SPOT RUSHERS
BRANDON McCALLA

▲
**IT CAN HAPPEN
IN A MINUTE**
S.M. JOHNSON

▲
LIPSTICK DIARIES
CRYSTAL LACEY WINSLOW
VARIOUS FEMALE AUTHORS

▲
LIPSTICK DIARIES 2
WAHIDA CLARK
VARIOUS FEMALE AUTHORS